# Frozen Conquest

Randall Krzak

# Frozen Conquest

*To Sylvia, my true flower of Scotland,*
*And to our son Craig, of whom we're very proud.*
*There's no doubt I have the best family in the world.*
*Thank you for loving me.*
*I love you.*

# Acknowledgments

Cover Design By: DarnGoodCovers.com

*Frozen Conquest* would not be a reality without those who helped me along my journey, including: T.J. Beach, Richard Bishop, Barry Campbell, Jeannie Delahunt, John Delaney, Jenny Foister, George Hulse, Mike Jackson, Pat Kane, Michele Kapugi, Michael Kent, Everett E. Kergosien, Sylvia Krzak, C.B. Laurence, Du-Marc Mills, Pamela Monson, Don Olivio, Desmond Orsinelli, Craig Palmer, Kristin Perry, Terry Pleasant, Glen Robinson, Vivienne Sang, Marie Souza, Richard Toole, Paul Wedel, Kelly Zimmer, and the Writer's Café-Mocha Team.

# Chapter One

U nnamed Ice Sheet
Antarctica

*Craack! Craack!*

A thunderous sound rolled over the ice and out to sea. Penguins and seals dove into the dark, icy water. Petrels and albatrosses screeched as they soared into the air to escape the impending doom.

*Craack!*

An extensive swath of the ice shelf slowly broke away, almost a kilometer deep and two kilometers wide, and crashed into the ocean, forming a new shoreline. It also generated an underwater tsunami, causing an impact on sea life. The ends of the ice broke away, thereby creating icebergs.

A man bundled in white cold-weather gear stared at his handiwork through binoculars. *Perfect. The boss will be pleased with the first test.* Samson turned and vaulted into an Arctic Sno-Cat. The vehicle trundled across the white expanse, powering over small frozen drifts while avoiding crevasses he had previously marked.

"Sam ... Can ... me?"

The man grabbed his handheld radio from the dash holder. "This is Samson. Please repeat."

"Ready ... test ..."

Samson sighed. "You're breaking up. Climb to the nearest high point." He yanked the radio from his head as the device emitted a piercing squeal.

"Can you hear me now?"

"Much better, Reginald. What's the status?"

"We'll be ready for test two in about twenty minutes."

"Where are you?"

"I'm b-bouncing across the t-tundra in your d-direction."

"Reginald, don't initiate the test before I arrive." *Bloody idiot.*

"Roger, wilco."

Samson replaced the radio in its holder and used a gloved hand to wipe the windshield, which had frosted despite the heater being turned to high. "Blasted weather. Why couldn't the boss pick a warmer climate for his test?"

His vehicle climbed a slight rise. The treads spun, but he didn't move. "Damn. Must have caught on something." He shifted the gears into neutral, activated the brake, grabbed a pickaxe, and ventured outside.

Samson knelt and glanced under the vehicle. *Just as I thought.* He crabbed under the Sno-Cat and used the axe to break up a large chunk of ice caught in the treads.

Back inside ten minutes later, Samson engaged the engine and continued his journey.

*Craack!*

Fracturing ice drowned out the engine's roar. In the distance, he spotted a towering plume of pulverized ice and snow. "Blast it! I told the damn fool to wait." He jerked the wheel to the right, gunning the engine to escape a thousand tons of ice and snow descending upon him.

Before he had traveled a hundred meters, the vehicle lurched to the left. Wide-eyed, Samson fought the controls. For a brief moment, the Sno-Cat righted itself. *Thank God!* He closed his eyes as he tried to calm his racing heart. *Thought I'd be buried in an avalanche.*

Without warning, the now-free chunk of ice overturned, taking Samson and his Sno-Cat to a watery grave. His screams went unheard except by the escaping birds.

\* \* \*

Diablo Headquarters
Miami, Florida


Walter Brown, the eighty-year-old founder, and CEO of the privately-held Diablo Corps, gazed out the office windows on the top floor of the company headquarters in downtown Miami. Favoring the color green, Brown had all of his offices painted in varying hues of the color, emulating nature. Although the headquarters was dwarfed by much taller buildings, Brown normally enjoyed the skyline view toward the ocean.

As one of the world's wealthiest men, he could have lived anywhere. Having grown up in the Miami area, he wanted to remain near his old stomping grounds. Few knew his name and even fewer could boast of meeting the recluse.

Angry rain lashed the windows as a sudden storm disrupted the otherwise hot and sunny day. He turned back to face a ninety-five-inch monitor mounted on the wall. Blinking red and green lights on the world map signified his worldwide operations.

He frowned. *What's taking so long? I should have heard by now.*

When his phone rang, he stabbed at the console and put the call on speaker. "What?"

"Sir, Reginald here. I've completed both tests."

"Excellent." A smile etched across his face. "About time I heard from you. Have the accountants arrived yet?"

"Yes, sir. They came yesterday and are becoming acclimated now. Several began work this morning, but ...."

"What's wrong?"

"Uh ... your nephew. He was caught on an ice floe after the second test. He's still missing."

Brown closed his eyes and pursed his lips. "Very well. Keep searching, but I doubt he'll still be alive in those conditions. However, my sister will want to give him a proper burial, so you need to find his body."

"Yes, sir. Our best search and rescue team is in the area now. When will you be returning?"

"I should finish what I need to do here by tomorrow morning. Expect me to arrive in the evening on the following day. Tell Chris to make sure everything is ready for me."

"Yes, sir."

Brown broke the connection and changed the monitor presentation. Blue lights signified the locations of the top one hundred banking and investment institutions, and orange showed the world's sixteen richest stock exchanges. "Soon, we shall make our requirements known. If the G7 doesn't bend to our demands, the might of Diablo will wreak havoc on their economies."

He stepped to a self-service bar in the corner of his office and poured himself a large Isle of Jura twenty-one-year-old single malt whiskey. After taking a slug, he logged onto his computer and created a message:

To: *The Chairs and Governors of the G7 Central Banks*
   From: *Nightmare*
   *Stand by for my demands, which will be released in the near future. Failure to comply will result in the destruction of your way of*

*life as you know it. The world cries out for truth, and I will be the sword of justice.*

A wheeze escaped from Brown as he clutched a hand to his chest. He reached into a drawer with the other, rummaging for his nitroglycerin tablets. *Where are they?*

His shaking hand found the elusive bottle. With agonizing slowness, he forced the cap from the top and placed two pills under his tongue. Before long, his chest relaxed. *Damn inconvenient getting old. Covid didn't get me, and I'm sure not going to let my heart pack it in either.*

He picked up his glass and took another sip of his whiskey. *Ah, the elixir of life. If some French nun made it to 117 drinking a glass of wine each day, why shouldn't I have my favorite beverage?*

Brown took a final drink before turning back to his computer. He reread his message and clicked send. *And so it begins. Who will be the first to crack? Not the British—too stoic. America? A possibility, but too politically divided to move fast enough.* He snapped his fingers. *My money's on the French.*

Enjoying the sound of his own voice, he uttered his thoughts to an imaginary crowd. "So what should my demands be? The G20 is unable to get climate change under control, and I need to push them. Perhaps if I confiscate the G7's gold stockpiles and share them with less wealthy nations to get climate change promises underway? Maybe push them to provide the rarest diamonds and artwork, either from private collections or museums and banks to those less fortunate?"

Brown stood and gazed out the window at the shimmering ocean. "Problem is, I don't really need anything, but I crave all the influence the G7 controls. As my father used to say, 'Power is everything. Without it, you're nothing.'" He laughed. "Once I have the power, I can do whatever I want."

Randall Krzak

His phone rang, interrupting his train of thought. He scowled and picked it up. "What?"

"Mister Brown, this is Jean-Luc. I wondered what you would like for dinner this evening and at what time?"

"Hmm." Brown tapped his fingers on the desk. "Mexican—not what you made last time. Even my dog wouldn't eat it. Order in—for 8 p.m. Make it for two—you will join me. Perhaps you can learn from the experience."

"But, sir, I have a late-night date with my fiancée."

"So? Cancel it. What's more important? Your private and personal life or taking care of my dietary needs?"

"But ... but ..."

"No excuses, Jean-Luc. If you're not in the dining room when the food arrives and I'm ready to eat, I suggest you pack your bags. You won't find another job in this city as a chef—I promise you." Brown hung up and sighed. "So hard to get good help."

He opened a drawer in his desk and pulled out an unlabeled bottle and a whiskey tumbler. He poured two fingers' worth of the golden liquid into the glass and brought it to his nose so he could savor the aroma. *My nephew is dead, and that fool wants to know what I want to eat. Suppose I should arrange a memorial for Samson—the least I can do for my sister.* He downed his whiskey in a single gulp.

# Chapter Two

Diablo Corps Secret Outpost
Near Prince Charles Mountains
Antarctica

A red, white, and blue de Havilland Canada DHC-6 Twin Otter aircraft hugged the ground as it flew over Antarctica before touching down on a makeshift runway near the Prince Charles Mountains. Plumes of snow and pulverized ice arched up and out from beneath the tires as the plane decelerated and continued toward a rocky promontory.

The pilot, Godfrey Fenton, compensated for a skid toward the rocks by steering into it and regaining traction. Hydraulic lifts raised a camouflaged door in the rocks, large enough to allow the plane to enter the hidden hangar.

Godfrey grinned. *Another perfect arrival. But I don't think Brown would have noticed or cared if he did.* Godfrey taxied inside and brought the aircraft to a gentle halt, the door beginning to close as soon as he cleared the entrance.

Once they stopped, a door opened, and a set of stairs extended. A short, mostly bald man rushed down. Liver spots covered his head and face. "Chris! Grab my bags and take them to my quarters."

"Yes, Mister Brown." Chris Handler, tall, slender, and sporting a thick, black beard, sprinted to Brown's side and handed him an over-stuffed legal-size envelope. "Here are your latest messages, sir."

Brown waved a hand. "Anything urgent?"

"No, sir. All routine. Everything is moving forward according to your plan."

"Excellent. Bring me a large cup of strong black coffee and a warm croissant."

"Right away, sir."

Brown turned and strode along a red all-weather carpet. As he walked, he glanced around the cavernous facility housing his hidden headquarters. Built in great secrecy near the Aramis Range in the Prince Charles Mountains at a cost exceeding five billion dollars, he considered it a masterpiece.

The original above-ground facility was constructed by the Russian Antarctic Expedition and nicknamed Soyuz Station and was officially closed in 1989. Brown's construction crew began two months later.

To ensure no one found out about his headquarters, building contractors lost their lives when one of his ocean-going vessels carrying them home after two years of work sank under mysterious circumstances during a storm, taking its cargo of innocent victims to their watery graves. Little did anyone know, it was explosives that sank the ship, planted by Brown's security team. Since it was assumed the storm caused the accident, when the vessel was refloated by a marine salvage company he owned, no one looked close enough to spot the areas where the explosives blew holes in the hull from the inside.

When he reached his office, Brown entered a five-digit code onto a keypad mounted by the door and gazed into a retinal scanner. He pressed his index finger onto another pad extended from the wall.

As soon as security protocols were completed, the door clicked open. Brown strode inside, tossing his Arcteryx Therma Parka onto a nearby coat rack. He slid into an ergonomically-designed chair behind a polished red oak desk and pushed a button under the lip of the top.

A panel opened on the left side of the desk, and a computer screen slowly rose and locked into position. He logged on as an inner door to the office opened.

Chris entered, pushing a cart holding a china coffee pot, a cup and saucer, a sugar bowl, and a covered plate. Each piece of the coffee service was trimmed in gold with a red D prominently displayed.

He placed the cup and saucer on a pull-out shelf on the left of Brown's desk and poured a black coffee. Using a pair of tongs, Chris deposited two sugar cubes into the steaming liquid. He uncovered the croissants, stepped back from the desk, and cracked his knuckles. "Will there be anything else, sir?"

Brown nodded. "Will you please stop cracking your knuckles? It sounds like you're breaking bones."

"Sorry, sir. Just a nervous habit."

"Well, once we launch our operation, go back to Miami and get that looked at without delay." *Drives me bonkers.*

"Yes, sir."

"I'll buzz if I need anything else. Dismissed." Brown sipped his coffee and turned to the computer screen.

Back in his own office, Chris eased into his chair, slamming a fist on the gray metal desk. Hired to handle Diablo's information technology and communications needs, he found himself working more and more as a personal lackey. *One day ... I'll make Brown pay for his callous behavior.*

Chris booted his computer and logged in. Staring at the ceiling, he tapped a finger against his lips. *Beware the Devil. Attack imminent.*

Focusing on a mental image of his message, he encoded it as he typed:

*To: Numerologist*
*From: Knuckle Cracker*
25220 42609 22071 92223 22051 81527 26070 72624 16221 41418 13221 30700

Chris read through it again, cracking his knuckles as he did so. Satisfied all was correct, he activated his Tor account, connected to the dark web, and sent his message.

He frowned. *Hope Matthew remembers our university code.*

A red strobe flashed.

Chris picked up the phone and hit the appropriate button. "Yes, Mister Brown?"

"I want an update from our test team. No one's answering the phone. Where are they?"

Chris closed his eyes. *The sooner I'm out of here, the better.* "I'll find out."

Brown broke the connection.

Chris hit another button on his console.

Reginald immediately answered. "What's up, Chris?"

"The usual. Why won't you answer when Brown calls?"

"You know why." Reginald sighed. "I told him it would be a few days before we can calve more ice. He doesn't want excuses—just results. I told him we had to wait for the arrival of a new demolitions expert since Samson disappeared—probably dead. All he could say was, 'It's damn inconvenient of Samson to kill himself.' So much for any concern about his nephew."

"I thought Samson's death was an accident."

"It was. At least, I think so. But as far as Brown's concerned, Samson was weak and couldn't handle the pressure."

"Okay, understood. But try to appease him and keep him off my back."

"Will do. We're almost finished drilling the holes for the explosives. I've told the others not to touch them or the explosives—no point in anyone else dying for this maniac. The money might be good, but I want to live to spend it."

"I agree with you, Reginald. Talk to you later."

\* \* \*

After snoozing on the sofa bed, Chris checked his computer. One new message:

To: *Knuckle Cracker*
 From: *Numerologist*
  15121 32007 18142 21312 19222 60900 04181 51520 22070 71922 07071 92204 12092 31206 07000

Chris translated the message in his head: *Long time no hear. Will get the word out.* He thrust a hand in the air. *Yes! He remembered! If only someone could stop Brown before it's too late.*

\* \* \*

Brown stormed through a door labeled *IT – Keep Out*. He stopped in front of the first desk. "Well?"

A young man with blond hair, thick glasses, and a scraggly beard jumped to his feet. "Mister Brown, w-we will be r-ready to conduct the first d-demonstration to shut down the electrical grid in Albany in a couple of hours."

"Excellent." Brown clapped his hands. "I want it shut down for ten minutes—enough to show what we can do—before I send out a warning of future shutdowns."

"B-But Mister Brown, a q-quick shutdown and r-restoration might c-cause damage."

"Who cares? It'll reinforce our demands when we make our presence known to the G7." Brown grinned. "Continue with your preparations. Hit the grid just after dark."

"Y-Yes, Mister Brown."

\* \* \*

Downtown Albany
New York

*Crash! Bang! Crunch!*

A packed Albany city bus smashed into a cement mixer as the lights flickered out and came back on green for every direction at the intersection. A delivery van added to the congestion, crashing into the side of the truck as it whipsawed from the impact.

Two police cars came to a stop near the partially overturned bus to protect the scene. While someone turned off the sirens, the overhead flashing lights remained on. Officers jumped out and dashed to the smoking vehicle.

Blood covered the cracked windshield. Screams and cries filtered out from the wrecked vehicle.

One of the officers knelt and peered inside. Ray pulled back and accessed his radio. "Dispatch, this is Metro 321, 10-33, possible fatalities. Expedite paramedics, and request CSI and supervisor. This involves a bus with multiple injuries."

"Metro, this is Dispatch. 10-4."

Lou glanced at his partner. "Looks like the driver's a goner—head crushed against the dash from the impact." He shook his head. "Wasn't wearing a seat belt."

"We need to get in there. I'll check the escape door at the back of the bus." Ray raced around the bus and tried the escape door.

It wouldn't budge.

He tried again with the same result and ran back to his partner. "Couldn't get in. Break the glass."

"Don't we have a glass breaker in the vehicle?"

Ray shook his head. "Didn't see one when I looked earlier." He looked around at the responding vehicles. "Fire department's not here yet either. They'll have a 'Jaws of Life.'"

Lou yanked his baton from the ring holding it on his duty belt. "We can't wait. There are kids inside." He whacked the glass several times before it gave way. "Hold on, kids—help's on the way."

Ray got back on the radio. "Dispatch, this is Metro 321. 10-33. Need Jaws of Life. Expedite the paramedics, too."

"Roger, Metro. Fire department and paramedics en route to your location."

Sirens eclipsed the cacophony produced by the arrival of multiple fire engines, ambulances, and police cars. A fire chief directed her men to hose down the vehicles' engines with foam to prevent any explosions.

Lou forced his way into the bus, crawling across a pile of bloodied and scattered schoolbooks and backpacks. He pushed on one of the emergency exit windows, managing to shove it far enough for the paramedics to gain access. He shouted, "In here." He turned and continued working his way along the aisle.

Two paramedics followed him. "We'll take care of the kids, Officer."

"Of course. Let's get moving." Ray remained stoic, demonstrating his professionalism. "I have kids at the same school. I don't see them—I hope they were on a different bus."

The paramedic, who happened to live next to Ray in the New Scotland area of Albany, clasped Ray's shoulder and pointed to his radio. "Additional first responders are heading to multiple crash sites. If their bus became involved in a collision, they'd be taken care of by my colleagues." He gave Ray a weak smile. "I better start working on the injured." The paramedic turned and knelt by the first motionless body. He checked for a pulse and shook his head before moving to the next child.

As the fire department and the paramedics performed their duties, the police kept onlookers at bay under the guidance of a supervisor. Eventually, things settled down as the injured and dead were whisked away in ambulances. Wreckers moved in and connected to the damaged vehicles.

Ray accessed his radio again. "Dispatch, this is Metro 321. Code Four." After informing Dispatch everything was stable at the scene, he headed back to his car to proceed to the hospital.

As he climbed into the vehicle, Lou joined him. "Just spoke to another officer who was on the bus call. He said everyone from Bus 547 was fine."

Ray closed his eyes and breathed a sigh of relief. "Thank God."

Barflies stared wide-eyed at the TV as they gripped their beer glasses. One finished his drink with a single swallow.

Someone handed the anchor a message, who read it before finding the active camera.

"In other news, local Albany hospitals have been overwhelmed by multiple accident victims caused during a total power outage in the downtown area. Over twenty-five men, women, and children died, while another sixty are being treated for injuries ranging from minor to life-threatening. The cause of the outage is still under investigation. We'll bring you more as soon as we find out."

The New York announcer stared into the camera, his lips pursed. "Such a tragedy."

# Chapter Three

B oard of Governors, Federal Reserve
Washington, D.C.

Ted Nicholson, chair of the U.S. Federal Reserve, studied a communique he had just received and shook his head. *What the hell? Is this someone's idea of a sick joke?* He picked up a phone and punched in a speed dial number. "Hey, Bruce. Did you just receive a strange warning?"

"Yeah ... but ... Sorry, I had a mouth full of apple—just eating my lunch." Bruce McDermott, governor of the Bank of England, cleared his throat. "Was going to ring you. What nutter dreamed this up?"

"I don't know, but telling the world's central banks to do as they say in respect to their climate change demands, or we'll be remorseful, doesn't come across as a serious threat. What would attacking the LME do?"

Bruce laughed. "I haven't the foggiest. The London Metal Exchange is better protected than your Fort Knox. Only a complete idiot would threaten the LME. Still, it's probably wise to notify a threat assessment team about this on the off chance it's genuine, and there's an unknown vulnerability that could cause future issues."

"Whatever they want—"

Warning alarms and shouting echoed through Ted's handset. "What the hell is going on?"

"You won't believe it—the LME just started shutting down their entire enterprise. I had a monitor tuned to activity on the floor. When I spotted people running around more than normal, I turned up the sound. Let me turn it off and see what I can find out."

"Can you tell what's happening?"

"No, not well. It's almost pitch black on the floor—mainly emergency lighting. None of the traders can do anything—their computers shut down. Even the backup power didn't come on. I'm sure every system crashed unless the UPC backups worked long enough to take the network offline."

"Hmm." Ted picked up the communique. "The warning did say darkness would descend. So what? The emergency generators should be kicking in now. As soon as the power's restored, the computers will be rebooted, and it'll be business as usual."

"I think that's the whole point, Ted. They, whoever they are, said it would be a warning of what's to come if we don't adhere to their demands. Wait a minute—looks like the LME's coming back to life."

"Excellent. So, Bruce. Should we pay attention to these crackpots? Obviously, they have a superb hacker or two in place."

"Well, Ted, we can always ignore the warning and see what happens. After all, they can't take on all of the G7 countries at the same time, can they?"

"I don't know." Ted rubbed a finger over his pencil-like mustache. "I just don't know."

\* \* \*

At the close of the European bourses, everything flatlined on the CAC40, FTSE100, and the DAX. Traders shouted as they anticipated the loss of hundreds of millions in various currencies and were powerless to do anything about it.

Less than two minutes later, everything returned to normal —almost.

Tuned to CNBC, Ted listened to a newscaster give an underwhelming description of what had happened and shook his head. *Not sure what's going on, but that guy doesn't have a clue.* His eyes bulged as a statement scrolled across his computer screen:

*You Have Been Warned.*

\* \* \*

Diablo Corps Secret Outpost
    Near Prince Charles Mountains

Emmanuel Durand, one of Brown's hackers, restored the European bourses to their pre-interference positions. He glanced at his counterparts and sighed. *Am I the only one who thinks Brown's plans go too far? Will they encourage others to do what is needed for climate change, or will they balk? If they do, what will Brown have us do next?*

He shook his head and continued typing as he prepared for the next phase in Brown's plans.

\* \* \*

Brown studied the results of his initial salvo. *Excellent. We'll start small and rattle their economic cages.* He gazed at the climate change map on one of the screens providing a localized picture of future global impacts and laughed.

"A perfect smokescreen. I don't care all that much about the climate, but it grabs their attention. If the experts are correct, I'll be

17

dead before an irreversible catastrophe occurs. But it won't hurt to use this as a diversion while I acquire what I want—more power." He leaned over and rubbed a statue of Kratos, the Greek god of power.

He hit an intercom button.

"Yes, Mister Brown?" Chris asked.

"Bring me another pot of tea. I want fresh croissants, too. Tell the chef what he sent last time tasted stale. Don't I pay him enough to do my simple bidding? Tell him if he screws up this time, he'll end up in the ocean."

"Yes, sir."

\* \* \*

Chris placed Brown's order, not bothering to pass along the threat. He frowned. *The old bastard's getting more deranged by the day.* He began typing another email.

To: Numerologist
    From: Knuckle Cracker

08261 42208 12060 92422 24260 60822 23071 22326 02080 80712 24161 42609 16220 71813 07220 90906 11071 81213 08271 10922 11260 92221 12091 41209 22071 22412 14222 70000

*I hope Matthew understands the seriousness of the situation and informs someone who can intervene. Otherwise, Brown might destroy the world's technology and major economies in his mad quest for power.*

\* \* \*

Jean-Luc knocked on Brown's door.

After a terse command, Jean-Luc entered, pushing a cart in front of him. "M-Mister B-Brown. I-I made new c-croissants." He frowned as he stared at his boss. *His liver spots are getting worse. So are the bags beneath his eyes.*

"Hope they're better than the last ones—they were terrible."

"Yes, Mister Brown." Jean-Luc avoided eye contact. *Too bad I didn't have any rat poison. Instead of just spitting in the batter, I'd add a small portion to his food every day—he'd never find out until it was too late.*

"Get out. I want beef stew tonight—and fresh biscuits—so get to work."

"Y-Yes, sir."

* * *

Brown's phone rang. *Another interruption. Don't these people realize I'm busy?* He picked up. "Yes, what is it?"

Sawyer Johnson, head of Brown's security team, chuckled. "Sorry to bother you, Mister Brown, but you wanted to be notified when the new demolitions expert arrived."

"Show him to my office in thirty minutes." Brown glanced at the clock. "No, make it an hour."

"Uh ... sir, he's a she. I mean, the bomb expert is a woman."

"So? I still want to meet her."

"Yes, sir."

An hour later, Sawyer knocked on Brown's door.

"Come in."

Sawyer and a petite brunette with large brown eyes and shoulder-length hair stepped into Brown's office. "Sir, this is Madeleine Fingerhut."

She brushed the hair from her face and gave Brown a half-smile.

He remained seated, reached over his desk, and shook hands with the young woman. He gestured toward a visitor's chair. "Please be seated, Madeline."

Sawyer closed the door and leaned against it, crossing his arms.

She took the seat. "Please, call me Maddie." A timid smile creased her face.

Brown nodded. "Is this your first visit to Antarctica, Madeleine—I mean, Maddie?"

"Yes. I find it hauntingly beautiful."

"I remember thinking something similar when I first came here. Just remember when you're outside, Antarctica is very dangerous, especially on the ice."

"Yes, sir." She smiled. "I'm looking forward to working here. If I may ask, what happened to your previous explosives expert? I understand his departure was rather abrupt."

A thin smile creased Brown's face. "I guess you could call it an abrupt departure—he blew himself up."

"Oh!" Maddie's right hand covered her mouth. "I'm so sorry."

Brown shrugged. "What are you sorry for? Did you know Samson?"

"Oh ... well ... no." Her face reddened. "That's what people say at unexpected news."

"Hmm." Brown picked up a folder from his desk and extracted two sheets of paper. "You have a very interesting resume, working in various exotic places around the world."

"Yes, sir. For the past six years, I've spent most of my time outside the U.S."

"I see." Brown rubbed his chin. "Any boyfriends, a husband, or significant other? Who's your next of kin?"

Maddie shook her head. "No, sir. Why do you ask?"

"Never mind—not important." He waved a hand. "Just wondered who we should notify if something should happen to you."

Maddie gulped. "I-I shall take all necessary precautions when I'm working."

"It's not just the ice that's dangerous." Brown stared at her.

"Danger comes in many forms." He stood and extended a hand. "Welcome to Antarctica. Do a professional job, and we shall get along just fine." He turned to Sawyer. "Escort her around the premises and show her to her quarters."

"Yes, Mister Brown." Sawyer opened the door to allow Maddie to leave first.

"One more thing, Maddie."

She stood. "Yes, Mister Brown?"

"Sawyer will point out areas that are off-limits to all but a select few employees. These areas are marked with skull and crossbones signs. For your own safety, never venture inside one of them unless you are summoned. If you require entrance, Sawyer will escort you." He studied her. "It could be very devastating—for you."

As they walked along the corridor, Maddie turned to Sawyer. "What did Mister Brown mean by his last comment?"

Sawyer shrugged. "Brown likes melodrama. However, in this case, I must second his warnings. Several people have disappeared—never to be seen again."

# Chapter Four

R amstein Air Base
        Rhineland-Palatinate, Germany

Streams of condensation whipped off the wings of the C-37A Gulfstream as it aimed for the small ribbon of tarmac where it was destined to land on runway 08/26 at Ramstein Air Base just after dawn. The 'thunk' of the landing gears locking into place ensured a safe, if not bouncy, stop before it rolled into a hangar reserved for executive aircraft. The pilot silenced the engine while his copilot unlocked and extended the stairs. Out of view of any onlookers, three occupants descended.

Two men dressed in Air Force fatigues sans rank and nametags approached.

One of them extended his hand to a woman with spiky blonde hair. "Welcome to Germany."

Evelyn took the proffered hand and smiled. "I'm Skylark. You must be Condor." She turned to the other man. "I assume you're Offender?"

"Yes, ma'am."

CC and Trevor stepped forward and shook hands with both men.

"Haggis, I knew you guys were special when we met in Peshawar. It wasn't until the chairman of the Joint Chiefs of Staff called and offered me a job did I realize how connected you were." Condor gestured toward Offender. "We were both speechless."

CC chuckled. "Aye. The admiral told me. He thought the call had dropped out because of the silence. Glad you both decided to join us."

Everyone laughed.

"C'mon, let's get you to the house." Condor gestured toward the exit. "It's out the west gate in Ramstein-Miesenbach on the road to K-Town. Offender will collect your luggage and join us later."

The foursome climbed into an Air Force vehicle and headed toward the west gate. Twenty minutes later, Condor pulled onto a side street lined with well-manicured lawns and single-story houses. He parked in front of a red brick double-fronted house with black asphalt roof tiles and white window trim. They descended and walked up the path to the front door.

Condor pulled a set of keys from his pocket, unlocked the door, and headed into the kitchen.

He returned and passed out cold beers to everyone now seated in the living room. "I don't know how to thank you for this opportunity. The pay might be less, but the opportunities are worth it."

CC smiled. "Aye. Glad you're on board with us. First things first. We can't keep using our callsigns. People might become suspicious. I'm Craig Cameron, although I prefer being called CC. I'm a former Army colonel who was also offered a job I couldn't refuse."

"Like CC, I was also offered a fantastic opportunity. I'm Colonel Trevor Franklin, and I retired a few years ago from the Paras." He raised a hand in greeting.

"And I'm Evelyn Evinrude, formerly of MI-6. So, we've revealed who we are. We know you're both former SEALs, but what do we call you?"

Condor glanced at the floor. He whispered, "Rufus T. Chopin."

"Aye. Nothing to be ashamed of—Rufus." CC struggled to smother a grin. He turned to Offender. "What about you?"

Offender stared straight into CC's face. "August Lewis. I was born in August, and my folks thought that was a good enough name. But they should have named me March because I became a soldier."

CC laughed. "Och, aye."

"Do you have any siblings?" Evelyn smiled. "Was there a name trend?"

"Yes, ma'am. Three sisters—April, May, and June. If I had a brother, I'm not sure what my parents would've called him."

"What about you—Rufus? Any siblings?"

"Yes. Two brothers—Jasper and Festus."

"Aye. Now that the secrets are out, I want to thank you for inviting us to participate in your selections. It's not easy picking a team."

"Got that right. We could have used Zoom to do this, but I thought it would be better in person, plus you could see our new digs." Rufus tilted his beer and finished it in a single go. "We received ten applications. While I think I'm an excellent judge of character, I don't know enough about Bedlam yet to make intelligent choices." He stood. "Anyone want a refill?"

Evelyn and Trevor shook their head.

"Aye. One more for me." CC tipped his bottle and drained the dregs.

Rufus came back with three beers. He handed one to CC, another to August, and kept the third for himself.

"Once we finish, shall we check out the warehouse the installation commander authorized for our use?" Rufus took a swig of his beer. "Afterward, we'll grab a bite to eat at one of the base's dining facilities."

Twenty-five minutes later, Rufus drove past a row of warehouses, stopping at the last one. The sign in front, usually used to identify the organization, was blank.

He pointed to the sign. "Any problem putting QRF on it? Lots of buildings on the base are identified by initials."

"Aye. Great idea. Putting quick reaction force on the sign should help quell any rumors rather than having people trying to guess who's inside."

They climbed out of the AF vehicle and headed to a pedestrian door. After Rufus unlocked it, he stepped inside and flicked a light switch. "Welcome to QRF." He smiled as he swung an arm to encompass the interior of the building.

Trevor wrinkled his nose. "Needs a bit of housekeeping, don't you think?" He studied the space, which was open to the roof, although part of it was subdivided into smaller cubicles. Boxes of equipment, books, and personal items littered the floor along the walls and covered the sole table.

"Yeah." Rufus chuckled. "I told August since he was number two, the cleanup fell to him."

"As soon as he said that, I volunteered to quit." August smirked. "The base is sending out some contract cleaners in the morning. In the afternoon, housing will deliver sofas, chairs, and other things we'll need."

CC nodded. "Aye. We brought a few items—computers and the comms gear you'll need to stay in contact with Bedlam. You'll need to understand a few things to make everything work, but we'll go over them before we leave."

"Sounds good." Rufus rolled his eyes. "Just what I need—more technology to learn. Why can't things be kept simple, or is it time for me to get a brain upgrade?"

Everyone laughed.

\* \* \*

After a quick meal, they returned to the off-base house and gathered again in the living room. This time, August retrieved fresh drinks from the kitchen.

Rufus unlocked a cabinet, pulled out his laptop, and booted it. While they waited, he turned to the others. "I placed all the applications on here. Eight are prior military, while the other two are FBI agents looking for a career change."

"Aye." CC sipped his dark German beer. "We'll give you our opinions, but in the end, the choice is yours."

Rufus nodded. "Admiral Blakely said we should pick four people for now, giving us a decent QRF staff as we could split into two three-person teams if necessary, although I think a total of eight would be better."

Trevor glanced at CC. "Fully agree with you. However, in our recent team build, the admiral indicated changes would need to wait for additional funding."

"Aye. If everything works out, we'll get the necessary financing in the next budget."

"I recommend picking four people you want right away." Evelyn sipped her white wine. "Choose two others as alternates—they can be added to the team when the budget is sorted." She smiled. "Of course, it depends on how many meet the threshold for being offered positions."

"Makes sense." Rufus clicked on the first file and opened it. "I've blocked the names and photos in case any of us know the applicants and might show inadvertent bias. For now, they'll be known as number one through ten."

"Aye. Excellent idea." CC scooted forward.

* * *

Over the next three hours, the five Bedlam personnel reviewed the files. Two were rejected outright due to a lack of operational experience. While well-trained, they were desk jockeys and had never served in a high-tension environment.

The Bedlam operatives took a short restroom break and replaced their empty drinks.

Rufus led them outside for a breath of fresh air.

"Will you keep this place when you've assembled your teams?" Evelyn glanced at the other houses on the street.

Rufus nodded and pointed to two properties, both larger than their current abode. "Yes. Those houses over there are available and each has three bedrooms. Each member would have their own bedroom but will share the common areas. Meanwhile, August and I will stay here. It's only two bedrooms but plenty of space for us." He yawned. "Shall we get back to it?"

Everyone agreed, and they returned inside.

After an additional two hours, they reached a decision: one, three, four, six, eight, and nine.

"Shall we uncover their names and faces to see if we know any of them?" Rufus unblocked the hidden information and stepped through the six applicants.

"Wait." CC raised a hand. "Number nine—I recognize his photo and name. In my opinion, you don't want him."

"Any valid reason? He seems very qualified." Rufus frowned.

"Aye. He's qualified on paper, but his emotional IQ is the problem. He's smart but resents authority from those he considers junior to his abilities. In Afghanistan, he killed an Afghan captain after a disagreement. Charges were never filed—I think the rest of his team didn't want to deal with any repercussions as they could end up like the captain."

CC gazed into each of their faces. "He also tried to kill an American army colonel looking into the Afghan captain's death—me."

# Chapter Five

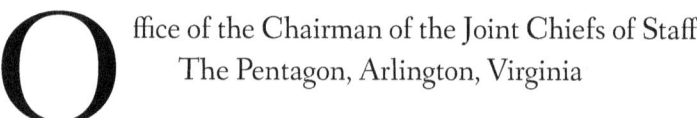

Office of the Chairman of the Joint Chiefs of Staff
The Pentagon, Arlington, Virginia

Leaning back and swiveling in his chair, Admiral Blakely hit a button on the telephone console. "Please send Matthew in."

Moments later, someone rapped on the admiral's door.

"Come in."

Matthew entered, a folder tucked under one arm and holding a Starbucks cup holder with two coffees in the other. "Ready for a refill, Admiral?"

The admiral grinned as he took one of the cups. "Did you install a camera in my office, Matthew? You always seem to know when I'm ready for a fresh coffee."

"I just figure when I'm ready, you will be too." Matthew smiled.

"Did you read the warning the Fed shared with the Intel Community?"

Matthew nodded. "I admire whoever was behind it. Although they targeted several bourses, no one lost a penny."

"In the world you live in, you'd probably admire the culprits." The admiral chuckled as he pried the plastic cover off his coffee and sipped. "Anyway, what do you think?"

"These are world-class hackers—no doubt about it." Matthew set his unopened coffee on a coaster placed on an end table and opened the folder he had brought with him. "I don't think they'll have any problem carrying out their threats—their warnings should be heeded. Did they provide any specific demands?"

The admiral shook his head. "No. I'm attending a meeting later at the White House regarding this warning. I'll give them your brief assessment."

"There's something else, Admiral. When I attended MIT, my roommate and I used a simple number substitution code to keep our text messages secret from any prying eyes. We would arrange where to meet, who was dating who, and things like that." Matthew removed a sheet of paper from the folder and handed it to the admiral.

"Aware of your love for numbers, I know you're Numerologist. Who's Knuckle Cracker?"

"He was my roommate. He sent this message last night."

"I assume you can still decipher this?"

Matthew nodded. "Yes, Admiral. His message reads, *Beware the Devil. Attack imminent*. I sent a response saying I'd get the word out." Matthew's face reddened. "Perhaps I should have waited to tell you first before acknowledging it."

"Not to worry." The admiral waved a hand. "Any idea what he's warning us about?"

Matthew shook his head. "Not yet. He sent it to me anonymously. I suspect he's trying to avoid detection."

"What's his name? Do you know where the hell he is?"

"His name is Chris—Chris Handler. He had a bad habit of cracking his knuckles whenever he was nervous, and in the past, he'd been known to hang around the wrong people and some of them terrified me. We kept in contact for a long time after we left MIT, but this is the first I've heard from him in a couple of years."

Matthew pulled a second sheet of paper from his folder. "Here's another one—he sent this yesterday a few hours after the first one."

The admiral shook his head after reading the decrypted message.

*Same source caused today's stock market interruptions. Prepare for more to come.*

"Still no mention of who's behind these attacks. Nor does Chris give his location."

"He did repeat his earlier reference to the Devil. I'm going to do some research, to include message boards and chat rooms, to see if anything pops up that we can use."

"Excellent idea." The admiral pursed his lips. "Could you send your friend a message and ask for specifics about who is behind this? Although I doubt he'll provide this information. Perhaps if we offered him protection? Tell him we'll try to help."

Matthew shook his head. "Since he's gone to great lengths to keep his communications vague and coded, he won't reveal the identities— at least in this method. I'll give it some thought to see if there's another way to get him to be more forthcoming."

"Yes, do more research and see if you can persuade Mr. Handler to meet you or contact you on a secure line so he can be more specific. We can't do anything with the information he's given us so far." The admiral glanced at the clock. "I better head to the White House. We'll talk again when I return."

"Yes, Admiral." Matthew picked up his coffee and followed the admiral out the door, turning toward his office.

\* \* \*

The Situation Room
   The White House

The security specialist manning the gateway to the White House returned Admiral Blakely's ID with a smile and snapped a salute to indicate he was cleared. Afterward, a secret service agent escorted him to the situation room.

The admiral took his customary seat next to Jonathan Meu, the national security adviser. "Anything new today, Jonny?"

"About the cryptic warning?" Jonny shook his head. "I was hoping you'd have some intel we could use from your Bedlam team."

"I might have something—"

Everyone stood as the president of the United States entered the room and took his seat at the head of the table. He cleared his throat. "Okay, who has something on this culprit taking down the European markets?" He glanced around the table. "CIA? FBI? State? Treasury? Pentagon?"

The NSA and the other representatives shook their heads.

Hortense Stonemason, the treasury secretary, half-raised a hand. "M-Mister P-President?"

The president chuckled. "Go ahead, Hortense. I don't bite."

"Not what I've heard." Longtime colleague and current labor secretary Hampton Merriweather laughed.

"Y-yes, M-Mister P-President. I-I spoke to m-my colleagues in E-England, G-Germany, and F-France. They are clueless about the a-attacks. As far as they can t-tell, everything was restored, and none of their c-customers lost a p-penny."

"Well, that's something." The president turned to Admiral Blakely. "Richard, anything from—" He glanced at Hortense. "From your, uh, special group?"

"We might have something, Mister President, but it's too early to tell. Do you recall the young man I introduced to you last year in the Rose Garden? I called him Grandson."

"Wasn't he the numbers guy from MIT? My daughter thought he was cute."

"Yes, that's the one, Mister President. I won't bore you with all the details, but it seems Grandson received a cryptic warning last week from his former roommate. He didn't think anything about it at the time, but in the message, there was a warning to 'Beware the Devil.' Grandson's going to run this down if he can."

"Anything else?"

The admiral shook his head. "Not at this time, Mister President. If anything further materializes, I'll inform Jonny straight away."

The president nodded and stood. "Well, everyone, shake the trees and see what falls out. We need to get on top of this before something more serious happens."

* * *

When Admiral Blakely returned to his office, he found Matthew waiting.

Matthew jumped to his feet.

The admiral waved him back to his seat. "Nothing from the White House meeting—just as I expected. Tell me you have some good news?"

"Nothing yet except for the good weather." Matthew smiled as he shook his head. "I sent Chris a message, but not sure when I'll hear back. I googled 'Beware the Devil.' There were over one hundred eighty million hits. I'll build some algorithms to whittle things down."

The admiral nodded. "I better notify the teams. Maybe someone has a contact they can reach out to and get more useful intel."

After Matthew departed, the admiral turned to his computer and began his normal index finger typing.

To: *Alpha, Bravo, Charlie, QRF-1*
   From: *Bedlam*

*Reach out to your contacts regarding strange events at the UK, French, and German bourses. Someone is attacking them and exhibits world-class hacking skills. This might be sponsored by one of the unfriendly countries, but no proof thus far. No specific demands yet, but we've been warned.*

After he sent his message, the admiral leaned back in his chair and stared at the acoustic tiles covering the ceiling. *What now? Whoever is behind this wants something big. I can feel it.*

# Chapter Six

D iablo Corps Secret Outpost
       Near Prince Charles Mountains

Brown marched into the cleanroom used by his team of hackers, slamming the door behind him. He glanced around the room, which was supposed to be kept as clean as possible to protect the electrical equipment from pollutants such as dust and aerosol particles.

Discarded snack wrappers, empty water bottles, and dirty cups littered most surfaces. Wrinkling his nose at an offensive odor emanating from a cigarette smoldering in an ashtray full of butts, he coughed. *So much for needing a controlled environment to work in. Looks more like a war room in the movies.*

Brown stomped to Emmanuel's desk and threw a newspaper at him. "What's this?"

Emmanuel lips moved as he read the news article. "Mister Brown, you said create a warning by shutting down the bourses. We did that."

"No, you didn't. You only shut down three, and I wanted more. What about Canada, the U.S., Italy, and Japan? They're all part of the G7 too."

"I was waiting for your approval to hit them next."

"This time, do it an hour before they close and make it last thirty minutes. Hit France, Germany, and the UK again as well."

"Yes, Mister Brown. Anything else?" A sneer crept across Emmanuel's face. "We're doing as you instructed."

"Don't get uppity with me. I'm working on another idea. Next, I want you to hit the G7 currencies. Buy and sell massive amounts and dump them on the markets. Push them hard, so the value of gold rises."

Emmanuel swallowed. "Yes, Mister Brown."

"Well, don't just sit there—get to work. You have your orders—I'll let you know when I'm ready for something else. And clean this place up." He glanced around the room with disdain etched on his face. "It's a pigsty." Brown turned on his heels and marched back to his office.

Emmanuel glared at the retreating Brown. *I need to keep that door locked so he can't barge in whenever he wants.*

\* \* \*

Maddie climbed into the passenger seat of the Sno-Cat next to Reginald. "With all these clothes, I now know what the Michelin Man feels like."

"Better to wear multiple layers that you can easily remove if you're getting too warm." He smiled. "Ready for your first sojourn onto the ice?"

"Why are we breaking off chunks of the ice sheet?" She studied the stark and rugged beauty in front of them. "It doesn't make any sense to me."

Reginald shrugged. "We do it because we're following Mister Brown's orders. He's a brilliant man and knows what he's doing."

"But when the ice melts, won't it raise sea levels? We should want more ice in Antarctica, not less."

"This is part of Mister Brown's master plan to promote the necessity for the world to make vital changes to stop the planet from overheating."

*Seems nuts to me.* Maddie shook her head. "I have my doubts about this."

Reginald glanced at her. "I suggest keeping your thoughts to yourself. Mister Brown's nephew voiced similar opinions—look what happened to him."

"What really happened to Samson?"

Reginald stopped the Sno-Cat and pointed to the right. "See that ridgeline? Samson set up the charges to calve a huge section. He was always thorough and didn't make mistakes. However, on the day he died, I spotted Sawyer Johnson, the head of security, lurking on the ice." He shrugged. "I don't know for sure, but Sawyer doesn't come out on the ice often. So, a word to the wise—be careful who you choose to share your thoughts with. Otherwise, you could end up in big trouble like Samson." Reginald shifted gears, and the Sno-Cat lurched forward.

Maddie raised her voice over the engine noise. "Why did you come to Antarctica? What was the big draw?"

"At first, it was the excitement of working in Antarctica. Of course, the money was twice what I would earn anywhere else in the world." He smiled. "I have a girl back home in Chicago. One day, I hope to save enough money and ask her to marry me. How about you?"

"Similar reasons. I've worked in all the corners of the world and many places in-between. When the opportunity to work in Antarctica came up, I leaped at it. I hope I haven't made a mistake." *Should I be saying this to Reginald? He might report me.* "But I don't have anyone waiting back home for me." She smiled.

Reginald chuckled. "Keep your nose clean and do as you're told, and you'll get along just fine." He tapped a mittened hand on her knee. "If you ever have any questions or concerns, bring them to me. I'll steer you clear of trouble—if I can."

Maddie smiled again. "Thank you, Reginald."

Twenty-five minutes later, they traversed a rise and down the other side. In front of them, a string of red flags—fifty yards apart—disappeared in the distance.

Reginald pointed to the flags and then the open sea. "This is the next section Mister Brown wants seeded and dropped into the sea."

"Who placed the markers?"

"I did—yesterday. There are one hundred of them. I'll begin drilling the holes. Each will be four feet deep. You can start placing your explosives and stringing them together once I dig a few holes."

Maddie raised a hand to shield her eyes from the intense sunlight as she strode toward the string of flags. "Okay, Reginald. It'll be the largest explosion I've ever done and never before in sub-zero temperatures."

"Not to worry." He smiled. "You'll be fine."

"When will we set the explosives off?"

"Not until after lunch. With what happened to Samson, I don't want to be anywhere near here when you detonate them." He gestured to the cargo area of the Sno-Cat. "We better get started."

Reginald and Maddie worked in silence as they unloaded their gear and the explosives they would need. Before long, the peaceful-ness of the ice sheet became lost under the noise of Reginald's diesel-powered generator driving his borehole digger.

Maddie placed an explosive package near each of the first ten flags. As she worked her way back to Reginald, she stopped and studied the ridge. *What was that flash?*

She spotted a dark shadow as it moved over the ridgeline and disappeared. She turned toward Reginald and waved her hands for him to stop drilling.

He cut the power to his drill, and the peacefulness resumed. "What's up, Maddie? Forget to bring something?"

She gestured toward the ridgeline. "No. I saw something flash off the top of the ridge. What would the sunlight catch out here?"

"Hmm." Reginald scanned the ice. "Are you sure your eyes weren't playing tricks on you?"

Maddie shook her head. "No, I'm positive about what I saw. I think I spotted someone walking across the top of the ridge and disappear. Who could it be?"

"I'm not sure, but we'll keep our eyes peeled for another visit. It might be one of Johnson's security teams checking up on us." Reginald pursed his lips. "The question is why?"

Sawyer slid down the escarpment toward his Sno-Cat. After climbing inside, he started the engine and reversed course back to the camp. *Mister Brown will be pleased with the latest calving, I think. Too bad if we lose Maddie—she seems like a kindred spirit. Still, I have my orders—Reginald must go.*

United Nations Security Council
    760 United Nations Plaza, Manhattan
    New York, New York

The UN Security Council convened after an emergency request by the UK and France. Although Germany was not a permanent council member, they were included in the request.

The monthly revolving presidency belonged to the United States. Sylvia Green, the U.S. representative to the UN, banged the gavel. "The chair recognizes the UK ambassador."

Bethany Williams smiled. "Thank you, Madame President. I will be speaking on behalf of my French and German colleagues." She sipped from a glass of water on the table in front of her. "Madame President, we are concerned that the unprecedented attacks on our bourses must be investigated. All countries with a stock market should be warned about the possibility of future attacks. We request the security council issue an appeal for any and all impacted countries, or those who might be targeted, to work together to identify the culprit or culprits behind these episodes."

She nodded, signaling the end of her brief speech.

Sylvia glanced around the chamber. "Any other speakers?"

In a rare show of unity, no one challenged Bethany's summary.

Sylvia banged her gavel. "The proposal is hereby passed and will be disseminated. We will reconvene at next week's regularly scheduled meeting. During the session, we'll discuss which UN agencies will conduct the investigation."

* * *

Treasury Building
  1500 Pennsylvania Avenue, NW
  Washington, D.C.

Hortense Stonemason sat at the rectangular table in the conference room near her corner office at the Treasury building on Pennsylvania Avenue. She reviewed a document in front of her as she waited for a technician to complete the arrangements for her virtual meeting with the other G7 members.

"All set, Madame Secretary." The technician gestured to the screen showing the muted and frozen photos of her counterparts before handing her a remote. "All you need to do is hit the unmute all button, and you'll be live with them."

She smiled. "T-Thank you." Hortense cleared her throat as she hit the button and gave a half-wave at the screen. "T-Thank you for joining me t-today. As you are a-aware, we are under a-attack."

"Yes, Hortense." The Japanese finance minister wiped a hand through his thinning black hair. "What do you propose?"

"I-I'm not sure. Somehow, we must increase the security of our markets and work together to ensure w-whoever is behind these ww-arnings and a-attacks is brought to justice."

"How do you propose to do this?" The Italian finance minister chuckled. "Even our intelligence services can't identify who is responsible."

"Gentlemen and lady, if I may." The French finance minister smirked, showing his pearly whites. "I believe a Russian hacker group, the Chinese, or the North Koreans, are behind this."

"But what do t-they w-want?"

"A greater hold over the rest of us," the UK finance minister said. "I think the G7 leaders should issue a statement to whoever is responsible to go ahead and shut down the stock markets if they want. It'll hurt them just as much."

"I-I hope we can—"

The screen blanked out.

* * *

Diablo Corps Secret Outpost
Near Prince Charles Mountains

Chris checked his dark web account for any new emails. There was one—from Numerologist. He opened it and studied the request. *Hmm. Can't tell him more about Diablo or where we're located in case Johnson finds out what I'm doing.*

He typed up a new message:

. . .

40

24261 31312 07092 20526 15141 22227 15182 11813 23161 32022 09272 52204 26092 22613 12071 92209 26070 72624 16081 21213 27000

Chris leaned back as he hit send. *This should get Matthew pointed in the right direction.*

# Chapter Seven

QRF Facilities
Ramstein Air Base
Rhineland-Palatinate, Germany

CC and the others lounged in QRF-1's new premises. Scattered sofas, chairs, and a variety of tables borrowed from base housing filled the break area. A large screen TV was suspended from the ceiling above a handcrafted teak bar surrounded by six stools. A fridge sat at both ends of the bar. One held beer and white wine, while the other was stocked with soft drinks, fruit juices, and water bottles. An old-fashioned jukebox leaned against one wall, ready to be used by the new inhabitants.

CC sniffed. "What's that smell?"

Rufus chuckled. "Pine-Sol. We had to fumigate the place and give it a good clean when we moved in."

"Hope it dissipates." CC wrinkled his nose.

"It will, given time." Rufus glanced at the TV, currently showing a welcome message from Admiral Blakely. "QRF-1 doesn't have a network—yet. I hope we can establish one in the future."

"Aye." CC drank from a bottle of orange juice. "The admiral will always include QRF-1 on anything he sends to the teams, so you'll be aware of our tasking."

"Do you need to respond to him?"

"No. He knows we're with you, and our seconds-in-command will pass the word."

Rufus nodded. "I see. So our orders will come out the same way, and you, Trevor, and Evelyn will see them?"

"Aye. Keeps everyone in the loop." CC frowned. "Of course, we don't know what will happen toward the end of the year when the admiral's stint as chairman runs out. We're hoping for one of two outcomes: the president extends the admiral's role as chairman, which requires congressional approval, or he becomes the deputy National Security Advisor and retains control of the teams. This will also require approval from Congress but might be easier."

"Which one do you favor?"

"I think his appointment as the Deputy NSA would be best, at least for us." CC interlocked his fingers and tapped them on his chin. "However, the president won't be asking for my opinion." He sighed. "As front-line operatives, we'll adjust to whatever changes come our way. After the next election, things might be better as long as the teams stay together."

Rufus glanced at a smiley face clock above the bar. "Time to head to the terminal and pick up our new team members. Care to accompany me?"

"Aye."

Fifteen minutes later, they climbed out of the van in a parking spot designated for VIP vehicles and stood waiting for the C-37A aircraft to come to a halt. As soon as the steps descended and locked into place, three men and a woman disembarked and stood on the tarmac.

Rufus raised a hand, and the four headed toward him.

The first two stopped in front of Rufus. Well over six feet, bald, with bulging biceps, they looked as if they were carved from the same mold.

The one on the left extended a massive paw. "I'm Maverick Kingfisher. You must be Condor."

"Call me Rufus." He introduced CC.

Maverick grabbed CC's hand and squeezed.

He smiled as he gritted his teeth to keep from yelping at the brutal grip. After pulling his hand back, CC tried not to wince.

The second man stepped forward. "I'm Quincy Kingfisher. Maverick and I are cousins."

The third man, short when standing next to Quincy and Maverick but the same height as CC, grinned as he introduced himself. "Many thanks for this opportunity. I'm Gordon Russell. I won't let you down."

The woman, a tall African-American with close-cropped hair and a scar on the left side of her chin, joined the others. "I'm Alexandria Steele, but I prefer to be called Alex."

After a round of handshakes, Rufus gestured to the vehicle behind him. "Let's store your gear, and we'll head to our headquarters."

When they arrived at the warehouse, August, Trevor, and Evelyn came out of the building and met them.

Rufus climbed out of the vehicle and turned to his new team. "Leave your luggage in the van. After we've shown you around the facility, we'll take you to your quarters."

They entered the warehouse and headed to the makeshift lounge area.

Rufus gestured at the new arrivals. "Take a seat. What you're about to hear is classified top secret, so keep your ears open and your mouths shut." He turned to CC.

"Welcome to the QRF. You beat out several well-qualified individuals to become part of this unit, so well done. I'm CC, also referred to as Haggis. I'm Alpha's team leader. You'll need to learn the callsigns of all team members because you'll usually hear from us in this manner. Real names will not be used in any emails, text messages, or voice communications. Alpha team uses callsigns associated with our countries of origin, while Bravo uses colors, and Charlie relies on birds of prey."

Maverick raised a hand. "How do we choose ours?"

"We'll discuss this later, Maverick." Rufus smiled. "Your name would be a good one, but you'll need to choose something else."

"Once the QRF becomes organized, we'll arrange individual meetings with the teams so you can learn how each one operates." CC gestured to Trevor.

"Good morning, lady and gentlemen. I'm Colonel Trevor Franklin, a retired member of the British paras. My callsign is Black. I would also like to extend my welcome. You'll find we train hard and play hard."

Evelyn stood. "I'm Lady Evelyn Evinrude, formerly from the British MI-6. I'm sure we'll all get along famously." She smiled. "However, don't assume any of us are pushovers. We'll expect a lot out of you, but at the same time, we'll help you in any way we can."

"How many women are in the teams?" Alex frowned.

Because of Alex's deadpan face, Evelyn chuckled. "An excellent question. With you, there are now three of us in the teams but more in the support units. The other woman on my team is Barbara Battersea."

"Just wondered how much competition I had."

Everyone chuckled.

CC glanced at his watch. "I'm afraid we'll have to cut the welcome short. Rufus, Trevor, Evelyn, and I have a meeting with the installation commander to iron out a few details. We'll catch up later on the obstacle course. Why not take it easy and check out your new workspace?"

\* \* \*

A technical sergeant showed the Bedlam team leaders into the installation commander's office. After a round of handshakes, they sat at a small conference table.

Brigadier General Frederick Rinehart, the Ramstein Air Base installation commander, puffed out his cheeks as he squirmed his rotund body into a chair. "I can give you ten minutes. I'm a very busy man and a group of local leaders are due to arrive soon for an important discussion."

"Thank you for meeting with us, General Rhinehart. We greatly appreciate all of the assistance you've provided thus far. I'll make sure to mention this to Admiral Blakely." CC forced a bland smile. *I think this guy's a windbag who probably never served a day in a combat role.*

Rhinehart nodded. "Not a problem. I've reviewed the memorandum of agreement again." He stared at CC and Trevor. "Colonels." He dragged out the words as if they were a curse while tapping the single star on his shoulder board. "I understand your QRF leader is a mere sergeant. He should be staying with the rest of the single NCOs on base."

"Actually, he was a master chief petty officer in the SEALs, equivalent to an air force chief master sergeant. Rank isn't important to Bedlam—being able to do the job is what counts." *What a pompous ass!*

"Well, you'll have to replace him. I insist every organizational head on this installation be the equivalent of a field grade officer. This fits with what I project to the local communities. Until such time as he's replaced, I'll require him to attend all installation meetings. Furthermore, should I need his services in whatever capacity I choose, he'll be required to comply."

CC shook his head. "You might think you're in control of everything on this base, but you're not." He turned to Trevor.

He opened the briefcase he brought to the meeting, extracted a folder, and handed it to CC.

Pulling out a multipage document, CC turned to the signature page before sliding it across the table. "Is that your signature under Brigadier General Frederick Rhinehart?"

The general scoffed. "Get to your point—I don't have all day to waste with you on this nonsense."

"Did you actually read the document before you signed it?"

Rhinehart stared at CC before giving a slight nod.

"Do you recognize the signatures of Admiral Blakely, Chairman of the Joint Chiefs of Staff, and General Claude Bouchet, the Air Force Chief of Staff?"

The general pursed his lips as he tilted his head.

"Well, General. When did your one star outrank their four stars?"

Rhinehart crossed his arms but remained silent.

"Let me fill you in on some reality. You are instructed by this MOA, which you signed, to render all assistance to the Bedlam Quick Reaction Force while they are housed on this installation. Furthermore, you agreed not to interfere in any way with the operation of this organization."

CC leaned forward. "There is absolutely nothing in the MOA indicating Bedlam is subordinate to you, nor is there a requirement for the QRF to participate in any installation meetings or events unless the QRF leaders choose to do so. Does this ring a bell?"

"Yes, but important things are missing from the MOA. I—"

"There are no buts, General. Details contained within an MOA are ironed out before the document is signed, not afterward. When I return to the Pentagon, should I inform Admiral Blakely and General Bouchet you agreed to comply with the MOA? Or would you prefer a transfer to a weather station in Alaska?"

Rhinehart tossed the document at CC and struggled to stand. "Get out of my office—now!"

CC, Trevor, and Evelyn stood and headed for the door. Before closing it behind him, CC turned back to Rhinehart. "By the way, General, as a member of the senior executive service, I hold an equivalent rank to you. So does Trevor in the British government. You might want to do a more thorough background check when you're wasting taxpayers' money conducting unauthorized investigations into people who aren't subordinate to you." He closed the door.

Once out of the building, the Bedlam team leaders burst into laughter.

"CC, I thought he was going to have a heart attack or stroke." Evelyn linked arms with both men. "He probably hasn't been put in his place for a long time." She glanced at CC. "I bet you play a mean game of poker."

He laughed. "Och aye. But a certain four-star warned me about Rhinehart and how he tries to intimidate people."

"Well, CC." Trevor smirked. "I think he just met his match."

# Chapter Eight

board *RV Aquavit*
Ushuaia, Argentina

Carina Eklund, a tall blonde from Sweden with deep blue eyes, leaned against the rail of the research vessel *RV Aquavit* as she studied Ushuaia. She smiled at the snow-capped Martial mountain range surrounding the city. *Reminds me of home. Wonder what it would be like to ski here? Perhaps when we return.* Raising a hand to shade her eyes from the intense sunlight, she continued to scan the city before their ship's scheduled departure.

Buildings ranging from one to three stories lined the street running along the harbor, ranging from hotels to shops with restaurants sandwiched in between. Two other ships were docked near their research vessel. One was a cruise ship from the Holland America line headquartered in Seattle, Washington, while the other was an Argentinian destroyer allowing guided visitor tours.

Pleasure craft crisscrossed the water, and laden trucks trundled along the streets to unknown destinations. Tourists stopped and took selfies posing in front of various locations of interest.

Carina jumped when two hands grabbed her shoulders. She turned and smiled when she realized who was behind her. "About time you got out of bed. I thought you were going to sleep away our last morning in port?"

"No way I would miss our departure from civilization." Gunner Bengtsson, also from Sweden and even taller than Carina, chuckled. "It will not be long before penguins and seals will be our neighbors."

"Yes, but our mission is an important one. Our soon-to-be neighbors will be grateful the Scandinavian Protection Agency is on their side. With the data we collect and share with the UN, we will have definitive proof of how Antarctica is being impacted by climate change."

Gunner, the team's research and data analysis assistant, nodded. "Very true. However, everything needs to be examined in perspective. Most countries will probably agree there is something to the claim about climate change, but there are plenty who disagree on the severity of the situation or how to deal with it."

"That's why our mission is so important. We must convince every country to support efforts to reduce greenhouse gases." Carina sighed. "No one said this would be easy."

Gunner pointed to two men approaching the gangway. "Hey, who are those guys?"

Both wore red and green boiler suits and had backpacks slung over their shoulders. After showing identification to the security officer, they were allowed to board.

"I thought all crew members were already onboard and preparing to depart."

Carina shrugged. "Might be part of the crew we haven't met. They probably aren't directly working on our mission. I guess if it's important, we'll find out later."

"I—"

A shrill whistle pierced the air.

Crew members ran to the mooring stations to release the massive ropes, freeing the ship from its berth. Others shifted the gangway before leaping back onto the ship.

Gunner tugged Carina's arm. "Come on. Let us join the rest of the team in the ship's mess."

"Wait." Carina jerked her arm free. "Remember, we agreed to keep our relationship secret from the others—at least until we return to Ushuaia."

Gunner grimaced as he stepped away. "I remember. I disagree, but I understand your caution. We do not want people to jump to conclusions."

* * *

The two men who boarded prior to the departure whistle worked their way into the ship's bowels.

Liam stopped at a door not far from the engine room. He fished a key out of his pocket and unlocked the door. Stepping inside the small crew quarters, he gestured for Winston to follow him. "Hurry up before someone spots us."

Winston closed the door behind him and sat on a small chair. "How did Mister Brown find us jobs with the crew?"

"Wasn't him." Liam shook his head. "Sawyer took care of things. I assume he paid a hefty bribe for us to be allowed onboard."

"When do we start our mission?"

"Shh." Liam put a finger to his lips. "We can't discuss our operation while we're on the ship in case someone's listening to us. We'll just keep a low profile and mingle as little as possible with the crew while we take care of business."

Winston smiled. "Understood."

* * *

The Scandinavian Protection Agency had chartered the RV *Aquavit* as a floating platform for their venture to Antarctica, complete with an experienced crew and a scientific staff.

Carina and Gunner joined the rest of the six-person SPA team, which would conduct their experiments on the mainland. They entered the mess and found their teammates: Ailsa Dahl, a petite blonde from Denmark who served as the team's project manager and was game for anything; Bertelot Gulbrandsson from Norway, the team's leader and an engineer by training; Eggert Falkenberg, another engineer, and a blond giant of a man with a quiet nature who came from Bavaria; and Rona Lundgren, a statuesque blonde well over six feet tall, originally from Sweden. Carina and Ailsa were climatologists, while Rona was a meteorologist. Everyone held mugs of coffee or hot chocolate.

"Where did you two go? Checking out the sights—or each other?" Bertelot chuckled.

Carina's face reddened. "If you must know, I was studying the landscape above the city. It's the last time we'll see anything but ice until we return."

"Should have taken some photos to remind you." Bertelot maintained a straight face.

Everyone laughed.

Rona stood. "Anyone for coffee? I'll put on a fresh pot."

Carina half-raised a hand. "Could I have a hot chocolate, please?"

Rona smiled. "Of course."

After a round of "yes" from the rest of the team, she headed into the galley.

Another whistle blew.

A vibration ran through the deck as the engine engaged. The ship swung away from the pier, heading in a southerly direction.

Rona returned a few minutes later, carrying a tray with a fresh pot of coffee and cups and a mug of hot chocolate. After everyone had a refill, she raised her cup in the air. "Here's to our next adventure—Antarctica, here we come!"

Eggert spoke in a deep bass voice. "I'm looking forward to my first time on the ice. I have dreamed of this since I was a child."

"Too bad you missed our Arctic excursion." Carina smiled. "What a time to come down with chickenpox."

"Yes, but it was a mild case since I was vaccinated as a child. They were a present from my niece." He thumped his chest and coughed. "But I'm in perfect shape now." He coughed again.

"Take it easy, Eggert." Bertelot grinned. "We do not have a doctor aboard—just a nurse."

"Is she attractive?"

Bertelot chuckled. "I guess you could say so. The nurse's name is Tim."

"Oh."

Everyone laughed as they stood.

"See everyone here in about three hours." Bertelot pointed at Rona. "We have a guest chef tonight."

Rona touched a finger to her cheek. "Oh. Not sure about being a chef, but I make fantastic spaghetti and meatballs."

"I'm heading out on deck. Anyone care to join me in bidding Ushuaia farewell?"

Ailsa nodded. "I'll join you, Carina."

\* \* \*

Liam edged the door open. "It's clear. Let's go."

"Just a minute." Winston shoved a set of lock picks and a Kizer Splinter folding knife into his pockets. "It's better to be prepared."

Liam shook his head. "This is a recon trip only. We'll sort out our plan later."

Winston nodded. "Just remember, we're to photograph everyone we can—especially if they're part of the scientific landing party."

"Sawyer said he's aware of six people associated with the SPA, which he's interested in, but there might be more of the regular scientific community staff planning on joining them."

Winston grinned. "We'll just have to convince them otherwise. C'mon, let's go."

* * *

Carina and Ailsa stepped onto the deck and worked their way to the stern. Both wore matching blue and yellow down-filled jackets with a SPA logo over the heart. As dusk descended, lights popped on throughout the city.

"What a gorgeous sight." Carina locked her arm with Ailsa's. "It'll be a while before we see Ushuaia again."

"You make it sound like we'll be gone forever. We'll only be in Antarctica for about six weeks."

Carina laughed. "I know, but I wish we were already there so I can skip seasickness. Someone said the ship has been known to roll as much as twenty-five degrees depending upon how rough the water becomes. I hope I brought enough scopolamine patches."

They remained on deck to watch Ushuaia shrink in the distance before heading back inside.

"I'll meet you in the mess." Ailsa unzipped her jacket. "I want to get my camera from the room so I can get some group shots."

"Okay, I'll let the others know."

* * *

Liam knocked on the cabin door.

No answer.

He tried again.

Still no answer.

Winston knelt on the carpet and examined the lock. He used a pick to move the cylinders and a tension tool to keep them from slipping back as they moved other cylinders.

"Hurry up before someone comes."

"Just a min—"

*Click!*

Winston tried the handle, and the door swung inward. He climbed to his feet and stowed his picks before entering the cabin.

"We better hide in case someone returns." Liam turned on the lights and gestured to the bathroom. "You duck in there."

Winston nodded. "Works for me. Better turn off the lights."

Several minutes later, Liam heard a key slide into the lock. He jumped behind the door, preparing to tackle whoever entered.

The door swung inward.

Ailsa stepped into the room and turned on the lights. As she turned to close the door, she hesitated.

Liam lunged and shoved her to the floor. With a hand over her mouth, he pinned her so she couldn't move. "Winston—a little help."

Winston rushed from the bathroom and grabbed one of Ailsa's flailing arms. He pulled a small club from his pocket and tapped the side of her head, rendering her unconscious. He yanked a roll of tape from another pocket and ripped a piece off, covering her mouth to prevent any screams.

"Quick. Let's get her back to our cabin before she comes to." Liam picked her up, throwing her across his shoulder. "Check for anyone outside."

Winston opened the partially closed door and peeked outside. "Coast is clear."

"Let's go. Gotta hurry. She's starting to move."

"Just a minute." Winston stepped forward and applied a choke hold until she stopped moving. He pulled a cloth from his back pocket and wiped some blood from her forehead. "That should keep her quiet. But we need her alive so she can tell us what her group is doing here. Let's just leave her here."

"I guess you're right." Liam nodded. "She won't be much use if she has a concussion but better to make it look like she passed out in her own cabin. I should have used an injection or given her a whiff of something. It works in the movies."

Winston stared at his partner before glancing toward the ceiling.

"Why me?" He turned back to Liam. "This ain't the movies, and we've done it my way."

# Chapter Nine

Diablo Corps Secret Outpost
Near Prince Charles Mountains

Felix Zimmermann pulled the sleeves of his flannel lumberjack fleece over his tattooed arms as he glanced around the cleanroom. *Good. Emmanuel must have gone to the canteen.* He turned to his computer, brought up his Tor browser, and maneuvered to the dark web. Once he logged into an anonymous account he hadn't used before, he began composing a message.

After re-reading, he fixed a couple of typos and pressed send. *Hope this gets the word out.*

"What you working on?"

Felix jumped as he turned toward the voice. "H-Hey, Emmanuel. I just finished that report you wanted me to do. I was about to find something to eat."

"Hmm." Emmanuel pursed his lips. "After you finish, come find me. I have an important matter to discuss with security, and I want you with me."

"Uh. Sure thing. Whatever you want, Emmanuel." Felix stood and headed toward the door. He glanced over his shoulder before leaving the cleanroom.

* * *

Emmanuel stared at the retreating Felix. A frown etched across his face. He sat at his desk and picked up the phone, tapping two digits. *I saw the blue notification indicating a successful process before Felix logged off. What's he up to?*

"Hello?"

Emmanuel cleared his throat. "There might be a problem."

"Who?"

"Felix. What should I do?"

The voice at the distant end chuckled. "Just be yourself. I'll sort things out—again. But, you'll owe me."

"Very well." Emmanuel hung up and grinned. *Won't be long before Brown will need to find some new help.*

* * *

*World Bank Headquarters*
  *1818 H Street, NW*
  *Washington, DC*

Douglas Walliams, president of the World Bank, rifled through the stack of mail dropped off by his secretary. *Nothing worth reading.* He switched on his computer and skimmed his new messages. *Routine, routine. Why can't I receive something exciting?*

He deleted the spam and filed trivial reports in their respective folders. The one-word subject of the next message from an unknown email address piqued his interest. *What's this?*

Douglas opened the message labeled *Beware* and studied its contents.

*To: Douglas Walliams, World Bank President*
*From: A concerned citizen of the world*

*Behold the beast, for he wants to destroy the world. He will stop at nothing to achieve his goals. Seek him where glaciers abound.*

Douglas scratched his chin. *Is this some kind of a joke? Why send it to me?* He picked up the phone and dialed.

A deep male voice answered after the first ring. "Hello."

"Hey, Jonny. Douglas Walliams here. I received a strange email today. It might be from a crackpot, but with recent viable threats against the stock markets, I thought you might be interested." He forwarded the message to Jonny. "Just sent it to you."

"Got it. Hmm. Just a minute—I'll be right back."

Douglas listened to the classical hold music performed by an orchestra while he waited.

Moments later, Jonny came back on the line. "Sorry about that. I wanted to compare what you sent me with some earlier information that came in. I just forwarded your email to an organization already looking into this issue. If you receive anything else, just send it to me, and we'll look into it."

"Will do, Jonny. Should I be worried?"

"You can share what you received with your counterparts in Japan, China, Germany, and the U.K., as they have the most voting power after the U.S. However, I recommend against sharing it with your executive directors and vice presidents. If I recall, that will push the word out to over fifty more people, and I think we should keep it contained—for now."

"Understood."

"Anything else, Douglas?"

"Not today. We need to arrange another outing on the Chesapeake."

"As soon as a quiet period appears on my schedule, I'll let you know."

\* \* \*

Office of the National Security Advisor
West Wing, White House

After breaking the connection, Jonny picked up a secure phone and dialed a number he knew by heart.

"Admiral Blakely here, Jonny. What's up?"

"Did you read the latest email I sent you?"

"Yep. Appears to be related to what Grandson has received through a coded message from his friend."

"Agreed. Beast is a synonym for the Devil. The references to glaciers could be either the Arctic or Antarctica, although there are dozens of countries where they're found."

"Great minds think alike." The admiral chuckled. "I'll instruct Grandson to work on this—he loves puzzles. Earlier, I notified Bedlam Alpha, Bravo, and Charlie to reach out to their contacts."

"Excellent. I'll tell some of my staff to give it a shot as well. We need to find out who is behind these threats." Jonny sighed. "I better brief the president. You know what he's like."

"Good luck. I'll keep you informed of anything we uncover." The admiral broke the connection.

\* \* \*

Diablo Corps Secret Outpost
  Near Prince Charles Mountains


Felix approached Emmanuel's door with apprehension. *Wonder what's up that he needs my help when he talks with security?* He rapped his knuckles on the door.

"Come in."

"You wanted my help?"

Emmanuel waved to a chair. "Take a seat. Sawyer will be joining us in a few minutes."

"Uh. I thought we were going to his office." Felix shut the door and sat in front of Emmanuel's desk.

"That was the plan, but it'll be easier here."

"Okay, whatever you think is best." *Why's he staring at me?*

"How are you settling into the job, Felix? This must be quite a transition for you after heading up your own team."

Felix shrugged. "You know how it is—need to go where I'll make the big bucks so I can retire early."

"That's why I took Brown's offer. I want to set up my own business in the future because I don't want to answer to anyone." Emmanuel chuckled.

"That's too much of an effort for me to take on. I always work better under a boss—but one who gives me the freedom to complete jobs on a timely basis without interference."

Emmanuel nodded. "Understood. I—"

Someone knocked and opened the door.

Sawyer, the head of Brown's security, sauntered in. He nodded at Felix as he sat in the chair next to him. "So what's up, Emmanuel, that requires my assistance?"

"I believe we have a security breach." He glanced at Felix. "An unknown individual is apparently using clandestine means to communicate outside the organization disregarding the nondisclosure agreement they signed showing they understood such communication is forbidden."

Felix swallowed. *I've only sent one message through the dark web. How did Emmanuel find out?*

"I'm pretty tied up doing some special projects for Brown, so I thought Felix would be the perfect candidate to help you."

"I-I am?" Felix glanced between the two men. "How?"

"Sure. Next to me, you're the best person on the team." Emmanuel smiled. "What do you think, Sawyer?"

"It's your call, but if you're satisfied with Felix lending a hand, I have no problem. Speaking of hands, I need some assistance on the ice with one of the smaller Sno-Cats. I skidded off the frozen path, and the machine is stuck. Could you both give me a hand? With three of us, it should only take a few minutes. The rest of the security team is tied up, or I'd get them to help me."

"Sure thing, Sawyer." Emmanuel stood. "We'll get our gear together and meet you outside in ten minutes."

"Excellent, thanks. We'll take one of the larger machines in case we need to tow the other one back."

\* \* \*

Fifteen minutes later, the three men climbed into a Sno-Cat, with Sawyer behind the wheel. "Should take about twenty minutes to get to the stuck machine. Hang on. I'm going to use a shortcut over the ice."

Maneuvering off the normal path, Sawyer gunned the engine as they bounced over the icy terrain.

"Is that your machine up ahead?" Emmanuel pointed to a dark smudge on the horizon. "You were well off the beaten path."

Sawyer laughed as he adjusted crampons onto his feet. "Brown pays me well to search for alternate routes around crevasses before crews go out on the ice. It's exciting work but can be a bit dangerous."

As they approached the abandoned Sno-Cat, Sawyer pointed to

the left of the machine. "If you look closely, you can see there's a crevasse not far from where I got stuck. I was trying to go around it when my little accident happened." He parked behind the first machine.

The men climbed out of their warm Sno-Cat and inspected the other one.

Felix pointed to the left side. "Looks like some damage—something fell off." He glanced around and spotted a red and white piece of metal near the crevasse. "There it is." He slogged through the snow toward the damaged part.

As he bent down to retrieve it, he slipped on the ice.

"Wait a minute, Felix. I'll help you." Sawyer stepped next to Felix. "Here, take this rope and tie it around your waist. I'll hold you while you step closer."

Felix did as instructed and inched his way forward. He began to turn toward Sawyer.

A dark shape hit Felix on the shoulder, propelling him toward the crevasse. "Hey! What are—"

Sawyer gave Felix a final shove, and he fell through the thin ice.

*Iaaaaaahh!*

In an instant, Felix was gone, his screams echoing as his body disappeared into the deep hole.

Sawyer turned to Emmanuel. "That's another problem sorted. At this rate, you'll have to keep working an extra five years for Brown to pay your debt to me."

# Chapter Ten

D iablo Headquarters
Miami, Florida

Brown stepped off the executive elevator and strode past his secretary without a word. He walked into his office, sat, and thumbed through the mail. *Nothing worthwhile here—just physical spam from charities looking for handouts.* He threw them into a wastepaper beside his desk. *Why do I receive so many requests for money? Everyone knows I never respond to cold requests. Waste of my time and theirs.*

Helen slid into the room and placed a cup of coffee on Brown's desk. "Sir, just a reminder about the board meeting in an hour."

He sipped his drink. *Perfect.* "Why do you think I came back from Antarctica? If I didn't need to be here in person to sign documents that couldn't be done electronically, I could've stayed there and done this over Zoom."

"Yes, sir."

"Helen, have you given any further thought to being with me all the time? I'd make it worth your while."

"Sorry, sir. I'm not too fond of the cold. Besides, I have my mother to think about as her health isn't good. However, if you ever move your operations to a warm climate, I'll take you up on the offer—as long as I can bring my mother."

Brown shook his head. "Can't blame me for trying. You're the best employee I've ever had." *Even if she does spurn my advances.*

"Thank you, Mister Brown." Helen blushed.

"I better prepare for the meeting. Remind me when I'm ten minutes late—we'll let the others squirm. I want you to take notes as usual."

"Yes, Mister Brown."

\* \* \*

As instructed, Helen waited until after the meeting was scheduled to start before knocking on Brown's door. She pushed it open.

Empty.

Puzzled, she headed to the board room, where she was the only one missing. Once inside, she eased into her usual chair, placing her tablet in front of her, ready to take notes.

"About time." Brown glared at Helen. "Now we can start." He glanced around the room at his vice presidents: marketing & promotion, finance & banking, consumer services, mining, energy, technology, and construction. He pursed his lips. "Where the dickens is Wendy? I made it perfectly clear I wanted her report on the push to increase our share of global risk management insurance." *Although I'll short the companies' stocks so I can make more money when catastrophes hit, and they have to make large payouts.*

A timid hand popped up. "Mister Brown, she couldn't make it today. One of her children is home with the measles."

"Harumph. Very well." He turned to a woman with blonde hair

and green eyes. "Rachel, what is the status of siphoning off two percent of all profit from each business segment?"

Rachel swallowed. "I-I met with everyone yesterday. We should start seeing a line item in the books for individual segments by the end of the month." She gulped and looked away. "However, we can only manage one percent at such short notice."

Brown slammed a fist on the table. "Why is everything so difficult? Just move the money to the account number I gave you as soon as possible. I want the amount increased to five percent by the end of the year. Call the line item Project Green Earth."

"Y-Yes, Mister Brown."

Once again, he glanced around the room, his stare lingering longer than before.

None of his vice presidents could hold his gaze. While some of them fidgeted with files on the table in front of them, others adjusted their clothing or scratched behind an ear. None of his vice presidents could hold his gaze.

"Make sure you provide the requisite amount on time. We need the funds to support worldwide climate change initiatives before it's too late. The UN held its first global climate summit twenty-six years ago, but things are moving slower than snails in wet cement. While there are plenty of individuals who truly want to see progress and are doing what they can, too many countries are refusing to hop on board with what needs to be done."

Brown sipped from a glass of ice water in front of him.

"I'm not getting any younger, and I can't wait around to see changes made. My time is too valuable to wait for others to do what they should already be doing. We'll use the funds in Project Green Earth to promote viable initiatives. I want each of you to examine your business segment and find out who is treating climate change with the urgency it deserves—that's who we'll support." He turned to a diminutive woman with thick glasses. "Queenie, I want you to start working on a global marketing promotion to push mitigation strategies. It's vital for every G-20 country to participate."

Queenie nodded. "At once, Mister Brown."

"Anything else?"

One by one, the vice presidents shook their heads.

"Excellent. I'll be attending next week's meeting remotely. Until then, I expect everyone to dig in. You have your guidance." Brown stood.

Helen raced to the door and opened it for him.

He brushed past without a word and headed toward his office. He stopped at the door, waiting for Helen to open it.

"Mister Brown, I—"

"I know I said let me know when the meeting was already underway, but I wanted to surprise them. Most weren't in their seats yet. It seems punctuality isn't a recognizable trait among my vice presidents." He shook his head. "If I didn't need them right now, I'd can the lot of them." He rubbed his temples. "Helen, bring me another coffee and some pain medication. My head hurts."

"Yes, Mister Brown."

* * *

Brown sat at his desk, continuing to rub his temples. *Everything checked out in my last physical. Hope the docs didn't miss something.*

A soft knock caused Brown to glance at the door. "Enter."

Helen stepped inside carrying a tray and set it in front of him. "Here's your coffee, some water, and aspirin. Also, I counted the number of nitroglycerin tablets remaining and requested a refill."

"Thanks." He took two pills from a small saucer, popped them in his mouth, and chased them with water. "Get me a chili dog with cheese, onions, and jalapenos. And a beer."

Helen glanced at her boss and raised an eyebrow.

"I feel fine. Just need something to eat." He waved her away.

"Yes, Mister Brown."

After Helen left the office, Brown picked up the phone and entered two digits. He waited for someone to answer. *Where is she? If her child is sick, she should be at home.* After the fourth ring, he broke the connection and redialed.

A person who seemed out of breath answered after the first ring. "Y-Yes?"

"Wendy—we missed you at the staff meeting today. How is your child?"

"Oh, Mister Brown. Didn't you get the message I left? I'm so sorry. Jennifer has flu-like symptoms, a temperature just over one hundred and two, and her face, neck, and chest are covered with a rash."

"Did you get her a measles, mumps, and rubella injection last year like I mandated for all employees' children at my expense?"

"S-She had the first shot, but I forgot to take her back for the follow-up."

"Have you taken her to the doctor?"

"Not yet—I'm taking her later today."

"Never mind—cancel the appointment. I'll send our doctor out right away. He'll take care of things."

"Oh, Mister Brown. Thank you!"

"Don't thank me, Wendy. I need you in the office as soon as possible. Do you have someone who can watch her?"

"I'll ask my sister. She lives in Orlando, and I know she's protected from measles, as is her family."

"Excellent. I expect you in the office first thing in the morning. Be ready to brief me on your efforts to increase our share of global insurance regarding risk management."

"But—"

"No buts, Wendy. If I don't have your report by noon tomorrow, you can begin looking for a new job—and it won't be in Miami." He slammed the receiver down. *It's so hard to get dependable staff. Perhaps in the future, all of my vice presidents should be childless. What's more important than what I want to be done?*

# Chapter Eleven

board RV *Aquavit*
Argentine Sea

Liam and Winston lifted the unconscious Ailsa from the floor and laid her on a bed. They arranged her arms and legs and put a pillow beneath her head to make it appear she wanted to rest and dozed off.

Winston bent down and poked a finger into a breast.

She didn't move.

He listened to Ailsa's chest. "Still breathing but not faking unconsciousness. Start placing the GSM bugs—they all have built-in batteries, so make sure they're well hidden. The cabin's small, so the bugs should pick up every conversation. Put two in this room and one in the bathroom." Winston located Ailsa's cell phone and tried to access it.

*Locked.*

He picked up her hand and swiped her fingers across the phone.

Nothing happened.

He tried again, this time using her right thumb and index finger. *I'm in.* "I'll download the spyware app to her phone. She'll never know it's there."

"Should I put a bug in the bathroom, too?"

Winston shrugged. "Why not? No telling what we'll hear."

Moments later, Liam stepped from the bathroom. "Done. Now what?"

"Let's get out of here." He used a software app on his phone to verify the signal and nodded. "We'll go back to our cabin and check the cables to make sure everything is connected."

Liam pulled the door closed as they left. "Psst, Winston. The door won't shut all the way. Something's sticking out from the lock."

"Hmm. Must have broken off when I forced the lock." He waved a hand. "Never mind. Leave it, and let's go."

Carina's eyes flicked from her watch to the companionway as she expected Ailsa to appear at any moment. She leaned forward in her chair.

"Something the matter?" A bemused smile flickered across Gunner's face.

"Yes. After Ailsa and I went on deck, she said she was going back to the room to retrieve her camera so she could take some group shots." Carina glanced at her watch again. "It's been almost thirty minutes—she should be back by now."

"Perhaps she needed to use the restroom."

"For that long? Maybe she's unwell. Perhaps I should check to be sure she doesn't require any assistance." Carina stood. "Something's wrong. I'm going to check on her."

Gunner drained the last of his coffee. "Wait a minute. If something strange is going on, I would feel better accompanying you."

"Me, too. Thank you, Gunner."

\* \* \*

Gunner and Carina left the rest of the team in the mess and made their way to Ailsa's cabin.

Carina reached for the door handle.

"Wait." Gunner pointed. "Look. The door is not shut. Let me go first in case someone other than Ailsa is inside."

Carina stepped aside.

He edged the door open and peeked through. Not seeing anyone, he entered.

"Holy smokes! Carina—it is Ailsa. Something has happened to her."

Carina rushed into the cabin and stopped by the edge of the bed.

Gunner had gone to the other side and cradled Ailsa's bloody head in his arms.

She started to stir. An eye slowly opened. "W-What happened?"

He turned to Carina. "Go into the bathroom and wet a cloth to wipe the blood from Ailsa's face."

She nodded and disappeared.

He helped Ailsa to a sitting position against the headboard with a pillow behind her. "The door was open an inch or so when we arrived, and you were on the bed. What do you remember?"

Carina returned and gently wiped her friend's face with a cool cloth.

Despite Carina's careful ministrations, Ailsa winced. "T-There were two men in the room when I entered. They wore clothes similar to the crew." She gasped as she felt her private parts. "Did they try to rape me?"

Gunner shook his head. "Not unless they are used to dressing and undressing women. Your clothing does not appear to be touched."

Carina held Ailsa's hand. "Do you feel bruised down there?"

Ailsa shook her head.

"Thank God. But what did they want? One of them held me

71

while the other hit me with some type of club." Her hand went to a lump near her temple. "Ow."

"We'll get you some ice or an icepack from the nurse to put on that." Carina rubbed a hand on Ailsa's arm. "Don't worry. We'll take care of you."

A slight smile creased Ailsa's face. "Thank you."

"I do not know. We must tell the rest of the team and inform the captain. As soon as you are ready, we will join the others. " Gunner frowned. "Someone also needs to check the cabin for anything that could be missing."

Carina nodded. "I'll go since I have an idea of what she had with her and will see if her camera is still there."

* * *

Gunner, Carina, and Ailsa joined the other team members and explained what they knew. As they talked, the chef clanged pots beyond the door to the galley. Silverware clinked in the holders while water sloshed back and forth in the bottles on the table.

Carina pulled back one of the curtains swaying in front of the port holes. She allowed it to drop back in place before standing by Ailsa and placing a hand on her shoulder.

"We must tell the captain." Bertelot clenched his fists. "Until whoever did this has been apprehended, I do not want anyone going around the vessel on their own. I propose Gunner escorts Carina, Eggert accompanies Rona, and I will keep an eye on Ailsa. Is this okay?"

Everyone nodded.

"Excellent." Bertelot stood. "I will find the captain now. Ailsa, please come with me so you can explain to him. Gunner, will you stay with Carina?"

"Of course."

Bertelot and Ailsa left the mess and headed up a flight of stairs to the bridge. They entered and searched for the captain.

"Over there." Ailsa pointed to the left.

They marched to where Paul Smythe, captain of the *RV Aquavit,* sat, a steaming cup of tea in his hand. "Hello, Bertelot. Are you and your team settling in?"

"Yes, we are fine, but Ailsa has been assaulted." Bertelot frowned. "Two men, dressed like your crew, were waiting in her cabin and attacked her."

"What?" He set down the cup, stood, and turned to her. "Are you all right?"

"Yes, at least I think so. It might be wise to have Tim check me over to be sure." Ailsa's face reddened as she glanced at the floor. "Do you think he has a rape kit? I want to be sure nothing happened."

"I'm sure he has one somewhere." Paul shook his head. "Never has anything happened like this on our previous voyages." He picked up an internal phone, put it on speaker, and hit two numbers.

"Hello?"

"Tim, Paul here. Will you come to the bridge? Ailsa is with me, and she's the victim of an attack. She might be fine, but it wouldn't hurt to give her the once over."

"Of course, Captain."

Paul broke the connection. "We have ten new crew members for this voyage. All the others have been with me for years. I can't imagine any of my regulars are behind this." He rummaged in a drawer and took out an incident report. "We'll talk with the new men and find out where they were when the attack happened. Of course, the makeup of the scientific team changes all the time, depending on which organization charters the ship. Wouldn't be hard for someone to blend in with them."

"We will leave things in your capable hands, Captain. In the meantime, we paired up so none of us are left alone—at least until whoever is responsible for this is captured."

Paul nodded. "We don't have many firearms onboard, but I'll arm the section heads until we know more."

Liam and Winston listened to the conversations taking place in Ailsa's cabin that were captured by the listening devices they installed there and on the bridge from the bug they planted on her phone.

Winston grinned. "Outstanding. The woman might have known what happened but she couldn't identify us." He glanced at Liam. "Good thing you didn't try to rape her."

"What next?"

"I think we should bug Bertelot's cabin. Since he's in charge of the SPA team, he's more likely to talk about their true mission." Winston rubbed the stubble on his face. "Sawyer thinks they have an ulterior motive for coming to Antarctica beyond their stated objectives. Until we uncover more information for him, we must continue to blend in with either the crew or the scientific team."

"It would be easier to pretend to be a scientist. Unlike the crew who wear various colored overalls, the scientists wear whatever they want. There are plenty of them, and they probably don't know everyone."

Winston nodded. "Good point. We'll need to find an empty cabin near the scientists since the crew is billeted on a lower deck of the ship. Perhaps there's an empty one near the SPA team. Let's go for a walk."

\* \* \*

After Tim examined the lump on Ailsa's head, ran a series of tests to check for concussion, cleaned up some blood seepage, completed a rape kit, and gave her some pain medication, the SPA team helped themselves to the spaghetti and meatballs Rona had whipped up earlier.

The once boisterous team was subdued after the incident. Rather than smiles and joking around, sullen looks appeared on each person's face.

Ailsa tapped a knife against her half-full water glass. "Listen, everyone. We need to put this behind us and get on with our mission. Besides, I can't stand the doom and gloom expressions on everyone's face. I've seen happier people at a funeral. It's time to liven up. Yes, I have a bump on my head, but the pain meds Tim gave me are working fine, and he said I didn't show any signs of concussion. Since the rape kit was negative, that's a weight off my mind."

"You're right, Ailsa." Carina smiled. "We have a few days left until we arrive in Antarctica, so let's make the best of things and enjoy ourselves. Does anyone have some dance music?"

Eggert pointed down to his backpack. "Ya. I never leave home without my music. I'll get the party started."

\* \* \*

Winston and Liam walked along the corridor on the deck above their cabin. They tried each door but found them locked.

"Hey! What are you doing?" A crewman dressed in black overalls held a wrench in his left hand and a radio in his right.

"Uh." A sheepish grin creased Winston's face. "I forgot our cabin number, but we left the door unlocked."

"You must be some of the new crew the captain mentioned. Since your overalls match mine, you're on the wrong deck. Go down the first flight of stairs to the crew deck." The crewman studied Winston and Liam as if trying to memorize their faces. "Be careful. Someone attacked a member of the SPA team."

"What? When?" Winston glanced at Liam. "Who was attacked?"

"About two hours ago. It was one of the women. She couldn't describe her attackers but said there were two of them." The crewman stared at them. "I don't recognize either of you. When did you join the crew?"

"This is our first time on the *Aquavit*." Winston gestured toward Liam. "We've served together on other ships."

The crewman stroked his straggly goatee. "Well, welcome aboard. Hope you find your cabin."

"If we don't, we'll check with someone on the bridge." Winston doffed an imaginary hat. "Have a great day."

The crewman shook his head and turned to leave. "You, too."

After he departed, Winston and Liam headed in the other direction.

Winston glanced at his partner. "Not sure he bought it, but he doesn't have to for long. We'll get the information Sawyer wants and get out of here as soon as we can."

# Chapter Twelve

D iablo Corps Secret Outpost
Near Prince Charles Mountains

Chris sipped from a Dr Pepper as he decoded Matthew's latest message:

*I need more guidance. My latest Google search on Beware the Devil showed over one hundred eighty million hits. My boss says we can protect you, but we need to know your location. Please advise.*

He pursed his lips as he pondered his response. *How much can I reveal? I think Sawyer is getting suspicious.* He logged back onto his dark web account via a TOR browser and typed.

. . .

*Cannot reveal any more about the devil except look at alternative words. Must add a log or two to the fire as I'm always cold. You've seen the attacks thus far—more to follow, so don't delay.*

After encoding the message, Chris hit send. "Hopefully, he can figure out where I'm at and who's behind the attacks." He retrieved his empty coffee mug and headed out of his office in the direction of the canteen.

When he entered, the snack bar was almost deserted. He filled his mug, grabbed a chocolate brownie, and stopped by the cashier. Once he paid, he turned and almost ran into Sawyer.

"Hey, Chris."

"Uh. Hi, Sawyer. How are things going in the security world?"

Sawyer shrugged. "Same ol', same ol'. Do you have a minute?"

"Sure." Chris pointed to a table against the wall. "Will that do?"

"Yeah."

After they sat, Chris turned to Sawyer. "What did you want to talk to me about?"

"Well, this is kinda delicate. As Brown's main aide, you have access to personnel records, right?"

Chris nodded. "But as head of security, so do you."

"Yes, but .... Each time someone accesses the files, a digital tracker makes note of it."

"So, what's the problem?" *What's he after?*

"As I said, it's delicate. I missed out earlier with another woman because of Samson's involvement. Can you scan Madeleine's file and check her personal information? I'm particularly interested in whether she's married or has a significant other in her life."

*Ah! He must be falling for her.* "Yes, I suppose I can do it for you, considering your position. However, you can't tell anyone I did this— everyone would be after me."

They shared a nervous laugh.

"However, you must understand no one can know, and not just so she doesn't get her feelings hurt. She might not take kindly to having me pass you private information about her, and I could get in a lot of trouble and even lose my job."

"I won't tell anyone. Many thanks, Chris." Sawyer stood and stuck out his hand. "Don't let anyone know I've taken a personal interest in her."

Chris rose and shook Sawyer's hand. "Of course." *But it'll be useful to have this over his head if I ever need his help.*

He bought another coffee refill before returning to his office. Chris checked his dark web account. *Nothing.* He logged onto his Diablo email. One from Brown:

*Prepare for my return—probably tomorrow night. Is our new explosives expert ready to calve the final section? Ask Emmanuel for a status report—he's late with yesterday's update, and he's not responding to my emails.*

Chris cracked his knuckles before typing a quick response:

*Everything will be ready whenever you return. Madeleine and Reginald are planting the explosives now. Will check with Emmanuel and sort things out.*

After sipping from his mug, he logged into the personnel files. Once he perused Madeleine's file, he made notes on a sheet of paper and stuffed them into his pocket. *Don't want to send it to him as it'll leave an electronic footprint. I'll give this to Sawyer later.*

\* \* \*

Maddie and Reginald climbed out of the Sno-Cat. After they pulled their tools and explosive packs from the cargo compartment, the engineers trudged across the tundra to the line of stakes they had placed along the edge of a deep crevasse earlier in the day.

Breathless, Maddie dropped her tools onto the ice and carefully lowered the explosives beside her. "This is hard work, Reginald. I thought it would be easier—just drive up to a spot, drill a couple of holes, drop in the fireworks—and bang, you're done."

"In your dreams." Reginald laughed. "The only thing easy about this job is selecting our way across the ice back to the facility."

As Maddie placed an explosive package into the first hole and filled it in, she studied the terrain. *Always seems peaceful, but I sense an underlying danger to being here.* She glanced around and shivered. *Don't know what's bugging me, but it must be my sixth sense.*

Satisfied with her placement, she moved to the next spot.

Without warning, the ice gave way, and a gaping chasm opened up.

"*Yeeeeah!*"

Maddie clawed with freezing fingers at the surface as she slid down a slope toward the crevasse. She pulled an ice pick from her belt.

"Reginald! Help!"

Her feet dangled over the side as she tried to stop her momentum by hacking at the ice with her axe. She screamed again. Her pick bit into the ice and slowed her progress as her feet dangled over the side. *God, help me! I'm too young to die.*

As she was about to disappear, two hands grabbed her.

"Hold on, Mad—"

Reginald tugged on the straps of her backpack, pulling her away from the chasm. "I—I got you." He fell backward as he yanked her clear of impending disaster.

Back on his feet, he inched Maddie further away from the hole until they were both a safe distance from the yawning crevasse.

Maddie threw her arms around him. "Thank you so much for saving me. My God. I thought I was going to die!"

"Aw shucks, Maddie. Can't have you doing that." Reginald grinned. "Besides, I'm enjoying being out here with you." He wrapped his arms around her and gave her a squeeze. "You going to be okay?"

Maddie pulled out of the embrace and nodded. "Yes. It was a bit scary, but I'm okay now—thanks to you."

"Think nothing of it. Besides, you'd do the same for me if the situation was reversed. I think in the future, we should always conduct surface tests to determine if there is any possible movement."

"Yes, I agree. I thought it would be okay since you said the previous test was okay."

He nodded and glanced at her belt. "Where's your linking cable?"

She felt along her side and pulled up a severed piece of the rope. "I-I don't know but look at this. Appears it frayed."

Reginald studied the strands and nodded. "Agree it does seem to have been tampered with. When we return, we'll let Sawyer know." He smiled. "Anyway, I'm glad I was available to rescue you."

"That's true, but I still owe you." She adjusted her sunglasses and grinned. "Perhaps I can buy dinner tonight?"

He smiled. "Oh, nice. You're rewarding me with cafeteria choices."

She grinned. "I know, very lame. But I promise we'll meet at some pricey location when we return home."

"I'll hold you to it." He pointed to the next hole. "Ready to continue?"

"Yes, let's keep going."

Three hours later, they completed their tasks and returned to the Sno-Cat. Maddie reeled out a cable connected to the explosive charges in a series.

After reaching the vehicle, Maddie hooked the wire to the electronic detonator. She turned to Reginald. "All set. Want to do the honors?"

He shook his head. "You do it—it'll be your revenge against the ice for trying to take you out."

"Okay." She activated the device and hit a flashing green button.

Within seconds, a series of explosions echoed across the ice.

*Craack! Craack!*

A large section of ice broke free from the shelf, plunging into the angry sea.

"Ready to go?"

Maddie nodded.

Reginald engaged the Sno-Cat's gears. He turned the vehicle around and followed their early trek back toward the facility.

Chris glanced at the time. *I better find Emmanuel. Brown will be more angry than normal if he doesn't get what he wants.* Chris left his office and padded along the corridor toward the cleanroom.

After knocking on the door, a click sounded as the lock was disengaged.

Chris pushed the door open and stepped inside.

"Hey, Chris. What's up?" Emmanuel looked up from his monitor. "No, don't tell me—Brown wants another situation report."

Chris shook his head. "I don't understand why he puts up with you."

"It's because I'm the best hacker he ever found." Emmanuel grinned. "Besides, I always get the results he's looking for, and I enjoy getting him riled up."

Chris sighed. "Will you just send him a short SITREP and get him off my back?"

"Sure thing." Emmanuel laughed. "If I forget to do it, you can let him know we'll be ready to hit the bank of his choice when he returns."

"Be better if we both tell him."

\* \* \*

Sawyer entered the snack bar to pick up a meal to take back to his quarters. He halted in his tracks when he spotted Reginald and Maddie sitting at a table in the corner of the room.

He cringed when he saw Reginald place his hand over Maddie's.

Sawyer ground his teeth as he turned back toward the door. *Perhaps it's time for Reginald to join Samson. Another competitor will be out of the way.*

# Chapter Thirteen

O ffice of the Chairman of the Joint Chiefs of Staff
The Pentagon, Arlington, Virginia

A hard knock on Admiral Blakely's office door disturbed his concentration. He frowned as he glanced up from his computer screen. "Enter."

Moments later, CC entered the admiral's office. "Tina wanted me to remind you about the upcoming teleconference with Sir Alex, Harrison, and the team leaders." He pointed toward the Marconi ViPr secure video conferencing system on the admiral's desk. "Tina said she's looking for a suitable replacement."

The admiral laughed. "I don't think Harrison has mastered this one yet. He'll be upset to find out there'll be a new system to learn."

"I'm sure Evelyn will be able to teach him." CC chuckled. "You might need to create some new signs to hold up for him."

Both men chuckled.

Low-volume gongs activated on the video conferencing system.

The admiral turned and accepted three incoming connections. "Welcome to Bravo, Charlie, and QRF. Glad everyone could make it. As you should all be aware, based on the status reports we've been sending, there's a major effort underway by an unknown individual or group to disrupt the financial markets and the banking industry. So far, no one has received any specific demands. However, National Security Advisor Jonathan Meu requested Bedlam unleash our best people to crack this."

Rufus raised a hand. "Sir, would you have someone send the earlier reports to us? With the QRF just going into operation, I want to ensure we receive everything about the current situation."

"Of course, and welcome to the party, Rufus." The admiral smiled. "We'll take care of it."

"Thank you, Admiral."

The admiral nodded. "Many of you met Matthew McMasters at our recent offsite. You may recall I dubbed him Grandson because of his youthful appearance. He's been receiving cryptic messages from an old university friend regarding the possible identity of the perpetrator. Unfortunately, this friend only referred to the person as 'the Devil.' So far, Matthew hasn't come up with any concrete identification. If anyone has any ideas, share them in the normal manner so everyone is kept in the loop."

"Why doesn't Matthew just meet with his contact to obtain more information?" Rufus pursed his lips. "Seems like an easy thing to do."

"It would be if Matthew knew his friend's location. The man is cryptic about his whereabouts as well, other than saying he's always cold."

"Being cold covers a large part of the planet." Rufus tilted his head. "Is he referring to somewhere like Alaska or parts of Canada? What about Greenland and Russia? All of these locations are cold."

"Or is he just someone with a low threshold for cooler climes?" Evelyn grinned. "Perhaps for some insidious reason, he's playing a game."

Sir Alex ran a hand over his clean-shaven chin. "Richard, how confident is Matthew about the validity of the information he's receiving from his friend?"

"I wondered about this as well. However, after every warning, an actual event occurred. Even the Albany power outage, which resulted in the deaths of over twenty-five people, was predicted by Matthew's friend."

"Admiral, we put the word out to our contacts when you first raised this issue." CC shook his head. "So far, we haven't discovered anything."

Trevor and Evelyn shook their heads.

"Understood. However, with the NSA now pushing this, it's a priority for us. I want everyone to start digging—use whatever resources are necessary. I'm also instructing Matthew to contact his hacker friends to see what they can come up with. If this devil succeeds, the civilized world will pay for his crimes."

"Whatever his reasoning, we need to identify who the devil is." Trevor nodded. "I, for one, want this sorted out. My pension's tanking with the economic tremors hitting the stock market."

Someone groaned. "Mine, too."

Everyone gave a nervous laugh.

The admiral's phone rang. "Just a minute." He spoke briefly into the handset before putting the call on speaker. "Jonny, I'm on a conference call with the rest of Bedlam. Could you please repeat what you just said so everyone hears it?"

"Sure. I received an email from Douglas Walliams, president of the World Bank. It was buried in my inbox, and I didn't see it until now, or I would have contacted you sooner. He forwarded a message he received from a concerned citizen of the world. I'm quoting the contents now: 'Behold the beast, for he wants to destroy the world. He will stop at nothing to achieve his goals. Seek him where glaciers abound.' Hopefully, this is some use to you."

"Thanks, Jonny. We'll add it into the mix and see what comes out."

"Glad to help. As you're aware, the president is afraid of a world economic meltdown with this beast hitting stock markets and banks, especially with an election on the horizon. What will come next— will this lunatic go after infrastructure or something else?"

The admiral shook his head. "Nobody wants that. Of course, the people behind this might decide to go after airline traffic control or missile control systems. They could also knock out satellite comms, which cover about forty percent of the world."

Jonny coughed. "Hadn't thought of those possibilities. Let's hope not."

"I'll keep you advised about anything we uncover. Anything else, Jonny?"

"That's all for now, so I'll let you get back to your meeting." Jonny broke the connection.

"Well, Admiral, it looks like this citizen is helping to narrow our search parameters. Unless, of course, he's a religious nutcase. Wonder if it's worth it to try to identify him, or will that be like a needle in a haystack?"

"Something to consider." The admiral turned to Matthew and nodded.

"On it." Matthew grinned.

CC glanced at the ceiling as if he was reading something. "If memory serves me correctly, glaciers are found at the two poles, Alaska, Canada, Greenland, Iceland, and about fifty other countries, although the areas I mentioned are the largest and the most stable. Guess we better start breaking out the cold weather gear."

Trevor half-raised a hand. "When I was with the Paras, we trained in the French, Austrian, and Swiss mountains. They have a number of glaciers, too, as does the Himalayas."

"Aye. Best if we check with the U.S. and British Geological Surveys, as well as with the Aussies and any other countries with survey capability to make sure we have a full picture of the problem."

The admiral nodded. "I want Alpha, Bravo, Charlie, and QRF-1 to put together an action plan to cover these locations and begin a search for Matthew's friend. I think locating him will be the best way to proceed. With the new name of 'the beast' to go with the devil, I'll have Matthew refine his parameters. I still think this is pointing to one individual or group, but only time will tell. I'll also have him contact anyone he knows who does satellite data analysis and has time to examine images of glacier areas. I'm sure he has a few friends who can do this. In the meantime, I'll put in a formal request for assistance."

"Aye. I agree with Admiral Blakley. Best to get Bedlam on the ground in likely remote places and leave the more populated areas to the satellite people."

"Admiral, I think there might be someone who will be able to help us out."

"Go ahead, Rufus."

"Well, since CC mentioned the poles, it got me thinking. My cousin is currently on the *RV Aquavit* on her way to Antarctica with a team from the Scandinavian Protection Agency. Perhaps we could have her look around for us while she's there?"

"Sir Alex and Harrison, what do you think? As you know, we normally don't use outsiders, but this may be an appropriate time."

"I agree, Richard." Harrison ran a hand over his hair as he yawned. "I think we can use any help we can find, but I think one of our people should be with her."

Sir Alex nodded. "I concur."

"It's settled. CC, Trevor, and Evelyn, work with Rufus on how to approach his cousin. Rufus, what did you say her name is?"

Rufus smiled. "It's Carina. She's a cousin on my mother's Swedish side of the family, but we're in regular contact."

"Okay, get your heads together and work something out. I want your proposal within twenty-four hours."

Rufus grinned. "Yes, Admiral."

The admiral glanced at the three connections. "Anything else at this time? If not, we'll break and meet again as soon as we have plans put together."

After a trio of negative responses, the admiral broke the connections.

"Admiral, I've been thinking about using non-Bedlam resources. What would be the probability of getting one of our team members onto the *RV Aquavit* to lend a hand?"

"You know, CC, I was going to ask you what you thought about it. Good to know we think alike. Who do you suggest?"

"Aye. I was going to say me, but Trevor has more experience in cold climates than I do. Let me review the personnel files and see if there is anyone else on the teams I can suggest."

"Get me a name by the end of the day, and we'll see what we can sort out."

"Aye, Admiral."

# Chapter Fourteen

Diablo Corps Secret Outpost
Near Prince Charles Mountains

Brown pounded on the cleanroom door. "Let me in, dammit!"

Moments later, a soft click indicated he could enter.

He shoved the door open and marched to Emmanuel's desk. "I told you before not to lock me out of your area. I own it."

"Sorry, Mister Brown. You agreed to the rules for the cleanroom when it was set up. I can give you the code if you want."

Brown pursed his lips. "Very well. Send the code to me. So, did you start on the bank yet?"

"No, Mister Brown." Emmanuel shook his head. "We expected you to return today, so I made the decision to wait."

"Good. Let's begin."

Emmanuel stood and indicated with his hand. "Right this way." He walked to an inner swinging door and pushed it open.

Inside, three men sat on either side of the room in front of computers connected to multiple screens.

Emmanuel pointed to a blue-shirted man and snapped his fingers.

The man stood and pushed his chair forward.

Emmanuel sat.

Another man offered a chair to Brown.

"Are you ready, Mister Brown?" Emmanuel gestured to the screens in front of him. "We've already defeated their IT defenses and firewalls in preparation for your arrival."

"Which bank are you going to target?"

"The Valkyrie Bank AG."

Brown, his brow raised, stroked his chin. "Never heard of it. Where the hell is it?"

Emmanuel smiled. "Liechtenstein."

"I wanted you to hit a major bank, dammit. How many people are even aware of Liechtenstein? Why did you select a backwater bank instead of one from a G7 country?"

"This bank is an excellent one to test our procedures before tackling a major institution." Emmanuel cleared his throat. "Besides, it's Liechtenstein's fourth largest bank with assets exceeding eleven billion Swiss francs or about eleven and a half billion dollars. Of course, we can only go after their electronic assets."

"But once this bank knows, won't they inform the larger banks so they can change their security protocols?"

Emmanuel shook his head. "I don't think so, as it would show their incompetence. Even if they do, we're smart enough to overcome any access changes."

"Hmm. Very well. Proceed."

Emmanuel turned and gave a thumbs-up to a subordinate. He faced Brown and gestured. "Watch the upper screen. See the balance listed?"

Brown nodded. "Yes. Three billion."

"Keep watching. You should notice a change in a moment."

The numbers blurred before stopping.

"Where did a billion go?"

Emmanuel pointed to the lower screen. "Should appear right about—"

The account balance changed from zero to one billion Swiss francs.

"Whose account is that?"

"I created it as a temporary stop for when we reallocate money from the rich and move it to a private account."

Brown blinked. "Who owns the private account?"

Emmanuel chuckled. "You do. However, before the money reaches you, there'll be at least ninety hops and several temporary accounts around the world with the intention of confusing anyone trying to follow it. There's a lot more to the process than I've mentioned, but I wanted to keep it simple for you." *He probably wouldn't understand the complex network of fake bank accounts and organizations I needed to set up first to get the money.*

"My God!" Brown rubbed his hands. "When the money eventually reaches the account, it's mine, and I can use it?"

"Of course. Just like any funds in your other accounts. Before the money reaches you, it'll be converted into multiple currencies but will end up in dollars."

Brown beamed. "I knew there was a reason I hired you."

*Guess I won't tell him about the few million I've siphoned off during the hops and currency exchanges. Must look after myself— Brown won't.* "You hired me because I'm the best."

Brown waved a hand in the air. "Just remember to keep doing my bidding, and we'll get along fine."

*If Brown doesn't keep protecting Sawyer, perhaps he can join Felix.* "Of course. I always do what you want." Emmanuel leaned closer to Brown. "Remember you asked me to check everyone's personal emails? There was a security breach involving Felix. Since every computer here has keylogging software installed, it's been pretty simple to keep tabs on everyone." Emmanuel chuckled. "As smart as Felix is, I figured he would find the software without any difficulty and disable it. However, he couldn't isolate the firmware I installed, which replicated the software's capabilities as he wouldn't know it was there."

Brown nodded. "What did you find out?"

"Felix thinks he's the smartest one here, but he's dead wrong. As well-versed in security systems as he is, I'm still smarter." Emmanuel nodded. "He was trying to dig up dirt on every employee for some nefarious purpose. I spoke with Sawyer about this, and we decided it would be best for Felix to meet with an accident—a permanent one."

"Hmm." Brown tapped his fingers on one of the chair's arms. "Just be careful—too many unexplained incidents might lead someone to become suspicious and contact the authorities." He frowned. "But in the future, don't make decisions and act upon them without my explicit authorization. I want to see your plans ahead of time so I can review them and make changes if necessary."

"Not a problem, sir. My software and firmware will keep me alerted to any external contacts." *No need to tell him about Chris using a childish code to communicate with his former university friend. He might be useful in the future.*

Emmanuel moved closer to the computer and began typing. His fingers moved so fast they appeared to be a blur.

"What are you doing?"

"Just hacking back into the email account of the bank's president. I want to find out if there's been any reaction." He pulled up the president's email. "Yep, he's panicking. Customers are trying to withdraw funds using various ATMs, and they're getting notices their accounts are empty. When word gets out about the bank crashing, major currencies might go into a freefall, at least the Swiss franc, the euro, and the dollar. This could have a detrimental impact on inflation rates, something you wanted."

Brown's forehead creased. "Yes, yes. But when does the money get to my account?"

"Patience is a virtue, Mister Brown." Emmanuel pointed to the lower screen. Once at zero, the numbers began to change rapidly, finally peaking at ten billion dollars.

"I thought you said there was more money in that bank. Where's the rest of it?"

"Yes, there is, but I wanted to do a second test to determine whether I could clean them out later if I'm interrupted." He turned and snapped his fingers.

The subordinate who began the initial withdrawal nodded and began pecking at the keys.

"The rest of the money will be on its way soon, Mister Brown. Before long, the Valkyrie Bank won't have a penny in its accounts."

"Excellent." Brown stood and slapped Emmanuel on the back. "Keep at it. In the meantime, I'm going to send an email to the *Washington Post*."

"Yes, Mister Brown."

* * *

Brown returned to his office, logged into his computer, and stared at the keyboard. *Did Emmanuel use his keylogging software and firmware on my computer?* Brown shook his head. *He wouldn't dare. Perhaps in the future, I'll dictate to Chris, and he can do my typing.*

*To: Editor-in-Chief, Washington Post*
   *From: Nightmare*
   *An open letter. Publish as soon as possible.*
   *To world political and financial leaders,*
   *If you have paid any attention to the temporary outages in Albany and the major international stock markets, you will heed this final warning.*
   *If I don't see the announcement of drastic changes to reverse the current climate crisis within fourteen days, what I did to the Valkyrie Bank AG in Liechtenstein will be like a human crushing a bug. An*

*immediate change to worldwide emissions controls on businesses and transportation would be a good start.*

*Otherwise, I'll begin shutting down all major G7 banks, taking their money for the good of humanity and the planet. The same will happen to the stock markets. Afterward, I'll tackle any infrastructure and communications systems attached to the internet. My organization will also issue reports on the effects of the environmental damage committed by businesses and governments.*

*As I previously told the G7 central banks, failure to comply will result in the destruction of your way of life as you know it. You must be held accountable. The world cries out for truth, and I am the sword of justice.*

As he logged off, a grin spread across his face. *The fat-cat financiers of the world are making our precious planet unlivable. Now I will do the same to them.* Let's see how they respond.

# Chapter Fifteen

board *RV Aquavit*

Southern Ocean

Carina stood at the stern of the ship, gazing out to sea. *Plenty of clouds but no stars. Nothing but eerie darkness.* She tugged her coat tighter around her to ward off the penetrating cold and pulled her lined woolly hat down to cover the tops of her ears. She turned and headed into the wind, hanging onto a safety rail with frozen fingers. *Should have remembered my gloves, but I'm glad Rufus suggested this headgear. I should call him and see how he's doing.*

Loose strands of blonde hair whipped across her watery eyes as she sniffed to control her runny nose. She edged her way along the ship's port side before returning inside. Joining her other team members, she scooted into an empty seat next to Bertelot. "Could I make my weekly satellite call now? Before we departed, my favorite cousin was hoping to land a new job, and I'm dying to find out if he got it."

Bertelot sipped his hot chocolate. "Okay. What job was he going for?"

"I'm not sure." She tapped the side of her nose. "Something spooky, I think. He's a former SEAL."

Bertelot pulled the satellite phone from his backpack and handed it to her. "No more than fifteen minutes, or you will pay the extra cost."

"C'mon, Bertelot." Carina batted her eyes at him. "I'll be as quick as possible." She stood and headed toward the exit. "I'll be right back."

He laughed. "Sure you will."

After zipping up her parka, which she had loosened when she joined the others, she donned her hat again and stepped back onto the deck.

She took one step and halted. "Need my gloves before I do this, but one of the guys will have to escort me to my cabin." Carina stepped back into the corridor, spotted an open door to a supply closet, and chuckled. *A convenient telephone booth.*

Following the procedures Bertelot taught the team for using the phone, Carina located the appropriate satellite and punched a series of numbers. She grinned when the phone began ringing.

A male voice answered. "Hello?"

"Hi, Rufus. Carina here. How are you doing? Can you hear me well enough? I have to speak quietly so no one can hear me or, if I must, I can take this phone on deck where hell has frozen over."

"Hey, Cuz. Glad to hear from you. Stay where you're at, as I can hear you fine. Where are you calling from? There's a pause between your sentences—you must be on a satellite phone. Are you on your way to Antarctica?"

"Yes, and your recommendation about the woolly hat is already paying dividends." Carina chuckled. "Too bad you couldn't come with me, you being a SEAL and all."

"Hardy har har! This SEAL doesn't want to play with the seals you'll meet. But, I suppose you'll find it quite an adventure."

Randall Krzak

"If you change your mind, I'll talk with Bertelot, our team leader. So did you get the job you were after?"

"Yes. An admiral made me an offer I couldn't refuse. The pay isn't as good, but the potential growth and job stability is much better than being a contractor."

"Can you tell me about it?"

"I can't reveal much, Carina, but I'm now working on an American base in Germany."

"Are you in charge?"

"Of the base—no. Of my unit? Yes. The only other thing I can mention is we're a quick reaction team, so we can be sent anywhere in the world at a moment's notice."

"Even to Antarctica if I run into trouble?"

Rufus laughed. "As long as my boss gives me the word to go ahead."

"I'm onboard the research vessel *RV Aquavit,* and we're in the Southern Ocean. I better give you the Scandinavian Protection Agency's number."

"Already have it. When you called, I recognized you were using a satellite phone—impressive. Your number's in my phone's log."

"It's not my phone, Rufus. It belongs to the SPA. Our team leader allows each of us one call a week, but only for fifteen minutes due to the cost. The one we're using costs two dollars a minute."

"Ouch. Pricey. I feel honored you chose to call me."

Carina chuckled. "You're my only living relative worth keeping in contact with, so who else would I call? I don't have a boyfriend—at least right now." She sighed. "I better go for now. Take care, Rufus. Speak to you next week."

"Sure thing, Cuz. Watch out for those seals—and the penguins. I hear the seals are slippery characters, and that tux on the penguin may look charming, but I hear they're cold and picky little buggers."

Carina laughed as she broke the connection and returned to the mess, carrying her hat and parka. She sat next to Ailsa and offered her sympathies to her friend. "How are you feeling?"

98

"Other than the bump on my head and a stiff neck, Tim says I'm fine. I wonder who those guys that attacked me were?"

Carina shook her head. "Hopefully, the captain will find out and deal with them. I heard he's planning to move us in with the scientists as they have some empty cabins. Bertelot said we'd be better protected with the scientists nearby."

"A great idea—some of them are cute." Ailsa grinned.

Carina laughed. "The men or women?"

"Both."

Carina rolled her eyes. "Whatever works for you."

"Aw, I'm just having fun with you. The guys, so far."

"Well, I did spot one of the female scientists checking you out."

"Probably thought I was a lab specimen."

Both women chuckled.

Carina linked her arm through Ailsa's. "We better find escorts to take us back to our cabins just in case those perverts who attacked you are still lurking about."

Rufus pulled his secure work phone from a desk drawer and dialed Admiral Blakely's number.

After four rings, someone answered. "Aye?"

"Admiral Blakely, please."

"Hey, Rufus. CC here. The admiral stepped out, so I grabbed his phone when it rang. Any problems?"

"Everything's fine so far. The team's shaping up, and so is our headquarters."

"Aye—good to hear. Any trouble from Rhinehart?"

"I saw him in the base exchange yesterday, and he just glared at me. Don't think he'll be any problem."

"Aye. Want to leave a message for the admiral or call back?"

"I'll leave a message. Please tell him my cousin, Carina, is onboard the *RV Aquavit*. They're in the Southern Ocean, en route to

Antarctica. I have her team's satellite phone number. The leader is named Bertelot." He rattled off the digits.

"Thanks, Rufus. I'll pass along the message as soon as he returns."

"Many thanks, CC. Catch up later."

"Aye." As CC hung up, the admiral returned. "Sir, Rufus just called." CC gave him the details.

"Excellent. If we want to put one of our people on board, I can contact this Bertelot and get his concurrence. Are you still up for it, should it be necessary?"

"Och aye, Admiral. After the video conference call, I spoke more with Trevor and Evelyn, and we decided I'm the best one to send. I've always wanted to visit Antarctica. I did a bit of research and found some interesting info which would support my cover story as an archaeologist."

"Hmm." The admiral scratched his ear. "Since your university degree proved worthwhile in our mission in Turkey, I assume you've conducted appropriate research. What did you come up with?"

"There are a number of historic sites and monuments I could check out from an archaeological standpoint. For example, the Soviet expeditionary cemetery, the Inexpressible Island Ice Cave, Shackleton's Hut, the Terra Nova Hut, and Wilson's Stone Igloo, to name a few. Plenty to establish my bona fides."

"Work up a plan, and I'll consider it."

"Aye, Admiral."

* * *

Liam knocked on the door and slid his key into the lock.

"Just a minute." Winston inched the door open. "Where have you been? You left more than an hour ago."

"On the deck where the scientists stay. One of them said there were still plenty of empty rooms, and he took me to one. It's much bigger than ours down here."

"Figures. We're on the crew deck. What do we have to do to move?"

Liam grinned as he fished a key from his pocket. "Not a thing— we're all set."

"Fantastic. Let's transfer our stuff."

Liam's grin grew wider. "There's more news. The SPA team is moving onto the same deck."

"Excellent."

"Only thing is, the word's out about the attack on the SPA woman. Rooms are being rearranged so there are men in cabins on either side of the women to provide some protection."

"Hmm." Winston pursed his lips. "We'll need to identify each of the SPA's rooms and try to plant some more bugs. Otherwise, we won't get the info Sawyer wants."

Liam tossed his bag on a bed and began packing. "I'll be ready in five minutes."

"Take your time. I'll be ready as soon as I can. I'm not a coward and don't just grab stuff from a drawer and cram it into my case before running away."

Twenty minutes later, Liam led Winston into their new cabin. He swept his arms through the air to encompass the area. "Ta-da! See, I told you it's bigger."

Winston nodded. "Yeah, it'll do. Let's unpack and go introduce ourselves to our new neighbors."

After settling in, Liam left the cabin, followed by Winston. He stopped at the first door and knocked.

No answer.

Liam knocked a second time with the same result. He pulled his lock picks from a pocket and knelt by the door. With his tools poised over the lock, he turned at the sound of footsteps.

"Hey! What are you doing at my door?" A short, squat man with the bulging arms of a bodybuilder approached them.

"Oh, sorry." Liam glanced at the deck. "We just moved from the deck below, and I thought this was our cabin."

The man shook his head. "Nope—it's mine. Say, aren't you in the room next door? I heard someone was going to move in."

Liam looked around. "Oops. Wrong cabin. Sorry. These cabins all look alike."

The man stared at them as if trying to memorize their facial features.

"Hey, man." Winston puffed out his chest. "Why not take pictures?"

"Do yourself a favor and check the cabin layout map at the end of the corridor. If I find you trying to enter my cabin again or anyone else's, there'll be hell to pay. But, I'll mention you being here to the captain—in case you don't belong."

"Whatever." Winston walked away. "Thanks, man. I'll do that. Sorry to disturb you."

Liam followed but not before glancing back at the man. He yanked a folding knife from his front pocket and clicked it open. He whispered, "If there's any hell to pay—you'll be the one doing it."

# Chapter Sixteen

D iablo Corps Secret Outpost
Near Prince Charles Mountains

Chris slouched in his chair, alternating between twiddling his thumbs and cracking his knuckles. *Why can't Matthew figure out Diablo from the clues of the beast and the devil? We used to play word games like this all the time. If I weren't afraid of Emmanuel catching me, even on the dark web, I'd come right out with it. Would he break the code? It's not complicated.*

He sighed as he leaned forward and grabbed his Dr Pepper. *Guess I'll check Google for some other synonyms. Perhaps Matthew will pick up on one of these.* His fingers flew over the keyboard as he ran a series of searches.

*Nope. Nope. Nope.*

At last, Chris smiled. *Don't have any idea if these will work, but they are the best I can find—Lucifer and Beelzebub.* He scooted closer to the keyboard, logged onto his dark web email account, and began typing:

*To: Numerologist*
  *From: Knuckle Cracker*
  07192 22322 05181 51808 25221 91813 23071 92224 09260
81912 21071 92215 18222 41907 22130 80722 18132 52613
16271 41209 22260 70726 24160 82609 22111 52613 13222
32724 12130 81823 22091 50624 18212 20926 13232 52222
15012 22506 25270

Chris reread the message a final time to check his conversion. He made a couple of corrections before reaching toward the send key.

*Knock! Knock! Knock!*

Chris swallowed as he hurried to send the email before rushing to the door and unlocking it.

Emmanuel stood in the corridor. "Can I come in?"

"Sure." *What's he want? Is he on to me?* Chris moved to the side and gestured for Emmanuel to enter. After reclaiming his seat, he nodded. "Have a seat, Emmanuel. What can I do for you?" He reached into a box of Kleenex, pulled out a tissue, and dabbed a trickle of perspiration from his forehead.

"Can't a fellow coworker drop by and say hi?" Emmanuel grinned. "After all, we both work for the same tough monster—I mean master."

A low chuckle escaped from Chris. "I suppose you're right. It can be difficult to keep on top of everything Brown wants—especially since he changes his mind all the time." *Is he trying to befriend me so he can learn more about what I'm doing and turn me in to Sawyer?*

"Got that right. I had my team hack into a small bank the other day and take most of their money. He complained because he wanted us to hit another big bank—even though we did as he wanted before he flew back to Miami. I wish he'd just stay there."

Chris sighed. "I suppose we're stuck with him—at least until our contracts expire."

"I guess." Emmanuel grimaced as he studied Chris' face. "I have a touchy subject to discuss with you."

*Uh-oh. He's definitely on to me.* Chris nodded.

Emmanuel shrugged. "It's like this. In addition to my hacking duties, I'm supposed to keep an eye on what everyone else is doing with their computers."

"Even Brown?"

"Except for him." Emmanuel chortled. "As if he'd catch on if I was perusing his activities. I think the original Pong game was too difficult for him."

"What about the other hackers? Won't they figure it out?"

Emmanuel smiled. "Why do you think I picked people who aren't as smart as me? Of course, Felix tried to put one past me, but he's been taken care of. Can't have anyone trying to take over."

"Indeed." *Why's he telling me this?*

"Anyway ... I've been checking employees' use of the dark web. Most of the staff aren't using it—just me, Sawyer—and you."

Chris gulped and cracked his knuckles. "Is there a problem with that?"

Emmanuel shook his head. "No problem, except who is Numerologist? There wasn't anyone by that name on your list of contacts."

"Uh ... he's a former university friend." Chris waved a hand in the air. "I forgot to include him on the form."

"I see." Emmanuel stared at Chris. "So, what's with the coded messages?"

Chris laughed. "Just something we used to do to fight the boredom of our classes. It's nothing, really."

"Yeah, I know. It took me about two minutes to work out your code." Emmanuel rubbed his right temple. "I understand what you're up to, and I approve."

Chris sat upright in his chair. "You do?"

"Sure. Why not? We're both working for a scumbag who thinks he's the planet's savior—while at the same time, he's lining his pockets. In fact, I used one of your references to glaciers when I sent a message from a concerned citizen to the president of the World Bank. I also mentioned the beast." *No need to let him know it was really Felix who sent the message since he's out of the way.* Emmanuel grinned. "Of course, if Brown's caught, I'll be able to prove I sent the message, which should keep me out of trouble."

*Emmanuel's probably skimming money from Brown, too. Even if he's not, I don't trust him.* "I'm not sure why my friend, Numerologist, isn't picking up on the clues I already sent him, so I came up with some new ones today right before you knocked."

"If he doesn't catch on soon, you might have to be straightforward. I assume he has a contact or two he can share the information with so it can be used?"

Chris nodded. "Yes, he's in some type of hush-hush think tank or something like that. I haven't been able to find out any specifics, and he's not saying." *I'm probably sharing too much information with Emmanuel, but I don't think I have a choice, or he might turn me in to Brown.*

"I can try to find out if you tell me his full name."

"No can do. We promised long ago never to share each other's names. Without his permission, I can't do it." *What's he after now?*

Emmanuel frowned. "Okay. I understand. In the meantime, I'll keep covering for you and won't let Brown or Sawyer know what you're doing. At the same time, you'll need to keep quiet." He grinned. "Otherwise, I know where your accounts are located and can wipe them out with a few keystrokes."

"No need to make threats. We both realize what's best. While I agree with Brown's desire to combat climate change, he's going about it the wrong way."

"Agreed. He keeps billions stashed in various secret accounts around the world. He could donate thirty or forty billion to help impoverished countries tackle climate change without missing a penny."

A buzzer sounded as a red light flashed.

Chris smiled. "Speak of the devil, and I've been summoned. Wonder what he wants now?"

"Best not to keep him waiting. Why not join me for dinner in the canteen—say, around 19:00?" Emmanuel stood.

The buzzer sounded a second time.

"Sure thing. I better go."

"See you tonight."

Chris slipped through the inner door into Brown's office. "Yes, sir?"

"What kept you? I don't like to be kept waiting."

"Sorry, sir. It couldn't be helped—I was in the bathroom."

"Well, I hope you washed your hands. Make me an Americano and bring some of those Jaffa Cakes I brought back with me."

"Yes, sir. Right away."

Chris returned to his office and began preparing Brown's snack. *Wonder if I should add a little extra to his coffee? Perhaps some of the arsenic crystalline Jean-Luc brought back with him?* Chris shook his head. *Not yet—need to coordinate with Emmanuel, although I still have my doubts about his opposition to Brown.*

After he finished making an Americano, Chris took it and a package of Jaffa Cakes into Brown's office and set them on the corner of his desk. "Will there be anything else, sir?"

"What? No. You're dismissed. I don't want to be interrupted for the rest of the day—unless there's an emergency. Understood?"

"Yes, sir." Chris left Brown's office, resisting the urge to slam the door.

\* \* \*

Just after the agreed-upon time, Chris entered the canteen. He glanced around, spotted Emmanuel at a table in the far corner, and approached. "What are the specials tonight?"

"Jean-Luc's meatloaf or salmon with radish and orange slaw." Emmanuel pointed to his plate. "I decided on a burger and fries."

Chris laughed. "Let me get something—be right back." He walked over to the hot food line and waited to be served. "I'll take the meatloaf with mashed potatoes and peas."

The server nodded and dished up the food.

Chris returned to Emmanuel's table with a tray and sat. "I've always enjoyed meatloaf since I was a kid. Jean-Luc's is far better than my mother's."

"Enjoy." Emmanuel sipped on his Coke. "What was so urgent for the high and mighty?"

"What? Oh. Brown wanted a coffee." Chris shook his head. "One of these days ... I'll do the unthinkable and poison him. Perhaps make him an Americano with a generous amount of a special ingredient —arsenic."

Emmanuel laughed. "Don't do it yet—wait until we steal more of his money."

# Chapter Seventeen

B edlam Headquarters
Joint Base Myer-Henderson Hall
Virginia

CC leaned back in the chair, hands laced together behind his head, legs crossed and propped on the edge of the desk. He studied the map of Antarctica on the computer screen and nodded. *Perfect.*

Dropping his feet to the floor, CC leaned forward and captured a screenshot of the display, sending it to a nearby printer. After reviewing the printout, he picked up the phone and punched in two digits. "This is CC. Is the admiral still here, or did he return to the Pentagon? I need a few minutes of his time before he leaves."

"Yes, CC. He has a phonecon scheduled with the NSA in twenty minutes, so if you hurry, I can fit you in before he departs."

"Och aye. Thanks, Janice. On my way." CC replaced the phone in the cradle, picked up the printout, and headed to the office the admiral used when he wasn't at the Pentagon.

Minutes later, Janice, who served as the admiral's secretary whenever he was at Bedlam Headquarters, ushered him inside.

CC smiled. "Thanks for the help, Janice."

She nodded and closed the door.

"Take a seat, CC. What's up?"

"Admiral, I've made a decision on the places I plan to visit in Antarctica, which would provide me with a plausible explanation for my participation with the SPA. Assuming you approve, of course." CC placed the printout in front of the admiral.

Multiple locations were highlighted in bold red. Two others were marked in green. "The red ones are the Soviet expeditionary cemetery, the Inexpressible Island Ice Cave, Shackleton's Hut, the Terra Nova Hut, and Wilson's Stone Igloo I mentioned to you before. The green ones are new—Scott's Discovery Hut and the González Pacheco Shelter."

"Will you survey all of them?"

"No. Only as many as needed to support my presence on the ship." CC grinned. "If we find what we're looking for, I might not need to visit all of them to cover my movements. Of course, my interest in archaeology suggests I should stop at all of them."

"Work together with Georgia and plot your itinerary. I'll let Bertelot know you're on the way. They should arrive in two to three days, so you'll need a plane to get you from Ushuaia to their location in Antarctica. I'll ask Bertelot for the coordinates so we drop you at the right place."

"Aye, Admiral. A question, though. When you say drop, should I assume the plane will land somewhere, or will I use a chute?"

Both men laughed.

"CC, if you want to use a parachute, I'm sure we can arrange something. However, I was thinking of a more traditional arrival. It'll also allow us to send some equipment and supplies with you."

"Whew!" CC wiped the mock perspiration from his forehead. "Aye. I agree with the traditional arrival—it's been a long time since I jumped out of a plane. I think my parachuting days are long behind me—I hope. Unless you'd like to come with me, sir?"

The admiral chuckled as he shook his head. "We'll make sure the *Aquavit* is docked somewhere before you begin the final leg of your journey. Have a safe journey." He waved a hand in dismissal.

*  *  *

CC hustled down the corridor to the office of Georgia, Bedlam's logistical whiz. She shared it with Antonia "Toni" Turner, Ph.D., their IT/Telecom consultant. He knocked on the door and entered.

Georgia sat at a cluttered desk, and her eyes were focused on a computer screen. "Have a seat. I'll be right with you."

"Aye."

She turned around. "Sorry, CC. I was concentrating so hard I didn't realize it was you." Georgia turned on her radiant smile. "So, where can I drop you?"

"Huh? Why does everyone want to drop me? First, the admiral, and now you." He smirked.

She laughed. "Just an expression. I hardly see you except when you need to be someplace in a hurry."

"Aye. I need transport to Antarctica."

"Don't think I'll find many scheduled flights." She grinned as her fingers flew over the keyboard. "Okay, while I can get you to Ushuaia, the closest city to Antarctica, it looks like all the charters depart from Punta Arenas, Chile. You'll depart Dulles tomorrow at 08:42, traveling via Panama City, Panama, and Santiago, Chile, with a final flight to Punta Arenas, arriving twenty-two hours later."

"Would it be possible—"

"Got you covered." Georgia chuckled. "Given the length of time for the trip, you're authorized business class."

"Let's go for it. Even if I have to spend a few days in Punta Arenas, it'll allow me the opportunity to acclimate."

"Sounds good." Georgia hit a few keystrokes, and her ticket

printer rumbled into life. "You're all set for your first leg. We'll need a plane equipped for ice landing strips to tackle Antarctica's rough conditions. Let me do some checking around, and I'll let you know when everything's sorted out."

"Aye. As soon as I receive the landing area coordinates, I'll pass them along. In the meantime, I'll draft a list of equipment and the supplies I want to take."

"Perfect. Send me your list, and I'll make things happen. Don't forget your tickets. And your rip cord."

"Aye." CC chuckled as he shook his head. "Everyone's a comedian these days."

After stopping by Starbucks for an Americano, CC returned to his office and fired up the Marconi ViPr secure video conferencing system perched on the edge of his desk. As soon as he logged on, incoming pings announced three connections.

"Hey, guys. Great timing—I needed a coffee before our session." He raised his cup in a toast to the others. "I propose we send two-person teams to check out the glaciers, staying away from more settled areas." CC pursed his lips. "The admiral managed to arrange a few hours of satellite time, so we can cover some of the remote locations when the satellites pass overhead."

"Isn't the admiral going to request their orbits be adjusted to do this?" Rufus scratched his chin.

"He did and was told no, as there are higher priorities. I suggest we get moving on this. If no one objects, I'll send Aussie and Kiwi to Oceania while Rebel and Mountie head to the Canadian wilderness."

"No objections from me." Trevor grinned. "Green and Red will proceed to Pakistan, while Blue and White will go to Svalbard in Norway."

"You guys are cherry-picking the best locations." Evelyn smiled.

"I tasked Nightjar and Raven to head to Franz Josef Land in Russia. Meanwhile, Falcon and Petrel will remain on standby while Petrel continues his recovery from the knife attack in India."

"I guess that leaves me." Rufus ran a hand over his head. "Since we've just stood up the QRF, I'll pick Offender and one of the new members to travel to Greenland."

"Aye. All good choices. While they're away, coordinate with Georgia regarding other locations for the teams to check out. The admiral gave the go-ahead for me to join the *Aquavit,* so I'll be heading to Argentina in a couple of days before transferring to the ship."

Everyone nodded.

"I also want everyone to give some thought about the identity of the group causing the disruptions. I asked the admiral if Matthew had heard any more from his friend, and he hadn't."

Evelyn pursed her lips. "We should conduct an analysis of what organizations would have the motivation and the technical abilities to cause such problems for the developing world."

Trevor tapped his scar. "I'm sure there are some criminal groups and foreign governments who could be involved, such as Russia, China, and North Korea, as they have hacking capabilities and a dislike for the developed countries of the West."

"Aye. Good points. Let's follow up on this. If there's nothing else, I need to decide what equipment and supplies to take with me."

After signing out from the conference call, CC checked his email—one from the admiral:

*Bertelot and his team will be expecting you. They'll initially dock not far from the German Neumayer III research station before they transfer to a location on the Ekström Ice Shelf. The research station is located at Latitude: -70° 40' 4.79" S Longitude: -8° 16' 1.20" W. Godspeed.*

He acknowledged the admiral's email and forwarded it to Georgia. He googled food, equipment, and supplies for forays into Antarctica. Finding a couple of useful links, he perused them.

He studied the food list first and wasn't surprised to find items high in fat were the first priority, followed by those providing protein, with carbohydrates coming in last. He sent it to Georgia, suggesting she work her magic to pick items that mirrored those on the list. He also pointed out a modern sledding box contained twenty person-days of food, so he requested she double it.

Next, he turned to the equipment and clothing lists. Nodding as he scanned the items, CC forwarded them to Georgia, again asking her to choose what she thought was best.

A two-word response came back from Georgia: *On it.*

CC smiled as he finished his review of the lists and read about earlier Antarctica excursions. He downed the remains of his now-cold coffee, stood, and stretched. *Everything's falling into place. Should be an interesting time.*

# Chapter Eighteen

Diablo Corps Secret Outpost
Near Prince Charles Mountains

Brown yanked his office door open and stomped inside. He kicked the door shut and threw himself into his chair before stabbing at the intercom button.

Chris rushed through the inner doorway. "Yes, sir?"

"Get me a coffee and be quick about it!"

"Yes, sir. Right away."

After making Brown's coffee, Chris took it to him. He set the cup and saucer on the edge of Brown's desk. "Will there be anything else, sir?"

Brown glanced up. "What?" He waved a hand in dismissal. "No. Get out."

"Yes, sir." Chris raced into his sanctuary.

Brown sipped on the hot liquid and burned his tongue. "Damn!

Can't anyone do anything right?" He put the cup down. *I've hired a bunch of nincompoops—I could train monkeys to do a better job.*

He pulled his keyboard closer and began typing an email. When he finished, he clicked send. *Emmanuel and his hackers better get their act together, or they'll be fish food. When I tell them to shut down more banks and steal their money, I expect my orders to be carried out.*

Brown leaned back and pursed his lips, his feet resting on the edge of the desk as he drummed a beat on the chair's arm. *What should I do next?* He took a deep breath, blowing out slowly, expanding both cheeks before he tightened his mouth in a flat line as he squinted at the ceiling.

He snapped his fingers. *I know.* He reached for the phone, stabbed three digits, and waited for someone to answer.

"Hello?"

"Xavier. Tell me how much money we've siphoned off with our current hacking operations."

"Just a minute, sir."

Through the phone, Brown could hear Xavier clicking on his keyboard.

"Sir? It's almost reached twenty billion. Do you want to do anything with the funds?"

"Not at this time. Inform me when it reaches twenty-five. I have an idea to use some of the money to attack climate change deniers."

"Yes, sir."

Brown broke the connection, grinning as he did so. *Why didn't I think of going after the deniers sooner? This should make for excellent press.* He made another call. "Sawyer? Come to my office. I need some guidance."

Several minutes later, someone knocked on Brown's door.

"Get in here."

Sawyer entered and took a seat in front of the desk. "You wanted to see me?"

"Yes." Brown twiddled his thumbs. "I want you to monitor the activities of Emmanuel and his team. They aren't following orders, and I'm afraid he's getting too big for his britches. He's overconfident, and I feel he's trying to undermine my position, even though he works for me. If it weren't for my largesse, he'd still be rotting in an Israeli jail for attempting to steal government secrets." *Emmanuel might think he's smarter than me, but I learned from my crafty old father to trust my instincts. They tell me Emmanuel is up to something. I don't know what it is—yet—but I'll find out and deal with him.*

Sawyer nodded. "Okay. If I find he's up to no good, what do you want me to do?"

"Good question." Brown pursed his lips. "If you catch him in the act, it might be time to make a public example. Execute him but film it so we can broadcast it to everyone here."

"Why not make them all attend in person?"

Brown nodded. "An excellent idea. I'll leave things in your capable hands." He glared at Sawyer. "Don't let me down."

"Have I ever?" Sawyer grinned. "I'll take care of things."

Chris finished the inventory Brown requested and emailed it to him. Picking up his empty cup, he left his office and headed to the canteen for a refill. After paying, he headed toward the exit.

A hand grabbed his shoulder.

He turned.

"Hey. I've been looking for you."

"Hi, Emmanuel. I was just going to your office."

"Let's go. You can fill me in on what you wanted to see me about."

When they entered Emmanuel's office, they took seats at a rectangular table.

"I wanted to follow up on our earlier conversation." Chris sipped his coffee and grimaced. "The canteen's coffee seems to be getting worse by the day."

Emmanuel laughed. "I don't think that's what you wanted to discuss."

"You're right. I'm concerned about Brown. He's getting more ill-tempered, and I think it won't be long before he totally loses it." Chris shook his head again. "When he wasn't looking, I removed the bullets from his pistol and replaced them with blanks. No telling who he might try to shoot."

Emmanuel rubbed his chin. "Not good. I suspect I might be the one in the firing line. He sent me a blistering email earlier today, complaining I'm not doing what he ordered me to do. Yet, I've made note of all of his instructions, and we're doing exactly what he wanted. Do you suppose he's developing dementia?"

"Only the doc could tell us. Perhaps it's worth a mention to him. I'll talk with Doctor Stine the next time we're in Miami. Perhaps he has a colleague who can examine Brown."

"Sounds like a winner. Anything else, Chris? If not, we're supposed to hack into some more infrastructure control systems—this time in Europe."

Chris shook his head and stood. "Thanks for listening. Catch up later."

\* \* \*

Brown started a new email addressed to the editors of the *New York Times, Washington Post, Wall Street Journal, USA Today, The Times (UK), The Guardian (UK),* and *The Telegraph (UK)*:

*Please publish this short open letter in your newspapers as soon as possible. The fate of the world could depend upon it.*

To: *Climate Change Deniers*
    From: *Nightmare*

*Wake up! Your refusal to accept scientific proof of climate change is causing irreparable harm to the planet. It is imperative we all take requisite action to protect ourselves now. Failure to do so will render Earth uninhabitable for future generations.*

*It is incumbent upon everyone to do whatever they can, no matter how small a gesture, to stop climate change. You're in my sights, so get busy before it's too late. Your lack of action will lead to your demise, so ignore my warning at your own peril.*

Brown reread his message and smiled before clicking send.

Maddie entered the staff canteen and glanced around. She spotted Reginald sitting at a table for two in the corner of the room. After buying a Mountain Dew, she took her drink and approached the table. She pointed at the empty seat. "Are you waiting for someone in particular?"

Reginald grinned. "Yes. I guess you haven't eaten yet."

She shook her head. "Not yet. I was hoping to bump into you." Maddie leaned closer, letting her fingers caress the back of his hand. She whispered, "Something's not right here. I keep getting strange looks from other members of the staff. Nothing threatening, but they give me the creeps."

"It's probably nothing to worry about. You haven't been with us long, and strangers are always checked out. New arrivals are always exciting as they break up the monotony."

"Perhaps so." She glanced around. "However, this morning, I did an inventory of my supplies. Six of the pre-made explosive packs are missing."

"Are you sure?"

"Positive. I just made them yesterday and haven't used any this week."

"Any idea who might have taken them?"

Maddie tilted her head. "Nothing concrete. But I hope to find the culprit before someone tries using them. They can be deadly, especially in the hands of a novice who doesn't know what they're doing. Someone could be maimed or even killed. Will you help me?"

Reginald smiled. "Of course. Just tell me what you want me to do."

"Keep your eyes peeled. If someone looks suspicious or is carrying a strange package, follow them."

"Is that all? Not a problem."

"Just be careful, Reginald." She squeezed his hand. "I don't want anything to happen to you."

# Chapter Nineteen

P residente Carlos Ibáñez del Campo International Airport
Punta Arenas, Chile

After spending almost twenty-two mind-numbing hours on airplanes since leaving Washington Dulles International Airport, CC's final flight began its descent into Presidente Carlos Ibáñez del Campo International Airport.

With a slight hop as the Airbus 320 touched down, the pilot hit the brakes.

CC and the other passengers braced for a quick stop using the seats in front of them.

The pilot slowed the aircraft before taxiing to one of the three ramps passengers used to enter the terminal. After the pilot turned off the *fasten seatbelt* sign, CC collected his belongings from the overhead bin. He followed others disembarking and climbing the ramp into the terminal.

He located the baggage claim sign and proceeded down a flight of stairs. He found an empty spot next to the luggage conveyor belt and glanced around.

A short, swarthy man pushing two luggage carts approached. He wore a black jacket and trousers. Perched on his head was a baseball hat with *SWOOP Antarctica* emblazoned across the bill.

Two porters followed, each pushing a cart.

The man stopped in front of CC.

"Aye. Are you Carlos?" CC asked.

The man's teeth gleamed when he smiled. "Sí. Carlos Alvarez. The email from Señorita Georgia said you had many boxes." He gestured toward the carts. "I hope this will be enough."

"Aye. Should be. How big is your plane?"

"It is a Beechcraft King Air 300—very popular with small groups visiting the White Continent."

"Excellent. There's only me and the luggage." CC glanced at the conveyor belt. "Here it comes now."

Twenty minutes later, the four carts were stacked high with duffle bags, various boxes, and hard-sided Pelican cases of different sizes.

The porters departed with two of the trolleys, leaving Carlos and CC to bring up the rear with the other two as they followed signs to the exit.

"How far to your plane, Carlos?"

"Not too far, señor. We shall leave the building through a staff exit and onto the tarmac. Someone will check your passport first, just to make sure you are not on any watch list."

"Aye. No problem."

They stopped at a desk by the exit where an airport official stood. "Passport, señor."

CC handed over his passport.

After a quick glance through the document, the official handed it back. "You may go. Enjoy your trip."

"Aye. Thank you."

Once outside, Carlos led the way to his blue and white aircraft.

"This is it." He patted the side of the plane as if it was a favored child. "I removed the extra seats to make plenty of room for your luggage."

The four men made short work of clearing the carts and securing everything in the plane.

CC pulled out his wallet as he glanced at Carlos. "How much of a tip should I give them?"

Carlos shook his head. "It is not necessary. Gratuities for them are part of the overall charter cost. They have already been paid. Shall we board?"

"Aye. Let's get going."

The men climbed inside, with CC sitting in the co-pilot's seat.

"Don't touch any of the controls." Carlos smiled as he ran through his departure checklist.

"You mean like this?" CC grinned as he feinted a move for the controls. "No worries. I have no idea how to fly."

"That makes two of us, señor." Carlos chuckled. After the twin turboprops were spinning, he keyed his mic. "Tower, this is SWOOP, ready for departure."

"Confirmed, SWOOP. The runway is yours."

The aircraft raced along the long stretch of concrete and seemed to jump into the air. "Sit back and relax, Señor Craig. We shall be landing next to your ship in about two hours."

As the temperature dropped, cold air seeped inside the aircraft. Noticing CC zipping up his parka, Carlos turned up the heat. "Have you been to Antarctica before?"

CC shook his head. "No, but there are several locations I want to visit from an archaeological perspective while I'm on the continent. I'll be using the *RV Aquavit* as my base."

"Sounds like a good plan. I hope you are met with favorable weather conditions."

CC grinned again. "Aye. Me, too." He gazed out the window at the sea below. *Never did like cold water. Glad I'm up here. Gives me time to think about the mission.*

Two hours later, Carlos pointed out the front of the aircraft. "Antarctica is before us. If you look closely, you will see your ship."

CC studied the view, finally spotting the RV *Aquavit*. "Aye. I see it."

Carlos keyed his mic. "*Aquavit*, this is SWOOP. We should be on the ground in about fifteen minutes."

"Roger, SWOOP. As requested, we fashioned a temporary runway for you. Be careful, as it might be a bit bumpy."

"Understood, *Aquavit*. SWOOP out." Carlos lined the plane up with the runway.

The snow and ice glistened in the bright sunlight.

Carlos began his descent. As the wheels were about to touch down, he turned and looked at CC. "Hold on, señor. I see a few rough areas." He clamped his jaws together. "But it is nothing I haven't faced before."

"Aye." CC checked his seatbelt.

The plane jolted as it landed.

Carlos hit the brakes to slow their speed as they raced toward a large pile of snow at the end of the makeshift runway.

*Bang!*

The left wheel hit something on the airstrip. The plane tilted toward the right before settling back on its wheels. Luggage and boxes rattled as they shifted.

CC bent forward, held in place by his seatbelt, before settling back in the seat.

Carlos stamped harder on the brakes, struggling to keep the plane in a straight line.

*Bang!*

The aircraft shunted to the left.

Carlos tightly gripped the yoke. "Hang on!"

The plane plowed into the snow along the edge of the runway and came to an abrupt halt.

Carlos glanced at CC. "Are you okay, señor?" A look of concern passed over Carlos' face.

"Och aye." CC grinned. "I once read if you can walk away from a landing, it was a good one."

Carlos chuckled. "Well, señor, we are in luck. We will walk away from this one." He switched off the engines and unbuckled his belt. "Shall we go outside and see if there is any damage?"

"Aye."

They disembarked and walked around the aircraft and inspected it.

CC glanced around at the whiteness of the continent. All looks the same. A perfect place to hide in plain sight. He turned to Carlos. "So, is there any damage?"

"I do not see anything of concern." Carlos grinned. "We will use the bulldozer to pull my ride back on the runway so I can depart. The ship's crew will help us."

Several people strolled down the gangway from the ship and approached. They all wore Arctic clothing, hats, gloves, and goggles to protect them from the elements.

A short and stout man with whisps of gray hair sticking out from under his *Brynje* hat stepped forward, a hand outstretched. "Welcome to Antarctica. I'm Paul Smythe, captain of the *RV Aquavit*."

CC grinned, shook hands, and identified himself. "I guess I'm a late arrival to your party."

"Yes. Bertelot said you missed our sailing from Ushuaia. You're the archaeologist, correct?"

"Aye. I'm looking forward to visiting several historical locations such as the Inexpressible Island Ice Cave and Shackleton's Hut."

Paul nodded. "We'll assist you as much as we can. C'mon, follow me, and I'll take you to Bertelot and the others."

"What about my cargo?"

"Don't worry about that." He pointed to the others who came with him from the ship. "They'll help unload the aircraft and get it back on the runway so the pilot can take off."

The captain turned to Carlos, a glint of merriment in his eyes. "Assume your hard landing didn't stress the plane too much?"

"No, Capitán." He grinned. "As I told CC, any time you can walk away from a landing, it's a good one."

The men laughed.

CC turned to Carlos. "Thank you for bringing me to Antarctica. Hope we'll meet again."

"Of course, señor." He smiled as they shook hands. "SWOOP is the only reliable service covering Antarctica." Carlos waved as he headed to his plane.

Paul and CC trundled through the snow and ice and reached the ramp leading to the ship.

CC gestured toward the orange and white research ship. "Very impressive."

Paul smiled. "Yes. We are very proud of our vessel. It was originally launched as an icebreaker before being refitted as a research platform. Someone will take you on a tour later."

Climbing aboard, Paul led the way to the ship's mess and stopped in front of the SPA team.

Bertelot stood and introduced everyone.

CC lingered over Carina's hand. "Aye. Rufus told me a lot about you." He studied the tall blonde with deep blue eyes. *What a looker.* He shook his head. *Probably has a stable of admirers.*

"Likewise, but he forgot to mention how handsome you are." Carina held his gaze with a smile on her face.

CC blushed as he finally dropped her hand. "Guess it's something guys don't usually talk about." He turned to the final member.

Gunner glared at CC. After a pause, he grasped CC's hand and squeezed.

*What have we here?* CC grinned as he matched the pressure Gunner used. *I've stepped into something, but what?* CC glanced at Carina.

An amused expression etched across her face.

Eggert clasped CC's shoulder. "Come. I'll show you to your quarters. I think afterward, Carina might be available to take you on a tour of the ship." Eggert grinned.

Gunner took a final look at CC before storming out of the mess.

"What's with him? We just met." CC shook his head. "Was it something I said? I mean, I've bathed and everything."

Carina laughed as she placed a hand on CC's arm. "He thinks we're a couple." An amused expression crept across her face. "But he's the only one who thinks we are."

# Chapter Twenty

O ffice of the Chairman of the Joint Chiefs of Staff
The Pentagon, Arlington, Virginia

Matthew leaned back in his chair and clapped his hands together, a grin spreading across his face. "At last! The answer's been staring at me all the time. If Chris is working for Diablo Corporation, no wonder he wouldn't share it. The CEO appears to be a mean and spiteful person based on the lawsuits mentioned in the press."

He checked his dark web account once again and smiled when he found another email from Chris. After reading it, Mathew picked up his empty cup and headed toward the admiral's office. *He should have fresh coffee.* After a quick knock on the outer door, Matthew stepped inside. He breathed in the aroma of newly-brewed coffee.

Susan raised her head and smiled. "Matthew, you always seem to know when a fresh pot is brewing. What's your secret?"

"Just lucky, I guess." Matthew smiled and filled his cup. "Is the admiral available?"

"He should be—he just came out for a refill, and no one is with him." She glanced at the telephone console. "He's not on a line." Susan stood and beckoned Matthew to follow. "Let me make sure he's not in the middle of something." She knocked on the admiral's door and opened it. "Sir, Matthew to see you. Do you have a moment?"

Admiral Blakely glanced up from his computer screen. "Ah, Matthew. Come in and rest your feet."

Susan smiled as she departed.

"Many thanks, Admiral." Matthew sat in a chair in front of the admiral's desk and put his cup on a coaster on an adjacent table. "I thought you'd like to know I finally solved the devil and beast riddle."

"Excellent. So, who or what are they?"

"Sorry it took me so long to figure it out. I was overlooking the obvious." Matthew picked up his cup and sipped on the now-cooling brew. "Both are aliases for Diablo. I also received a new message from Chris. He said the devil was behind the Liechtenstein Bank crash and provided two additional aliases for me to consider: Lucifer and Beelzebub."

Matthew shook his head. "I searched on the terms and came up with what I think is the answer: Diablo Corporation. The CEO is an eighty-something-year-old multi-billionaire by the name of Walter Brown. He's purported to be one of the top ten richest people in the world, and he's a real piece of work with dozens of former employees filing workers' rights violations, harassment, and misconduct."

"Doesn't sound like a pleasant place to work. So, where is Brown?"

Matthew pursed his lips. "That's what makes this such a difficult puzzle to crack. His headquarters is located in Miami—no glaciers there."

"Have the teams had any success?"

Matthew shook his head. "Not yet. At least, not so far. I'll be talking with them later."

"Tell them we haven't had any luck with the satellite search either, but I've requested BlackSky and Planet continue to scan the more remote areas so the teams can concentrate on viable locations. Of course, it'll depend on any constraints the companies have with their National Reconnaissance Office contracts."

"Yes, Admiral." Matthew stood. "I better get ready for my meeting. I'll keep you updated with any progress."

The admiral smiled. "I know you will. I'll pass your information to NSA Meu."

"Thank you, sir."

Back in his office, Matthew fired up the video conferencing equipment. Before long, the faces of Rufus, Trevor, Evelyn, and Aiden, who was filling in for CC, came onto the screen.

After brief greetings, Matthew dived into his report, bringing everyone up to speed from headquarters. He provided what information he had gleaned from public records concerning Diablo and the company's CEO. "Sorry, I don't have more details to provide. Other than required tax documents filings with the IRS and pending lawsuits, there isn't much information available. Even Diablo's company website is devoid of any specifics. Does anyone have anything else to add?"

Unfortunately, no one had any positive news to report.

Evelyn poked her tongue against her cheek. "There are more locations with glaciers than what we were first briefed on. It'll take some time to get the teams into the most promising locations as there are over two hundred thousand glaciers in the world." She tapped a finger against her lips. "During my search, I recall reading most of the world's largest glaciers are located in Antarctica."

Matthew nodded. "The admiral said he was requesting additional satellite coverage to scan the remotest locations so the teams could concentrate on more likely places. Also, we need to look for locations associated with Diablo Corporation. I'll send you a note regarding this."

"Well done, Matthew." Trevor rubbed his facial scar. "Look forward to reading your assessment."

"I haven't had a status report from Maverick and Quincy yet." Rufus crossed his arms and frowned. "We keep trying to contact them every hour, but so far, no success."

"Okay. If there's nothing further, I'll let you get back to your work." A slight grin crept across Matthew's face. "It's a bit of a stretch for me to be hosting a meeting—usually, I'm a silent participant."

"You've done just fine." Evelyn smiled. "When you next speak to CC, tell him to be careful when he heads to Antarctica."

"Will do." Matthew broke the connections and captured the meeting in an email, which he forwarded to Admiral Blakely.

\* \* \*

Jakobshavn Glacier
   Near Ilulissat, Greenland

Maverick groaned as he opened his eyes. He glanced around the dimly lit area before looking up, focusing on the hole in the ice he had fallen through. He licked his dry lips. "Quincy, can you hear me?"

Silence.

Maverick struggled to an upright position and leaned against a pile of fallen ice and snow. He took a deep breath. "Quincy, where are you?"

The sunlight beaming down through the hole fifty feet above cast a shadow on Maverick as Quincy leaned in to answer. "Hang on, Maverick. I'm dropping you a rope. I need to anchor it, so it'll take a few minutes."

Maverick coughed. "No worries, Quincy. I'm not going anywhere." Maverick coughed again and winced, holding his side. "I think I broke a couple of ribs in the fall."

"Be right back."

Maverick pulled off a glove and let it dangle on the hook attached to his clothing as he unfastened a pouch on his belt. Pulling out a penlight, he switched it on and cast the beam around the cavern.

Two eyes stared at him.

Startled, he scampered back against the ice and snow.

Dark, beady eyes, almost like slits, kept staring at him.

He focused the beam on the creature.

Long frozen and interred in the ice, the unknown animal maintained a silent vigil.

Maverick relaxed. *Not sure what it is, but I hope Quincy can get me out of here. I don't want to spend the rest of my life stuck in this place with you.*

A few minutes later, several small chunks of ice and a shower of snow dropped on him.

"Hey! Watch it."

"Sorry. Incoming. Here comes the rope and a harness."

Maverick watched as the rope slithered toward him. "Got it."

"Put the harness around you and let me know when you're secure. I have the other end connected to the winch on the front of the SUV, and I'm attached to the rope, too. When you're ready, brace for impact, and I'll get you out of there."

Maverick struggled to slip the harness over his clothes.

"Ow!" He grimaced as he tightened the cinches around his broken ribs. When he was ready, he gave the rope a tug. "Let's go—pull away."

The rope jerked as Quincy activated the winch.

Maverick suppressed a scream when he was yanked into the air.

Foot by agonizing foot, he inched his way toward salvation. At last, he neared the opening. "Quincy! I'm just below the edge."

Footsteps crunched on the surface. "Hold on." Quincy knelt and reached into the hole, his fingers finding a metal ring attached to the harness. "Ready to come up?"

"You bet. I'm tired of hanging around."

Quincy reached down and grabbed Maverick's outstretched hand. With a grunt, he pulled up and away.

Maverick popped out of the hole and hung onto his cousin.

"We better get you to a doctor. Your head's covered with blood, and you might have a concussion."

Maverick grinned. "At least I'm back among the living. Don't have any coffee or a shot of liquor by any chance?"

Quincy laughed. "No, but I'll see what I can arrange."

# Chapter Twenty-One

board *RV Aquavit*
Off the Coast of Sanae IV, South
African Research Station, Antarctica

After a short tour with Ailsa, they returned to the crew's mess. She opened the door and stood aside while CC stepped inside and surveyed the service wall. They had the space to themselves.

CC glanced around. "Any chance of a coffee?"

"How do you take it?" Ailsa smiled.

"Hot, black, and no sugar."

She grinned. "Same as me. Coming right up." She returned minutes later with a pot and two cups. "It might be a bit strong as it was made earlier."

"No problem—the stronger, the better." CC studied Ailsa's profile while she took a tentative sip of the hot brew. "How long have you been associated with the SPA?"

"This is my first excursion with them. When did you become interested in archaeology?"

"A long time ago. I went to Turkey with my parents, and they took me to a Phrygian excavation outside Ankara. It fascinated me so much I chose archaeology as my minor at Michigan State University."

Ailsa flashed her eyes at him. "How wonderful to do something you enjoy."

"Aye." A smile crept across CC's face. "I don't get to do as much crawling around ruins as I'd like because my regular work keeps me busy."

"Oh! I thought you were a full-time archaeologist."

CC shook his head. "Perhaps one day." He sipped the coffee while looking over the rim of his cup.

"What do you do when you're not visiting the past?"

"Nothing much." CC waved a hand in dismissal. "I work for an obscure government agency." He yawned. "Don't suppose you could point me in the direction of my cabin?"

"Of course. Yours is only two doors from mine."

They stood and headed toward the exit.

Ailsa linked her arm through CC's. "We're down a deck."

After descending, she led him to his cabin. "Knock on my door if you need anything." She pointed. "My cabin is that way."

CC held out a hand. "Aye. Thank you for the tour and the company."

She reached past his arm and pecked him on the cheek before stepping back and smiling. "Welcome aboard."

"Och aye." CC rubbed his cheek. "Thanks."

"Any time."

CC stepped into his cabin and closed the door. Picking up his rucksack, he pulled out his belongings and placed them in the three-drawer dresser. When he finished, he stripped, grabbed his shaving kit, and walked into the bathroom.

After a shave and a shower, CC wrapped a towel around his waist. As he headed for the bathroom door, he heard muffled whispers. *Damn. Wish I had my SIG Sauer.* He shut off the light and eased the door open a crack.

Shadows danced on the far wall as two people moved in front of the bedroom lamp.

CC closed the door and glanced around the bathroom. *Nothing to use as a weapon.*

Footsteps approached the bathroom door. The handle turned, and the door swung inward. A man stepped through the doorway.

CC grabbed the man's arm and tugged, propelling the intruder against the sink. A leveraged kick to the man's groin dropped him to his knees.

A second kick, this time to the man's jaw, rendered him senseless as he collapsed to the floor.

"Psst, Liam. What's taking you so long? Did you break something, or have you stopped for a leak?" A drawer squeaked shut in the bedroom as the second intruder finished his search. "Hurry up, Liam, before the guy returns."

CC reached around the corner and flicked the bedroom ceiling light off.

"Hey. What ya doing? Turn the light back on."

After CC's eyes adjusted to the darkness, he crept from the bathroom, following the sound of the man's voice. When he neared the man, CC lashed out with a sharp kick, striking his kneecap.

"Aaaaah!"

The man screamed as he fell onto his other knee.

CC reared back and threw a punch catching the intruder on the side of his head.

The intruder collapsed and remained still.

CC reached toward the light switch and clicked it on. After determining the man was out cold, CC went to the top drawer of the dresser, removed several zipties, and secured the man's wrists.

Entering the bathroom, CC did the same with the first intruder. He linked several zipties together, making a long enough length to wrap around the man's ankles. Once CC finished, he did the same to the second man.

Grabbing his keys, he stepped into the corridor and locked the door. He went to Ailsa's cabin and knocked.

Moments later, she unlocked the door and peeked outside, keeping a foot behind the door in case the person who knocked was unknown to her. "CC, what's wrong? Come in."

"Sorry to disturb you, Ailsa. Two men broke into my cabin—"

"What? Where are they? Are you okay?"

CC smiled. "Aye. I'm fine. I subdued both men and trussed them up like chickens. Could you notify Bertelot and Captain Smythe while I go back and check on my guests?"

"Yes, of course. I'll bring them to your cabin."

"Great." CC returned to his cabin and let himself in. After checking the men were still secured and breathing, he sat in a chair and waited.

A few minutes later, someone knocked on the door. "CC, it's Ailsa. I've brought help."

CC unlocked the door and pulled it open.

Ailsa entered the cabin with Captain Smythe, Bertelot, Gunner, and a bodybuilder named David Tennent, who worked for Smythe as the ship's security officer.

The captain nudged the man on the bedroom floor with his foot and turned to CC. "You certainly took care of him. Where's the other one?"

CC pointed to the bathroom door. "In there."

The captain motioned toward David. "Drag him out and drop him next to this one."

"I will help." Gunner stepped forward.

The men entered the bathroom and dragged the bound man. They dropped him on the floor next to his accomplice.

Both men began to stir.

CC yanked the second intruder's foot. "What's your name? I know you called out Liam, so I assume that's your partner's name."

The man spat. "I know my rights. I don't have to give my name to you."

Captain Smythe laughed. "You're an intruder on my ship in international waters. You don't have any rights unless I give them to you. Answer the man."

Liam glanced at his partner. "Tell them. They'll have to turn us over to the authorities."

"Are you both stupid?" The captain shook his head. "There aren't any authorities in Antarctica to turn you over to. You'll remain onboard as my prisoners until we return to Chile, where you'll be turned over as criminals. In the meantime, you will answer our questions."

"Captain, do you have a hammer I can borrow?" CC smacked a fist into the palm of his other hand. "I'm sure a bit of gentle persuasion will loosen their tongues."

The captain gestured to David and whispered in his ear.

David nodded and left the cabin.

The captain turned to CC. "David will bring a hammer and a few other tools that might be useful. Of course, as the captain of the ship, I cannot condone torture." He winked at CC.

"Aye. I'm sure they'll be singing like canaries—at least one will. We need to find out why they're on the ship and who they work for."

When David returned, he carried a toolbox. He handed it to CC. "Happy persuasion. I'll wait in the corridor in case you require assistance."

"Aye." CC grinned. "It's best if everyone leaves while I question our intruders. I'm sure they'll have an interesting tale to tell."

Everyone departed but Ailsa.

"You, too, Ailsa. I don't want any witnesses to what I'm about to do."

"Okay, CC. I'll join the others."

"Wait. Tell David to come back in."

Ailsa studied CC's face. "Okay. Do you want me to return?"

He shook his head. "Better if you don't witness what's going to happen."

She nodded and left.

Moments later, David reentered the room. "Ailsa said you wanted to speak with me?"

"Aye. Stay a couple of minutes. After I start talking with them, I want to keep them apart. You can grill one of them."

David grinned. "Okay, I can do that."

After she departed, CC opened the toolbox. He pulled out a hammer, pliers, and a cordless drill. He squeezed the drill handle, and the bit began spinning. "Aye. This'll do."

He gathered the tools and knelt next to Liam. "If you tell me what I want to know, you won't be hurt."

Liam's eyes grew wide as his head rocked from side to side.

After untying Liam and kneeling on his right arm, CC reached for the hammer. He raised it in the air and aimed at Liam's hand.

"Aaaiih!"

Liam screamed as the hammer thudded into the floor, narrowly missing his hands. "D-Don't. I'll tell you what you want to know."

The other intruder scowled at Liam. "Keep your mouth shut. They can't do anything to us."

CC turned to David. "Take Scowling Face into another room. Do whatever you need to find out what he knows."

David marched over to Winston, grabbed him by the arm, and hauled him out of the room, slamming the door shut.

CC raised the hammer again. "What's your friend's name?" The hammer thudded into the floor a second time.

Liam jumped. "I-Its W-Winston."

"Tell me his name again." CC pursed his lips.

Liam sucked in a breath before exhaling. "Winston."

CC nodded. "Who do you work for?"

Liam shook his head. "You don't know what they'll do to me. I can't help you, or I'll end up dead."

CC swapped the hammer for the drill. "Tell me now, or I'll put a hole through your hand before we boot you off the ship without Arctic clothing. You'll be dead in minutes." He squeezed the trigger, causing the bit to rotate. CC brought the whirring drill toward it. "Who do you work for?"

Liam screamed as he thrashed about, trying to escape from his tormentor. "D-Don't. We work for Sawyer Johnson."

"Where is he?"

Liam shook his head. "I-I don't know."

CC grabbed Liam's hand and lowered the drill toward Liam's hand. When it was just above the skin, CC activated the trigger. "Last chance."

Sweat poured off Liam's face. "H-He works for Diablo Corporation."

"Where?"

"In a special base here in Antarctica."

"Where do I find this base?"

"I-I don't know." Liam shook his head a final time as he passed out.

CC jumped to his feet and dropped the tools on the bed. He strode to the door and opened it.

David, Bertelot, and Gunner stepped into the room.

Bertelot glanced at CC. "We heard screaming. What happened? I assume everything went well?"

"The power of suggestion caused him to pass out." CC shrugged. "He said his partner's name is Winston."

David grinned. "The other guy wasn't so tough. It took about thirty seconds to get his name—Winston Applegate—after I pulled out my old Ontario MK 3 Navy knife and threatened to castrate him." David chuckled. " He said his friend is Liam Dawson. They work for Diablo's security office and were sent to the ship to find out what the SPA was planning."

"Aye. I need to send a message to Washington. With what you obtained, I have some of the intel I wanted, although they didn't reveal the specific location of Diablo's base. I'll require some additional assistance to find it. Can you remove these two clowns and stuff them somewhere?"

"I have just the spot—a small place we use as a brig next to the engine room."

\* \* \*

Once the intruders were secured in their new home, CC returned to his cabin. He fired up his computer and composed a message:

*To: Alpha, Bravo, Charlie, QRF-1*

*From: Haggis*

*Suspected location of target is a secret base in Antarctica controlled by Diablo Corporation. Recommend one person from each team be sent to me ASAP. Request Grandson continues digging into this corporation to determine if they've acquired rights in Antarctica. More intel to follow as it becomes available.*

# Chapter Twenty-Two

Diablo Corps Secret Outpost
Near Prince Charles Mountains

Sawyer stomped into the staff canteen, bought a Diet Coke to calm himself, and tossed a crumpled bill at the cashier. Scanning the room, he spotted the source of his irritation. *I should deck him.*

Gritting his teeth, he marched to a table at the end of the room where Harold sat. He yanked out a chair, the legs screeching on the floor as he sat and stared at his nemesis. *I want to reach across the table and strangle him.*

Harold raised a brow. "Hey, Sawyer. What's up?" Harold took an enormous bite of a bagel covered with cream cheese and washed it down with his tea.

Sawyer slammed a fist on the table. "I suspect you're not so stupid that you imagined I would stand by as you romance my girl?"

"Who?" Harold laughed.

"Maddie. I saw you talking with her." Sawyer whipped his head around to a nearby table where two employees snickered.

Harold waved his hands in front of himself as if warding off an attack. "Whoa, Sawyer. You got the wrong impression. She asked me to join her. We're only work colleagues and friends, nothing more. She was telling me she found the explosives she thought were missing. They were in a box in the back of the storeroom where we keep them, but she had thrown a tarp over the box and forgot about it."

"Liar. I don't believe you. I spotted you holding hands." A thunderous expression creased Sawyer's face. "I'm warning you. Stay away, or you'll be sorry."

"If you must know, she had caught her heel and grabbed me for support, which I was happy to supply." Harold pushed himself to his feet. "Maddie is a grown woman and is free to make her own decisions and do whatever she decides to do. If she wants to meet with me, what's it to you? You don't own her."

*But who is he to tell me whether I own her or not? I hate Harold's condescending attitude.* "Oh, yeah?" Sawyer clenched his fists. "It's a lot to me, she means everything, and I wouldn't want to be you if you drive a wedge between us with your antics. To you, she's just another pretty thing to chase. She's a game, one you won't win."

"Just because you're in charge of security doesn't give you the right to tell me what to do regarding her. If I want to talk with Maddie, I will. After all, we work together on the ice."

*That better be all they do together.* "I'm warning you." Sawyer lunged across the table, grabbing Harold by the throat.

Harold's face turned red as he tried to push Sawyer's hand away. "H-Help ... he's killing—"

Sawyer released his hold and rushed around the table. He shoved Harold backward hard enough to topple his chair and pushed him to the floor.

Harold's head bounced with the impact.

Sawyer smiled as he straddled the dazed Harold and pinned him to the floor with a flurry of punches.

Again and again.

Blood spurted from cuts around Harold's eyes and nose and splattered his clothes and the floor.

Two men rushed from the opposite end of the cafeteria. They struggled with the flailing Sawyer to pull him off Harold.

"Dammit! Let go of me!" Sawyer tried to break free without success.

One of the men assisted Sawyer to his feet and shoved him toward the exit. "Get out of here—now! You've caused enough of a scene, so don't make it worse."

A female employee dabbed napkins on the blood to wipe it away and helped Harold to sit again, staring at Sawyer as she did so.

Both men stepped back, standing between Sawyer and Harold.

Chest heaving, Sawyer glared at Harold. "Don't for one minute think this is over. You'll regret the day you crossed me." He turned and stormed out of the cafeteria, knocking over chairs and slamming the door behind him.

Chris sat in his chair, cracking his knuckles as he studied the screen. *How do I pass more info to Matthew without endangering myself? Brown's gotta be stopped before it's too late.*

Giving his knuckles a final crack, he stood, pushed his chair back, and began his daily one hundred pushups.

Sweat pouring off him when he finished, Chris grabbed a towel from over the sink in the corner and dried himself. *I should just tell Matthew and let things fall where they will.*

Throwing the towel toward the sink, he sat back and composed a message:

*Difficult to send this as my life could be in danger. My earlier clues didn't seem to help. I'm in the iciest place in the southern hemisphere.*

*Look into Diablo. I can't tell you any more as security is watching—everyone—and they would kill me.*

After he hit send, Chris picked up his empty Dr Pepper can and left his office in search of a new drink.

\* \* \*

Brown pointed at an empty chair. "Sit!"

Emmanuel sat, an irritated expression crossing his features.

"What's with the downtrodden face? I'm the one who's upset because you and your team aren't doing what I told you to do. Do you think I spent billions to create this secret place and hire everyone who wants a job to let them do whatever they want?"

Emmanuel slumped over and studied the floor. He whispered, "No, sir."

"Be a man, for goodness sake." Brown slammed his fist on the desk. "Speak up. I can't understand you."

Emmanuel straightened, cleared his throat, and stared at his boss before raising his voice. "No, sir."

"Good." A self-satisfied smile spread across Brown's face. "In the future, I expect you and your team to follow all of my instructions without even the tiniest deviation. This is my organization, and everyone must do as I say." Brown drew a finger over his throat. "Otherwise, people will be joining Samson in a watery grave. Do you get my meaning?"

Emmanuel swallowed. "Yes, sir. I understand."

"Well, don't just sit there. Go back to your office. Energize your people. I want to hear more news about disruptions to the banking industry. And start hitting the electrical grids across the G-7 countries."

"Yes, sir. Right away, sir."

"Now." Brown waved a hand in dismissal.

Emmanuel stood, opened the door, and walked out, pulling the door behind him until it clicked.

\* \* \*

After stomping down the hallway, Emmanuel stepped into his office. He gave a sharp whistle and waved his hands in the air to get the attention of his team.

They focused on him and slid forward in their rolling chairs.

A one-armed man named Dudley, who spoke with a Cockney accent, grinned at his colleagues. "So what did our octogenarian want today?"

"What do you think?" Emmanuel laughed. "Normal stuff. I'll tell you in a minute. First, how is the data mining going, and are we still stripping money from Brown's accounts?"

Dudley smiled. "Yes, boss. About two million a day from Brown, but he's so rich he'll never miss it. The Bitcoin operation is in full swing. We'll have an update later for you."

"Excellent. Remember, all the money we skim will be divided into equal shares. Today Brown complained he wanted to see more disruption in the G-7 banking industries and their power grids. Here's how we'll do this: I want to hit Wall Street, London's Square Mile, the European Central Bank, and the Bank of Japan and issue statements calling into question the competency of central bank policies. Another area we'll attack is the domestic financial institutions and put out reports they're reneging on their debt payments. We'll disrupt concurrent foreign markets and push a run on major currencies and send them into free-fall."

"On it, boss." Dudley turned back toward his desk.

"Wait a minute. When it gets dark in these same countries, I want blackouts in Montreal, New York, London, Frankfurt, and Tokyo." Emmanuel glanced at a wall clock. "In fact, someone can hit Tokyo now."

Everyone nodded.

Emmanuel slapped his hands together. "Right. Let's get on it. Brown will be watching the news to see what we've done. Let's give him a show and get him off our backs." *If he doesn't stop pestering us, there's no telling what might happen to him.*

\* \* \*

Three hours later, Brown turned on the news. He watched the talking head turn to someone who handed her a sheet of paper.

"We have breaking news, folks. This afternoon, the American dollar, the British pound, the euro, and the Japanese yen all shed ten percent of their value. So far, there aren't any explanations for why this happened."

Brown clapped his hands with glee as he continued to study the reporter's words. "I know the reason behind this—it's my hackers and me."

Another presenter waved a paper in the air. "More breaking news. It seems someone is attacking the electrical grids in various locations, but our network has an excellent backup system, so we're not impacted—at least so far. The entire east coast of the U.S., along with most of Eastern Canada, is experiencing its worst blackouts for decades. The same thing is happening in other G-7 countries. Speculation is rife about the Russians, China, North Korea, or Iran orchestrating these attacks. There are multiple reports of serious accidents, with several deaths and injuries."

She stared into the camera. "A word to the wise. If you're out and about in an area without working signals, remember to treat them as four-way stops." She frowned. "We'll update you on both of these stories as more information becomes available. In the meantime, we'll pause for commercials from our sponsors. After the break, the latest on the Iowa primary and a crucial defeat for the Tigers."

Brown continued clapping as he spilled wine on himself and the carpet. He toasted the television and chortled. "Excellent. My threat to Emmanuel is working. Soon, things will get worse, and then I'll swoop in for the kill."

# Chapter Twenty-Three

J akobshavn Glacier
Near Ilulissat, Greenland

Quincy half-dragged and half-carried Maverick to their rented SUV near the base of the Jakobshavn Glacier, where they had been searching for possible clues related to the location of Diablo Corporation's hidden outpost. He placed Maverick in a sitting position next to the passenger door as he struggled to open it. Eventually, Quincy helped his cousin inside.

Going into the cargo area, Quincy rummaged around in a box of supplies. *Where is it? I thought we brought a bottle.* As he shifted things around, he heard a welcome clink.

He searched for the source of the sound, and his hand found the bottle. *Perfect.* Quincy returned to Maverick's side, opened the bottle, and raised it to his lips.

Maverick sought the bottle, raising weak arms to bring it closer. He sipped and pushed it away. "Ugh, peppermint."

"Yes, peppermint schnapps to help ward off the cold."

"Okay."

Quincy reached over Maverick and hooked the seat belt. He grabbed a couple of blankets from the rear seat and tucked them around Maverick to keep him steady. "Let's get you strapped in. It'll take about thirty minutes to the hospital in Ilulissat."

Maverick slumped toward the door.

"Hold on, Cuz. Here we go." Quincy rushed around to the driver's side and climbed in. He started the engine and headed down the faint path they had initially followed to the glacier. As the SUV skidded over the icy terrain, Quincy fought to keep the vehicle on the road. Several times he brought the SUV to a standstill moments before they would have plunged over the embankment.

He glanced at his cousin and spotted some vomit on Maverick's lower lip. "Hang on, Cuz. You'll make it." *I hope.*

Quincy skidded a final time as he turned onto a paved road leading to Ilulissat. As he sped by two-story dwellings on Nuisariannnguaq, he zoomed past the Hotel Hvide Falk, where he and Maverick had adjacent rooms on the top floor.

With a final push along Napparsimaviup, he pulled up at the three-story red and white hospital. As he parked near an ambulance, a black police SUV with flashing blue lights and *Politi* prominently displayed on the hood and the doors pulled in behind him, blocking any exit.

A tall, stocky policeman climbed out of the vehicle and walked toward Quincy's SUV.

*Now what? Is he going to give me a speeding ticket?* Quincy leaped out of his SUV and gestured toward Maverick. "Help me, please. I think my cousin has a concussion."

The policeman nodded, yanked a radio from his belt, switched channels, and uttered a few words in Greenlandic. After replacing the radio, he turned to Quincy. "We will assist your friend from the vehicle. Emergency personnel will be here in a few moments."

Quincy nodded and stepped toward Maverick.

The policeman raised a hand. "We must wait. Let the doctors and nurses help."

Moments later, an orderly pushing a gurney appeared, followed by a nurse and a man wearing a white coat. They brushed past Quincy and the policeman.

After examining the now-unconscious Maverick, they eased him out of the SUV and onto the gurney. The orderly and the nurse rushed him into the building.

The doctor turned to Quincy. "Your friend is in good hands now. Please go to the waiting room, and I will give you an update as soon as I can."

Quincy sighed with relief. "Thank you, Doctor." He reached inside the vehicle and grabbed his backpack.

The doctor nodded and gestured toward the door. "This way, please. I must hurry to attend to your friend."

Quincy located the waiting area and helped himself to a coffee from a blackened pot sitting on a warming plate. He took a sip of the thick, tepid brew and grimaced. Putting the cup down by the pot, he sat in a chair against the wall. Quincy found a pack of chewing gum in his backpack, stuck two pieces in his mouth, and chewed.

After pulling his iPad and secure communications gear from his bag, Quincy connected everything and composed a message:

*To: Alpha, Bravo, Charlie, QRF-1*

*From: Cheetah*

*Sorry for delay with SITREP. Unexpected incident on glacier. Leopard suffered possible concussion. At local hospital, waiting for update from the emergency doctor. Will update Leopard's condition when known. To date, found nothing of interest.*

. . .

Just as he put away his iPad and the other gear, a shadow loomed over him. Quincy glanced up.

Standing over him was the policeman he met in the parking lot. The man sat in a chair beside Quincy. "As you know, Ilulissat is a small town, although it is the third largest location in Greenland. I am required to provide reports on all incidents in our area to police headquarters in Nuuk. Please tell me what happened to your friend."

Quincy took a deep breath. "We were exploring on Jakobshavn Glacier when my cousin disappeared in a crevasse covered with ice and snow. When he fell, he yelled. I inched forward on my stomach and peered down.

"Maverick was about fifty meters below me, and there wasn't any way to reach him. I ran back to our SUV, which had a winch on it, and lowered the cable and a rope I had attached to it until there was sufficient length to reach him. He was able to fasten it around his waist. When I pulled him up, his head was covered with blood, and he staggered as if he was drunk. I thought he would pass out. After I secured him in the vehicle, I drove straight here."

The policeman finished making notes on his iPad before staring at Quincy. "Have you forgotten anything?"

"No." Quincy shook his head.

"The reason I asked is because the orderly said your friend smelled of alcohol."

Quincy snapped his fingers. "Yes, I forgot to mention after I pulled my cousin from the crevasse, I gave him some peppermint schnaps to warm him up."

"Yes. The orderly said your friend's breath was like peppermint." The officer typed a final note before closing his iPad. "I have enough information to complete my report. Should you need any further assistance while you are in Ilulisaat, just come to the police station and ask for Mârio. If I am not present, someone will know how to contact me. I must remind you speeding is an offense here, and the next time you will receive a ticket." He held out his hand as he stood.

Quincy rose and shook hands. "Thank you, Mârio. I appreciate your help."

As Mârio departed, the doctor approached. "I have an update on your friend. He is suffering from a grade-three concussion. During the examination, he woke for a few minutes before becoming unconscious again. When I looked into his eyes, one pupil was larger than the other. His speech was slurred, and he complained of a severe headache. He also vomited twice and couldn't remember anything about the accident. He also has three broken ribs. In the past, we would have used a compression wrap on them but no longer do so as the wraps can restrict breathing, which might cause a partial lung collapse."

"Will he be okay, Doctor?"

The doctor raised a hand level to the floor and rocked it back and forth. "It is too early to know for sure. Right now, I think his chances of a full recovery are fifty-fifty. He will need to remain in the hospital for at least a week. Will you or someone else be able to stay with him? When he regains consciousness, a familiar face can help with his recovery."

"Thank you, Doctor. I will remain with him until a colleague arrives and stay with him as long as necessary."

The doctor nodded. "Very good. The on-duty nurse will be available to answer any questions." He pointed to the nurse's station. "I must continue my duties. Someone is on the way to the hospital—he drove a screwdriver through his hand at a construction site." He turned and hurried away.

Quincy resumed his seat and pulled out his iPad and communications gear again. He stared at the ceiling for a few seconds before he began typing:

To: *Alpha, Bravo, Charlie, QRF-1*
    From: *Cheetah*
    Update on Leopard. Stage three concussion and three broken ribs.

*Will require at least a week in the hospital. Assistance required. Send Bobcat or Panther to assist with monitoring Leopard until he is released. Upon arrival, I will proceed to the next glacier on the list.*

After packing everything away, Quincy sat back and closed his eyes. *I hope Maverick will be okay. If he isn't, what will I tell his momma?*

# Chapter Twenty-Four

board *RV Aquavit*
Off the Coast of Sanae IV, South
African Research Station, Antarctica

CC smiled as he read the responses to his request that each team sends someone ASAP to help him in Antarctica. *Jake from Alpha, Gerhard from Bravo, Alf from Charlie, and Rufus from QRF-1. Perfect. Och aye, they'll do.*

He reached for the coffee Carina brought him and sipped the lukewarm brew. CC grimaced and set it down. *Must have been made yesterday—worse than navy coffee.*

David Tennent, Captain Smyth's security officer and a former SEAL, opened the door to the mess. He poured a cup of coffee and tasted it. "Perfect! Just how I like it." He used his cupped hand to point to CC's. "Want a refill?"

He shook his head. "No thanks—a bit strong for me."

"I can understand that." David chuckled. "Ever since my stint in the navy, I developed a hankering for two to three-day-old navy coffee. The stronger, the better."

"Anyone else on board drink this?"

"Of course—most of the crew are former navy personnel, and Carina likes it too."

*Figured she'd like it.* "Well, I was in the army, and I'm used to something with a bit of flavor but not as bitter."

David drained his cup and set it on the table. "Ready to grill our captives again?"

"Lead the way." CC picked up his backpack and slid his arms through the straps.

They left the mess and headed below decks to the engine room.

David pulled a set of keys from his pocket and selected one. Shoving it into a massive Yale high-security padlock, he unlocked it and unwrapped the chain holding the mesh door secure. He turned to CC. "After you."

CC nodded and stepped inside.

Liam and Winston sat on a disheveled bed. Their arms rested on their knees as they held their heads in their hands. They glanced up.

"So, are you ready to talk, or do we need to separate you again?" CC crossed his arms. "Where do I find this secret base?"

Liam gestured toward Winston. "He knows—I don't."

"Shut up!" Winston glowered at Liam. "What have you told them?"

Liam gave a sideways glance at the floor. "Not much. I—"

Winston came off the bed, his hands reaching for Liam's throat.

CC and David rushed forward, separating the two men.

David grabbed Winston in a bear hug before throwing him back on the bed.

Meanwhile, CC pushed Liam into the sole chair in the small room. "Stay put."

CC motioned David into the corridor. "I don't know if keeping them apart is going to give us any more than what we learned when we separated them the first time. What do you think?"

"Agreed." David rubbed his chin. "The ship was never intended to be a place to hold prisoners, so it's better to keep them here."

"Aye. Let go back in."

They reentered the room, with CC sitting on one side of Winston and David on the other.

"So, tell us where this secret base is located." David grabbed Winston's forearm and squeezed.

Winston tried to yank his arm free without success. "Let. Go. Of. Me."

"Not until you tell us what we want to know. You'll remain locked in this room until we check out your information."

Winston continued to struggle. "You're all gonna die. Mark my words."

"And how is that going to happen?" CC grabbed Winston's chin and pulled his head toward him. "You're the one in trouble, not us."

Winston laughed. "Diablo will take care of all of you. Soon, the West will be a shell of its former self."

David twisted Winston's arm behind his back.

"Ow! What the hell are you doing?"

"Listen, asshole. Start answering our questions, or things are going to become a lot worse for you." David tightened his grip on Winston's arm, bending it upward.

"Ow. Shit! You're hurting me. You'll be in legal trouble if you injure me."

CC raised a brow. "Tough. Start talking. Otherwise, I'll use the drill on your knees and hobble you for life."

"All right, already. Sheesh! I'm not paid enough to be tortured."

Winston took a deep breath. "Walter Brown, the head of Diablo Corporation, purchased a former Soviet weather station in Antarctica from the Russians. He spent hundreds of millions of dollars to build a secret installation underneath the old weather station. Brown wants to punish the G7 countries for the damage done to the planet. I think he's dying, but he plans to wreak as much havoc as he can before he goes."

CC pursed his lips. "So, where is this facility?"

Winston glanced at Liam. "He doesn't have any idea, and I don't want him to know, so he can't tell anyone. Let me whisper it to you." Winston leaned toward CC. He whispered, "Near Prince Charles Mountains."

CC nodded and leaned back. He gestured toward David. "Keep them together. They stay under lock and key until I can verify their information." CC stood and retrieved his bag.

David released Winston and followed CC out of the room, resecuring it.

The two men returned to the mess and sat at the same table they had used earlier.

"At least we have a general idea of where to look." CC pursed his lips. "I think they both caved too early, but as Winston said, they aren't being paid to be tortured." He grinned. "Not that I would have carried out my threat."

"I wondered about that." David chuckled as he refilled his mug and offered the pot.

CC shook his head. "Go for it."

"He mentioned the Prince Charles Mountains."

"Aye, but there are numerous mountain ranges in the area."

"Hmm." David stood and walked across the mess to a wall where a map of Antarctica was taped. He pointed to a red cross. "This is the *Aquavit*." He took a step to his right and gestured to several peaks on the continent's eastern side. "The Russians referred to this area as MacRobertson Land. It covers several ranges, including the Prince Charles Mountains."

David nodded as he studied the map. He drew an imaginary line from the ship to the mountains. "From the *Aquavit* to Mount Menzies, the highest peak, would take four to five days by Arctic Sno-Cats but not long if a fixed-wing aircraft or a helicopter could be arranged."

"Perhaps SWOOP Antarctica would be able to assist."

"Great idea. They've been most helpful since our ship arrived."

CC returned to the table and opened his backpack, pulling out his secure comms gear and iPad. Once he connected everything, he located a satellite constellation and logged into his email. One waited for him:

To: *Alpha, Bravo, Charlie, QRF-1*
From: *Bedlam*
*Aussie, Green, Falcon, and Condor now en route to Punta Arenas. Once they all arrive, the same company that transported Haggis will bring them to you, along with some additional supplies. Will provide ETA when available. Grandson authorized to contact his hacker friends to counter Diablo's efforts and begin disrupting legitimate businesses.*

CC nodded as he typed a response:

To: *Bedlam, Alpha, Bravo, Charlie, QRF-1*
From: *Haggis*
*Acknowledge information. Please contact company and inquire if they can provide in-country transportation services from the ship to the Prince Charles Mountains, which may hold the key to locating target of interest.*

CC shut down his equipment and stowed everything away.

The door opened, and in strolled Carina. "Hey, CC. Care to join me for a walk around the outer deck? I make three or four laps every day to keep fit." She ran a hand down her thigh as she grinned. "The ship has a workout room, but I prefer to be outside even though it's so cold—it's always invigorating."

When CC nodded, she reached for his hand. "C'mon. Let's go.

When we finish, if you'd like a shoulder massage, I'm pretty decent with them." She flashed her eyes at him.

They headed to the changing room to don Arctic gear.

Holding hands, they pushed out the door and circled toward the port side.

Gusts of wind whipped the snow around them, making it almost impossible to see, even with the goggles protecting their eyes.

Carina leaned into CC as she handed him a carabiner from her belt. "Attach this to your harness so we don't become separated."

He took the device and connected himself before gesturing for her to lead the way.

As they reached the shelter of the superstructure, the wind tapered off, making it easier to walk and talk.

They both raised their goggles.

"We may not be able to chat much during our walk because of the wind, but when we return inside, I'll make both of us a nice cup of hot chocolate."

"Aye. Sounds good."

As they rounded the stern and headed forward on the starboard side, the wind resumed its onslaught, and they repositioned their glasses. Water sprayed over the deck, forced by the increasing wind.

Heads bent down, step by step, they tackled the gusts.

Carina clung to CC's arm as they moved forward.

*Bang! Bang!*

Two shots echoed across the ice.

*Bang!*

A third one followed.

CC yanked Carina behind a lifeboat and covered her with his body, keeping a hand over her mouth. When there weren't any additional shots, he inched up and peered over the lifeboat before glancing back at her.

When she nodded, he removed his hand and used it to shield his goggles from the pelting snow. He inched his way to the rail and glanced over.

A body lay unmoving on the ice, not far from the ship, with blood staining the surrounding area.

# Chapter Twenty-Five

board *RV Aquavit*
    Off the Coast of Sanae IV, South
    African Research Station, Antarctica

Captain Smythe, accompanied by David, CC, Bertelot, Eggert, and Gunner, rushed down the gangway to the shore. The SPA men carried lanterns while everyone else held heavy-duty flashlights.

CC and David also carried Glock pistols and night vision goggles taken from the ship's armory.

Spreading out in a half circle, they approached the body lying face down in the snow.

CC and David knelt, and together they turned the corpse over.

*Liam.*

CC shone his light on Liam's chest. *Thought they were locked up on the ship. How'd he get loose?*

There was a small hole in the back, but the front of Liam's chest exhibited a ragged exit wound. Blood spray dotted the snow and ice around his body.

CC shook his head. "One shot killed him. Is anybody else betting Winston is the shooter?" He scanned the area, his pistol arm following the movements of his head. "We better find him before he zeros in on one of us."

"Whoever it was, the shooter was on the ground." David glanced back at the ship. "There'd be a different angle to the shot if someone did this from the *Aquavit*."

"Aye." CC climbed to his feet and used a gloved hand to swipe away the snow from his knees.

David joined CC. "He can stay here for now. I'll send some lads out to secure the body." He turned to Captain Smythe. "Nothing we can do for him."

"Wait a minute." Bertelot walked away from the others and gestured to Sno-Cat tracks leading away from the ship. "These tracks appear to be fresh. Who would be out at this time of night?"

"David."

He turned at the sound of Captain Smythe's voice.

"Check the Sno-Cats to see if any are missing."

David touched a finger to an imaginary cap and set off for their makeshift depot. Moments later, he returned. "Bertelot's correct, Captain. We brought six, and only five are there."

The captain nodded. "Very well. Too late now to give chase, so we'll wait for morning."

"Captain, if I may suggest, David and I can follow the path tomorrow." CC gestured toward David. "We must assume whoever took the vehicle will either be heading to one of the occupied research stations or Diablo's hidden facility. My money's on the outpost. However, the blowing snow may hide every trace of the Sno-Cat's path."

"Yes, I concur."

Tim, the ship's nurse, raced down the gangway and rushed forward. "Captain Smythe, there's been another accident. I've just treated Oskar Johansen, one of the engine room mechanics, for a severe gash across his head. He's conscious and asked to speak with you."

"Understood. Lead the way."

Tim led the group back onto the ship and into the infirmary.

A battered Oskar sat on one of the four bunks, his head wrapped in a bandage. One area of the dressing was soaked with blood, and a black bruise covered his chin. When the captain approached, he tried to sit straighter.

Captain Smythe raised a hand. "Hold still, young Oskar. Take it easy. How are you feeling? Tim said you have a nasty wound."

Oskar nodded and winced. "Yes, Captain."

"Tell me what happened, son."

"Yes, Captain. I took food to the two prisoners like I did this morning. They didn't cause any problems earlier. I unlocked the cage and stepped inside. All of a sudden, they both rushed at me and knocked me to the floor. The big one kicked me in the jaw, and I became woozy. He pulled the gun from my belt and hit me across the head—twice. They locked me in the cage and left."

"Captain, if I may." CC gestured toward Oskar. "I surmise after Winston freed Liam, they fled. Once off the ship, Winston turned the gun on his partner and shot him. Perhaps he was afraid Liam might know more than he's revealed, and if we caught him again, he might tell us everything. This could have been pay-back."

"Hmm." Captain Smythe scratched his chin. "I think you're correct." He turned to Tim. "Take care of Oskar and keep him here overnight for observation."

"Of course, Captain."

"Excellent. Let's leave them alone and see if any more of David's special coffee is available. I could use a cup or two."

* * *

Queen Maud Land
   Antarctica

. . .

The following morning, CC and David set out in one of the remaining Sno-Cats, following the trail from the previous evening. Parts of it were now snow-covered, making their journey slow as they attempted to follow the tracks.

As they trundled along, CC drove while David periodically got out of the Sno-Cat and traveled about a hundred yards to verify if they were still on the trail. From time to time, he would raise a hand in the air to signal CC to remain where he was while David moved to his left and right until he picked up the faint marks again.

During a short rest stop to stretch their legs, CC turned to David. "We know Winston's armed and willing to kill."

"Yeah. But, we're armed, too." David patted his Glock. "We're also trained in dealing with scum like him."

"Aye." CC gestured to the Sno-Cat. "We better keep moving."

Hour after hour passed, with CC and David changing roles.

So far, Winston appeared to be heading in a more or less straight line.

\* \* \*

Winston finished the last of the water he had taken from their temporary cell after hitting the crewman over the head. He tossed the bottle behind him, watching it roll to the rear of the Sno-Cat before he engaged the gears again. *No point trying to hide my tracks. The wind should blow snow over them.*

He tapped the fuel gauge, which hovered over empty. *Should have checked for a machine with more fuel. Don't think I'll have enough to get back to the outpost.*

Fifteen minutes later, the Sno-Cat lurched as the last of the fuel worked its way through the engine. After coming to a complete stop, Winston climbed over boxes of tools and equipment to reach two red and yellow high-density polyethylene (HDPE) fuel containers fixed to opposite walls near the rear doors.

He tapped on the first one.

A hollow tone reverberated through the Sno-Cat.

*Empty.*

Winston tried the second one with the same result. *Shit. Have to walk. Can't be too far. Hope I'm going the right way.* After donning additional Arctic gear over his existing clothes, he climbed out of the vehicle and headed in the same direction he had been traveling.

An hour later, he stopped behind a stone outcrop that provided some shelter from the increasing wind. He scooped snow into his mouth and let it melt, trickling down his parched throat. *Need to rest for a few minutes. Not long.*

Winston pulled out the pistol he had taken from the crewman and examined the magazine. *Nine rounds. Wonder if he had extra magazines with him. Why didn't I check after I knocked him out?* He shook his head. *Too late now, but I should have waited until we were away from the ship and only used one shot to kill Liam. Don't think anyone heard the shots with the storm, but I better keep moving.*

Three hours later, David brought their Sno-Cat to a halt. He pointed out the windshield. "Check out the footprints. Someone's been going in circles."

CC nodded and gestured out the passenger side of the vehicle. "Aye. It appears to be an abandoned Sno-Cat over there. Keep an eye out for Winston and be ready to shoot if necessary."

David pulled out his pistol and kept it in his hand. "Ready."

They climbed out of their vehicle and followed the footprints to a sheltered area.

In a corner, now almost covered with snow, was a frozen body.

CC glanced at David, gesturing for him to approach from a different vector.

David stepped to his right, separating his distance from CC.

They moved forward toward the body.

*Winston.*

CC checked for a pulse. He shook his head. "The Sno-Cat must have broken down or run out of fuel. Let's check it out."

"Before we do that, let's put the body in our vehicle so we don't have to come back for it."

"Aye. Excellent idea." After forcing Winston's stiffened body into the back of their Sno-Cat, David drove to the other vehicle.

CC climbed out and circled the abandoned Sno-Cat. "No sign of any damage." He opened the cargo area and shook the fuel containers. "Empty."

David approached, carrying a heavy-duty chain. "These vehicles cost a lot of money. We've enough fuel, so we'll haul it back with us."

"Aye. Let me check the coords since we can assume Winston was going to rejoin Diablo." He pulled out his satellite phone and obtained the coordinates before turning back to David. "Got them. No point in us searching for their hideout at this time. Not much the two of us could do against an unknown number of people."

"Agreed. Let's head back."

After securing Winston's Sno-Cat to the back of David's vehicle, CC climbed behind the wheel to steer while David pulled them.

With a gentle tug, they turned in a circle and began their trek back to the *Aquavit*.

\* \* \*

Finbul Ice Sheet
  Antarctica

After CC and David departed, the SPA team finished their breakfast in the mess before donning their Arctic clothing and heading to three of the Sno-Cats to commence their mission. They planned to drill ice cores in three different locations on the Finbul Ice Sheet.

The three red vehicles were lined up in a convoy. Red and white trailers were connected to each one, holding fuel containers, core drilling equipment, tents, and supplies.

Bertelot and Ailsa climbed into the first vehicle, with Gunner and Carina in the middle one and Eggert and Rona bringing up the rear. The women slid into the driver's seats while the men sat beside them.

"How deep will we drill the ice cores?" Ailsa started the engine and engaged the gears.

"Eggert, Gunner, and I discussed this last night. Since our goal is to find out about recent changes, we agreed we would do nine centimeter-diameter cores for a maximum of twelve meters. Each core will be about a meter in length. Even at this depth, they should contain ice-layer accumulation ranging from a few years and might go back a decade or two. Those close to the surface are of the most interest to the SPA since they will represent more recent snowfall events. The more snowfall, the better opportunity to obtain more recent concentrations for us to study."

Ailsa nodded. "Makes sense. How do we sample the atmosphere?"

"The ship contains all the necessary equipment to allow us to do this. We will drill holes into small air pockets in the core samples. The air will be extracted, and we should be able to measure the past concentration of gases, including the ones we are most interested in: carbon dioxide, methane, and nitrous oxide."

"Gotcha. That's why EPA provided the specialized equipment."

Bertelot grinned. "As one of our climatologists, I knew you would catch on."

Ailsa yanked the wheel as she shimmied the Sno-Cat to the left to avoid a depression indicating a possible fissure. Once she bypassed the crack, she resumed her trek across the ice sheet, keeping a close eye on the surrounding area for additional depressions.

\* \* \*

While Carina followed Ailsa, Gunner donned his earbuds and listened to his favorite Norwegian 1980s rock bands: DumDum Boys, DeLillos, Raga Rockers, and Jokke and Valentinerne. He had his feet propped on the dash, his eyes half-closed as he nodded in time with the music.

"Watch it!" Gunner sat upright and leaned toward Carina. "Looks like Ailsa found something to avoid. Give her a chance to maneuver and follow in her tracks."

"Okay, Gunner." Carina eased off on the accelerator and coasted in position.

\* \* \*

A gust of wind stirred up powdered snow in front of Rona's windshield, blinding her access to what was happening in front of her Sno-Cat. Rather than easing up on the clutch, her foot slipped, and she rammed the accelerator to the floor.

The additional power propelled her machine forward.

Rona compensated for the boost as she used her skills to adjust the Sno-Cat's momentum. She managed to avoid catching Carina's trailer but still careened past straight toward the fissure.

After a reverberating crack, the crevasse widened.

With a thump, the Sno-Cat tipped into the opening and settled with both sides of the vehicle jammed in the hole.

The trailer separated and disappeared into the widening gap.

Rona screamed.

Eggert yelled.

They grabbed each other as the Sno-Cat settled in the hole inch by inch until only the vehicle's roof remained visible.

# Chapter Twenty-Six

board *RV Aquavit*
Off the Coast of Sanae IV
South African Research Station, Antarctica

Three days later, an orange and white Basler BT-67, a modified DC-3 with *SWOOP Antarctica* emblazoned in black letters, roared along the makeshift runway. Plumes of powdered snow and pulverized ice kicked up from the tires as the pilot brought the plane to a stop before turning and heading back toward the welcoming committee.

CC, David, Bertelot, Gunner, Eggert, and three others waited next to two red and white trailers to be used to store the cargo coming off the plane. They also held equipment that would be loaded onto the Basler.

The BT-67 pulled off the runway and parked behind the trailers.

Moments later, a SWOOP Beechcraft King Air 300 came in for a landing. As with the Basler, the tires forced up a flurry of snow and ice. After the aircraft turned around, it came back along the runway and stopped in front of CC.

Carlos Alverez, the SWOOP pilot who brought CC to Antarctica, was the first to descend from the King Air. He walked to CC with his hand outstretched. "I brought some strong hombres who said they work for you."

CC nodded and clasped hands. "Aye. There should be four of them."

"They have funny names—I don't think they are real."

CC smiled. "They probably gave you their radio call signs. It's normal practice." He grinned when he spotted the men stepping out of the King Air.

First to disembark was Jake, a black-haired, brown-eyed man well over six feet. "G'day, mate." He walked toward CC and shook his hand. "Great to see you again."

"Aye. Glad you made it, Jake."

The second Bedlam operative to leave the plane was built like a heavyweight wrestler. Gerhard lowered his Ray-Bans over his eyes as he glanced around. "Ag, man. Too much snow and ice for my liking."

Alfred, known as Alf, but often called Alfie by his teammates, was an average-height man with brown curly hair, dark eyes, and a wiry build. He tapped Gerhard on the shoulder. "What about Tiffindell Ski Resort in South Africa? Don't you go there all the time?"

"That's different. The resort is located high on Ben Macdhui. Besides, the whole country isn't covered in snow and ice, just the mountain."

The last passenger disembarked and approached CC. At six-foot-six inches tall, the bald Rufus carried his bodybuilder's physique with ease. He grabbed CC in a bear hug and lifted him off the ground. "Look forward to working with you again, CC."

"Aye. But put me down—the others might become jealous."

Rufus laughed and dropped him. "So what's the mission?"

"The five of us and David, the ship's security officer, and like you, a former SEAL, will fly to an area near the Prince Charles Mountains and set up a base camp. We have intel indicating the Diablo

Corporation has a secret underground site near the mountains where they're conducting their attacks against the G7. Our mission will be to put an end to their operation."

"Is that all?' Rufus grinned. "Sounds like a piece of cake."

"Aye. It might be, but first, we have to find them, which won't be easy."

\* \* \*

While CC met with the other Bedlam operatives, Salazar organized the offloading of the King Air. After they finished, he boarded the plane and took off, heading back to Punta Arenas.

David led the others to the Basler. They made short work of offloading cargo destined for the *RV Aquavit* and shifted the equipment going on the aircraft. Carlos supervised the loading and unloading before joining CC in the cockpit.

When they completed their task, the SPA men and the crew members returned to the ship while David joined CC.

\* \* \*

CC introduced David to the new arrivals. He turned to Carlos. "Are we ready to go?"

"Sí. From here to our destination is over one thousand four hundred nautical miles or about two thousand six hundred miles. We fitted the Basler with a long-range fuel tank which increases the distance we can travel without refueling, so getting there won't be a problem. We'll be carrying fuel to pump into the tanks for the return journey."

"Aye. How long will it take to get there?"

"Depending upon weather conditions, our cruising speed will be no more than three hundred eighty kilometers an hour, so it'll take about seven hours."

CC nodded. "Since it's summertime and there's daylight twenty-four hours a day, I suggest we leave in the morning as soon as everyone's awake. That should give us time for the flight and to unload before we're worn out."

"Sí. I concur."

David gestured toward the ship. "I suggest we move any further discussion into the mess. I told the guys about my coffee, and they can't wait to try it."

"Try not to kill any of them." CC grimaced. "I think I'll stick to hot chocolate."

David chuckled. "You army guys are just too weak."

Everyone laughed.

The following morning, the Bedlam operatives and David followed Carlos from the ship and climbed aboard the Basler BT-67.

CC joined Carlos in the cockpit while the others found seats among the various crates, boxes, barrels, and six Ski-Doo Alpine 640-ER snowmobiles in the rear of the aircraft.

After they buckled in, Carlos turned the aircraft and taxied to the end of the runway. Once he aligned the plane with the runway, he engaged the power.

The Basler bumped along the airstrip until it reached take-off speed.

Carlos engaged the throttle, pulled back on the yoke, and the plane lifted into the clear, blue sky. "Next stop, the Prince Charles Mountains." Carlos glanced at CC and grinned. "Take it easy and enjoy the flight. Should be smooth sailing."

"Aye."

Hour after hour passed with little change to the terrain below: ice, snow, a few crevasses, and small rock outcrops.

About six hours into the flight, Carlos made an announcement to those in the rear of the aircraft. "For those with a window view, the mountains are in front of us. We should be on the ground within forty-five minutes."

The mountains appeared to grow in size as they flew closer.

Carlos banked the aircraft and lowered the landing gear.

Moments later, they touched down. The plane bounced several times over ice protrusions and shallow snow drifts along the rough surface before Carlos brought the Basler to a standstill. He glanced at his satellite phone and noted the latitude and longitude before turning to CC. "Fifty meters off our estimated landing spot. Not bad, eh? But I'll do better next time."

"Aye. Well done." CC grinned as he opened his harness and joined the others in the rear of the aircraft. "Let's get things unloaded ASAP. Carlos will spend the night with us, so we'll need to put up seven of the Béche tents."

"Hey, CC. What about these?" David pointed to a large crate labeled *Jamesway*. Nearby were several smaller containers with the same label.

CC nodded. "Aye. That's the Jamesway hut that'll serve as our operational HQ. Once the tents are set up, I suggest you and Gerhard assemble the hut. Alfie, get the weapons loaded and passed around—except for Carlos. Jake, will you get the snowmobiles started and shifted to a departure point? Rufus and I will start unloading the smaller crates and boxes of supplies and equipment."

He glanced around. "When everyone finishes their tasks, you can help us. We'll also assist Carlos with refueling so he's ready to depart in the morning. Any excess fuel containers will be offloaded here as we'll need the contents for the generator and to refuel our transportation."

David and Gerhard tugged the ropes attached to the trailer holding the 1,200-pound Jamesway hut with a quick push from the others. They manhandled the hut to where they planned to erect it.

David turned to Gerhard. "Ever assembled a Jamesway hut before?"

"Ag, man. No." Gerhard shook his head. "But I've slept in them before. Does that count?"

Both men laughed.

"We need to be careful opening the crates." David pulled a small crowbar from the utility belt he had donned before they left the plane. "The exterior crates are used for the hut's floor."

While they worked on the hut, CC and Rufus brought two snow shovels from the plane and cleared an area for locating the remaining supplies and equipment. When they finished, they cleaned spots for the seven Béchervaise tents, each about a meter from one another. Before erecting the tents, they covered the areas they cleaned with tarps. They also ran stakes from tent to tent as they were assembled to keep them from being blown away in strong winds.

Alfie pried open the crates labeled weapons. He checked each Glock pistol before inserting a fifteen-round magazine and making sure there was a round in the chamber. After shoving them into holsters on extra-long web belts to go over their Arctic clothing, he added two additional magazine pouches. Alfie pulled four Mossberg 590A1 shotguns from another crate and loaded them with twelve-gauge shells containing double-aught buckshot.

Satisfied with his progress thus far, he nodded and turned to the final weapons crate. After prying off the top, he picked up one of the twelve H&K G36 assault rifles and attached thirty-round box magazines. When he finished with all of them, he strapped on one of the web belts, slung two others over his shoulder, and picked up three of the rifles before joining David and Gerhard.

As the others finished their assigned tasks, they joined David, Gerhard, and Alfie. Before long, they assembled the hut and prepared to set up the generator and comms gear.

As the temperature dropped and the wind and snow increased, the men worked fast to complete their preparations.

CC turned to Jake. "You're up for tonight's chow. What are you planning?"

"Since we have plenty of Dinty Moore Beef Stew, we'll start with that, followed by canned peaches. Unless, of course, you want me to fry some Spam."

CC chuckled. "Aye. Go ahead and get started but keep the Spam for yourself. Alfie, will you lend Jake a hand in getting the kitchen area squared away?"

"Sure thing, CC."

"Righto, boss." Jake grinned. "Grub coming up as soon as."

Diablo OP
    Near Prince Charles Mountains

Gerald Jerry, a member of Sawyer's security team, clutched his binoculars close to his eyes as he pointed them away from his hidden observation post. *Where is it? I thought I heard a plane.* He yanked his radio from its pouch and depressed the transmit button. "Security, this is OP-One. Come in."

A burst of static was the only response.

Gerald tried again and received the same results.

A third time: "Security, this is OP-One. Come in, please."

"OP ... This ... Sec ... You're break ... up. Say again ..."

"Just a minute." Gerald shifted his position by six feet. "How about now?"

"You're five by five, OP-One. What's up?"

"Are you expecting any aircraft today?"

"Negative. Brown's plane won't arrive until tomorrow. Why?"

"I thought I heard an engine and saw a glint of sunlight off a possible wing."

"Roger, OP-One. Might be one of the scheduled flights going to the year-round weather stations."

"It's possible, but it seemed too low to cross the mountains."

"Okay, OP-One. Keep a close ear and eye on the situation. I'll send one of the others to join you as soon as possible. Perhaps you've stumbled over someone who has learned about our facility."

"Yes, sir. What if a plane lands and men start searching the area?"

"If that happens, and someone approaches the OP, shoot to kill. Understood?"

"Yes, sir. Shoot to kill. Understood."

# Chapter Twenty-Seven

D iablo Corps Secret Outpost
Near Prince Charles Mountains

The strains of "The Gael," the theme song from *Last of the Mohicans*, echoed through Chris's room, shattering an early morning dream.

He glanced at the red flashing lights on the bedside table clock: 5:00. *Oh my God. Who's calling now?* Chris fumbled for the light switch as the music continued to play. Once he clicked on the light, he grabbed the phone and groaned. *What does Brown want at this ungodly hour?*

He accepted the call. "Yes, Mister Brown. Do you realize it's five in the morning?"

"Of course, I do, Chris. Why are you still in bed? I've been at work for an hour."

*Figures.* "Some of us require more sleep than others, Mister Brown." Chris exaggerated his yawn. "So what can I do for you at this early morning hour?"

"What did I call you for?" The sound of Brown snapping his fingers filtered through the line. "Oh, yes. I'm delaying my return from Miami for forty-eight hours. Godfrey wants to take care of some essential maintenance on the plane before we head back.

"Is there anything you require from the U.S.? Jean-Luc is putting together his list of supplies for the kitchen. Check with Emmanuel and Sawyer and find out if they need anything."

"Yes, Mister Brown." Chris yawned again and rubbed his right eye. "The canteen is running out of soft drinks and munchies—"

"Yes, yes. Don't bother me with their trivial requests. Tell them to send a list of what they want to Jean-Luc. The canteen and my over-paid and pampered employees will have to wait for the next flight if there isn't room."

"Yes, sir. Anything else?"

"Yes. Don't dilly-dally. Wake Emmanuel and Sawyer and tell them I expect their requirements within the hour."

*Good grief! Most stores in Miami will still be closed.* "Yes, Mister Brown. Anything further?"

"As a matter of fact, there is. Maddie's birthday is this week. I want to surprise her with flowers, chocolates, and a cake. Work with Jean-Luc to pick out something appropriate but not too expensive. I don't want to overindulge."

Chris stifled a laugh. *A multi-billionaire worried about the cost of flowers, chocolates, and a cake? Ridiculous! What a cheapskate.* "I'll take care of it."

"Excellent. Don't let me keep you, my boy. Time is money."

Before Chris responded, he heard a click and the dial tone.

\* \* \*

Diablo Headquarters
Miami, Florida

. . .

An hour later, as Brown sipped his morning tea, his phone rang. He glanced at the caller ID and let the phone ring again while he consumed more of his beverage before he accepted the call. "I haven't received your requirements yet. Why not?"

"Good morning, Mister Brown." Sawyer sneezed. "I wanted to speak with you first to get your approval."

"What needs my approval now? What's so urgent you couldn't follow established procedures? Have your men returned yet?"

"No, Mister Brown. Liam and Winston are still missing. It's been days since they last checked in—I think something happened to them while they were on the research ship."

"What do you want me to do about it? You're in charge of security. Get cracking and find out what happened."

"I'll take care of it, sir. It's my problem, and I'll deal with the situation. However, there is another issue you will want to know about."

"Well, what is it? I don't have all day."

"Gerald, who is working at the observation post, thought he heard a plane—"

"So? Planes fly around Antarctica all the time."

"But he also spotted a reflection off a wing."

Brown laughed. "Fits with a plane going by. Tell me something worthwhile."

"H-He thought it was landing."

"Hmmm. Did he check for any aircraft on the ground?"

"No, sir. I told him to be careful and remain at the OP."

"What do you want from me?"

"I want your permission to contact a former army buddy who runs a small mercenary outfit. He can provide a dozen men—"

"No. Maximum of six. Who are these people?"

"My buddy served with all of them in Afghanistan and Iraq. He'll vouch for each one."

"He better. Their cost will come out of your security budget. They must be at the airport by 10:00 in two days, or they'll have to make their own way to the site."

"Of course, Mister Brown. As soon as we finish, I'll call him and make arrangements."

"Do it now." Brown hung up.

* * *

Diablo Corps Secret Outpost
  Near Prince Charles Mountains


Sawyer punched in his buddy's phone number and listened to the rings. After the sixth ring, he was about to hang up when someone answered.

"Hel ... lo." A deep male voice, punctuated by deep breaths, responded.

"Sawyer here."

"How's it going, buddy?" Ben 'Ned' Needham, the leader of the Brotherhood of Vengeance, coughed.

"You okay, Ned?"

"Yeah, I'm fine. Gotta quit smoking. The coughing's always worse in the morning."

"Understood. My health's improved since I stopped. Anyway, remember our conversation last week about the possibility of needing your assistance?"

"Yeah. You said something about a dozen men for a job where it's cold."

"That's right, but my boss will only pay for six." *Ned doesn't need to know I have to pay for their services from my budget.* "Another stipulation is they have to be at the Miami Airport in two days to catch a flight or make their own way."

"No problemo, buddy. I'll pick five of my best to accompany me. How long is the job, and what do we need to bring?"

"I'd say at least three weeks, but it might be longer." *We'll probably have to take over that research ship as well and deal with anyone looking for us.* "I'll provide all the weapons and ammo you'll need. But if you have Arctic clothing, bring it. You'll be joining me in Antarctica."

"Holy shit! Are you for real?"

Sawyer chuckled. "As sure as what we did to those Afghans when we were searching the caves in the Tora Bora region for Bin Laden."

"We'll be ready. I already teed up Carter, Hudson, Lucas, Mateo, and Wyatt as my A-team, so I'll contact them, and we'll be at the airport in two days. What time and what kind of plane?"

"Perfect! My boss plans to depart at 10:00. When you arrive, go to the general aviation center. The plane you're looking for is a Gulfstream G550, painted red, white, and blue, with Diablo in black block letters. Can't miss it. This'll take you to Chile, where you'll switch to a DHC-6 Twin Otter aircraft painted in the same colors."

"Gotcha. Anything else? If not, I'll contact the team, and we'll relocate to Miami ASAP."

"That's it for now. I'll meet the plane when you arrive and get you squared away. Oh, one thing. My boss is always called Mister Brown. He's a bit eccentric, but don't let him fool you, as he's sharp as a tack underneath his bluster."

"Understood."

* * *

General Aviation Center
Miami International Airport

At 09:30, six burly men, each over six foot tall, with thick beards and dressed like lumberjacks, approached the loading area under the aircraft. Each man carried two over-stuffed duffel bags and hoisted them onto the small conveyor belt as if they were empty.

Led by Ned, they boarded the private executive jet. He stopped in front of a mostly bald elderly man sitting behind a desk. Liver spots adorned his head, face, and arms, while a red birthmark covered part of his neck and double chin. Heavy pouches sagged beneath his eyes.

"Excuse me. Are you Mister Brown?" Ned held out a hand.

"Yes, I am. I guess you're Sawyer's friend?"

"Yes, sir. I'm—"

Brown waved a hand in the air. "Your name is unimportant to me. When we're in Antarctica, we'll only have contact via Sawyer. Is that understood?"

Ned nodded as he dropped his hand by his side. "Yes, sir."

Carter nudged Wyatt. "What a jerk," he whispered.

Brown's head whipped toward Carter. "I might be getting on in years, sonny, but my hearing is as good as when I was your age. How dare you come on my plane and insult me? I should have you tossed out without a parachute when we're at thirty thousand feet."

"I'm sorry, sir." Carter dropped his head.

"You certainly are." Brown turned back to Ned and pointed to the rear of the aircraft. "There are seats for you and your men and keep them in line. When it's time for me to eat, Jean-Luc, my chef, will serve you the same food—no deviations. No alcohol—what's on board is my private stock. Am I understood?"

Ned and his team nodded.

"Well, don't just stand there. Go!"

The men trooped to the rear of the plane and claimed seats.

"It's going to be a long flight, and we better get whatever sleep we can since we don't know for sure what the situation on the ground will be like." Ned glanced into the face of each of his men. "As with any mission, one man will remain awake at all times. I'll take the first two-hour shift, and we'll rotate in alphabetical order."

"Excuse me, gentlemen." Jean-Luc appeared pushing a trolley. "We have a selection of soft drinks, fruit juices, and water. Mister Brown informed me you may each have one beer with every meal. He always eats the same thing on these flights—chili cheese dogs covered in jalapeno peppers, Lay's potato chips, baked beans, and coleslaw. He told me you will eat the same. However, if you don't want the peppers, please let me know."

Ned made a command decision. "We'll eat the same as Mister Brown."

"Very good, sir. I'll serve the food in about two hours."

* * *

Diablo Corps Secret Outpost
Near Prince Charles Mountains

Seventeen hours after leaving Miami and switching aircraft in Punta Arenas, Chile, Brown's Twin Otter descended and headed toward the mountains.

Godfrey hit a switch on the control panel. Hydraulic lifts raised a camouflaged opening in the rocks as he landed, allowing enough space for the plane to enter the hidden hangar.

As soon as they stopped, the opening closed again.

Men rushed forward to unload the aircraft.

Chris held a cup of tea while waiting for Mister Brown to disembark.

Sawyer stood next to Chris, expecting to see his new personnel.

Brown finally left the plane and marched toward Chris, holding his hand out for the tea. "Been a long trip. Plenty of work to do, so come with me, Chris, and I'll give you new instructions."

Ned and his men exited the aircraft, duffle bags perched on their shoulders. He looked around as they waited for Sawyer.

Brown glanced at his security chief. "Don't forget to brief your new team about the rules." He turned and walked away.

Chris and Jean-Luc followed.

"What rules?" Ned frowned.

Sawyer laughed. "Nothing we haven't faced before. There are

two rules: the first is to follow all guidelines issued by management and security."

"So, what's the second one?"

"Always obey rule one or face the consequences."

"Which are?"

"Depending upon the severity of the infraction, punishment can vary from instant dismissal, imprisonment in the security stockade or—"

"Don't tell me—same as in Afghanistan."

Sawyer nodded. "Yep. Death by firing squad."

# Chapter Twenty-Eight

D iablo Corps Secret Outpost
　　　　Near Prince Charles Mountains

Brown slipped on his red fleece-lined silk pajamas and added a matching robe. After checking himself out in the mirror and doffing an imaginary hat, he slid his feet into black Crockett & Jones Lion Rampant black velvet slippers and padded into his living room.

He stepped to the bar, poured a double shot of Glenfiddich Grande Couronne twenty-six-year-old single malt scotch whisky, and climbed into his Ananda massage chair. He selected the desired speed and intensity levels, picked up the remote for his home theater system, switched it on, and hit play for John Wayne's *Hondo*.

After taking a gulp of his whisky, Brown spat it out as he began choking. Panic set in as he clutched his chest, attempting to ease the seizure. He fumbled in a pocket on his robe for his nitroglycerin pills. No sooner had the container cleared his pocket than he dropped it on the floor.

Brown thumped a small device in the chest pocket of his robe.

The Quicksafe V3 Man Down alarm activated, sending a text to Chris and Diana, Brown's private nurse.

Chris responded first to the device's unique ringtone audio alert. He grabbed his phone and accepted the call. "Yes, Mister Brown?"

"H-Help m-me. C-Chest pain."

"On my way." Chris disconnected the call and jumped out of bed. Dressed in his pajamas, he threw on a hooded beige robe with oversized pockets, flung his door open, and raced down the corridor to Brown's suite. He fished a key from a pocket and accessed the area, leaving the outer door open, knowing Diana would arrive soon.

Chris entered Brown's living room and found his boss leaning to the side of the chair, still clutching his chest. His tumbler rested on the thick shag carpet, damp where the whisky had spilled.

Brown turned his head toward Chris. "H-Help. I-I can't breathe."

"I'm here, sir. Diana will be here soon." Chris helped Brown to sit upright and switched off the buzzing massage chair.

Brown's face was drained of blood and contorted with his effort to breathe.

A flurry of activity announced Diana's arrival as she pushed an emergency medical trolley in front of her. She placed her stethoscope on Brown's chest and listened before turning to Chris. "Place two of his nitro pills under his tongue. His seizure should ease."

Chris nodded and followed Diana's instructions.

Before long, the color returned to Brown's face. "T-Thanks. D-Dropped my pills."

Diana wiped the perspiration from Brown's forehead and handed him a towelette to wipe his hands.

Meanwhile, Chris picked up the empty glass and medicine bottle and secured the rest of the spilled pills.

Diana motioned for Chris to follow her to the other side of the room. She whispered, "I'm worried about Mister Brown. These attacks are becoming more frequent and are going to kill him one day.

He needs a full-time cardiologist and perhaps another doctor who deals with neurology."

"Understood. I'll raise this with him later today. Can I help him to bed now?"

"Yes, but can you stay with him? I'll take over in a couple of hours."

Chris nodded. "Not a problem."

"Fantastic. I'll check out a few doctors and email you the names."

"He already visits a cardiologist from time to time in Miami."

"Do you think this doctor would come here to check him out?"

Chris laughed. "I'm sure he would if the price was right."

"Well, Mister Brown has the money to pay for his treatment even here in Antarctica." Diana smiled. "When it comes to his health, he's willing to spend whatever he needs to get the best."

"I know. That's how he pulled you away from Johns Hopkins."

She chuckled. "It was hard to say no to double my salary and a bonus."

"That's how he got me to walk away from my job, too."

"Can you do me a favor? Talk with Jean-Luc and ask him to go easy on sugar, rich and spicy food—at least until the cardiologist is onboard."

"I'll do that, but who is going to explain this to Mister Brown? Not me—I'd prefer to keep my head on my shoulders."

Diana laughed. "No worries. I'll mention this to him later when he's up and about."

They helped Brown into his bed and made sure he was comfortable.

Chris sat in a bedside chair, pulled his Kindle from his robe pocket, and returned to the thriller novel he had been reading.

An hour later, Brown interrupted Chris. "Water. I'm thirsty."

He poured a glass of water and gave it to his boss. "Yes, Mister Brown. You sound like your normal self."

"What's that supposed to mean? And why are you in my bedroom?"

"Did you forget you had a seizure? Your Man Down device alerted Diana and me. We thought it best if one of us stayed until you returned to normal."

Brown waved a hand in the air. "Yes, yes. I'm fine now. Go back to your bed. I expect you in the office at your normal time."

Chris sighed. "Yes, Mister Brown."

Chris entered Brown's office at 06:00, carrying a cup of tea for his boss and a coffee for himself. He sat in his regular chair on the right-hand side of the desk.

Brown glanced around. "Well? Where are my pastries? Did you forget them?"

Chris shook his head. "No, sir. I didn't forget them. Diana and I had a discussion this morning, and she suggested you cut back on sugar as well as rich and spicy food until a specialist examines you."

"What do I need a specialist for? I pay her enough."

"She thinks you should have a full-time cardiologist here and perhaps another doctor who deals with neurology."

"Hmm." Brown sipped on his tea as he beat a rhythm on the desktop with his right hand. "I suppose so. Have her recommend a neurological specialist, but I want Doctor Stine as my cardiologist. Make it happen."

"Uh, yes, Mister Brown. What about salaries?"

Brown pursed his lips. "Find out what the annual average salaries are. Offer the specialist double for a year. But, offer Doctor Stine the same for three month-stints. I need him more."

"Yes, Mister Brown. I'll make the calls today."

"No!" Brown shook his head. "I don't want the word getting out. Fly to Miami and see Doctor Stine in person. Perhaps he can recommend a neurologist."

Chris nodded. "I'll leave right away."

"Yes and bring Doctor Stine back with you. I don't want to

survive on oatmeal and whatever else Jean-Luc comes up with. And bring me one pastry instead of two."

Chris struggled to contain a grin. "Yes, sir." *Hope the doc can do something with him. Too much to ask for a lobotomy. I'm sure he suffers from schizophrenia.*

* * *

Doctor Stine's Office
    Downtown Miami

Two days later, Chris entered Doctor Theodore Stine's office as scheduled for his appointment.

After they shook hands, Stine raised a brow. "So, where's Brown? I thought this was for him."

"It is, but things are complicated. As you're aware, Mister Brown visits Miami on a regular basis. However, his seizures are becoming more frequent."

Stine nodded. "I suppose he's still eating food I told him not to."

"Yes. Anyway, he wants to offer you a temporary job looking after him as his private cardiologist."

Stine rubbed a hand over his chin. "Where would this be? And for how long?"

"He'd like your services for the next three months at least. He's willing to pay you up to five hundred thousand dollars for the first three months and every six months afterward."

"What?" Stine almost bolted from his chair. "Where will we be? The Arctic?"

"The opposite end of the world, Doctor Stine." Chris grinned. "Mister Brown has a facility in Antarctica and expects you to join him there. He wants you to return with me."

Stine beamed. "For that kind of money, I'll do it. I'll be able to buy the yacht I've always dreamed of owning." He glanced at his computer screen. "My secretary will need to clear my schedule. Will Mister Brown cover the cost of having another doctor look after my most important patients while I'm gone?"

Chris nodded. "Yes. At least, I think so because he really wants you."

"Okay. When do we go?"

"Is tomorrow morning too soon? Also, our nurse recommended he have a neurologist."

"I can make a suggestion or two." Stine stood, a grin stretching from ear to ear. "What are you waiting for? Let's get the show on the road."

\* \* \*

After Chris left Stine's office, he went to a nearby strip mall and entered a Best Buy electronics store. Inside, he weaved his way through the crowded aisles as he headed toward the cell phone section.

As he stopped near some of the phones, a staff member approached. "May I help you, sir?"

"Uh, yes. I want to purchase a phone for temporary but anonymous use."

The staffer smiled. "You mean a burner phone. Come this way." He pointed down the corridor. "The less inexpensive phones used as burners are down here."

"Are there any you can recommend?"

"Any of the Nokia phones will work well." The staffer glanced around. "In fact, I use two of them."

"Can I purchase prepaid minutes?"

"Yes, sir. No problem at all. I recommend you purchase A Tracfone basic no-contract phone plan. It lasts a year and comes with four hundred minutes for only one hundred dollars."

Chris smiled. "Perfect. I'll go with your recommendations."

"Excellent. Come this way, and I'll get you fixed up."

Fifteen minutes later, Chris left the store and headed to a nearby Costa. After purchasing a medium-sized latte, he sat at a corner table. Prying off the lid of his drink, he let it cool while he entered a ten-digit number into his new phone.

When the fifth ring echoed down the line, someone picked up. "Hello. Matthew McMasters speaking. How may I direct your call?"

"Matthew, it's me—Chris. How are you doing?"

"Chris? Where are you, man? Why didn't you call earlier?"

"Couldn't call before because everything is monitored by Brown's security. I'm in Miami for a couple of days and wanted to reach out to my old roommate."

Matthew laughed. "I was wondering if you'd surface. Aren't you afraid your conversation will be overheard?"

"Naw. I bought one of those anonymous phones."

"You mean a burner? Good on ya. We have a team on Antarctica now searching for Diablo's specific location."

"After we finish talking, I'll text you the coordinates."

"Fantastic. Listen, do you have time to get together while you're in CONUS?"

"Sorry, Matthew. Not this time. I'm only here to fetch a cardiologist. Brown isn't doing too well. I'm not sure how much longer he'll be around."

Matthew chuckled. "From what I've learned about him, his demise couldn't happen to a nicer guy."

"Well said. Listen, I better go, and we'll catch up another time."

"Sure thing."

As Chris disconnected and prepared to send a text, two burly men dressed in dark suits, ties, and white shirts, approached his table. Chris pursed his lips. "Can I help you?"

"Chris Handler?"

"Who wants to know?"

The first man pulled out a leather wallet containing his identification and a badge. "FBI."

# Chapter Twenty-Nine

B edlam Base Camp
Near Prince Charles Mountains

CC yawned as he opened his laptop and accessed his email. A shadow loomed over him while he typed. He turned.

"Morning, boss." Jake handed CC a steaming cup of black coffee. "You're up earlier than usual. Couldn't sleep?"

CC shook his head. "No. Had a premonition during the night and thought I better act upon it."

"That's what makes you such an excellent leader."

"Uh-oh." CC chuckled as he sniffed the air. "Did you burn breakfast already?"

Jake cringed. "I'll have you know I've never burned breakfast in the past—"

"Except one time where we ended up with nothing to eat and had to throw out the pans."

"C'mon, CC. That was years ago. I've improved since then."

"Aye, you have. Just jerking your chain. So, what's for breakfast today?"

"Beef hash and scrambled eggs. Most of the eggs arrived in the padded boxes in excellent condition, but enough were cracked, so I'll use them up for breakfast and not waste them."

CC nodded. "Sounds like a plan." He blew on his mug and took a tentative sip. "At least you still know how to make a good brew."

"I guess that's the best compliment I'll get from you this morning, so I'll head to the kitchen area and let you work on your messages."

CC returned to his email and opened one from Captain Smythe:

To: *Haggis*

   From: *Aquavit*

   *Storm front moving in and should reach you later today. Hunker down as best you can. Will send you additional supplies via SWOOP after it passes.*

CC acknowledged the message and began composing his own:

To: *Bedlam, Alpha, Bravo, Charlie, QRF-1*

   From: *Haggis*

   *Request Red, Nightjar, and Panther pack their gear and be forward deployed to Punta Arenas. No specific threat at this time, but premonition and self-preservation warrant additional support be available should the need arise.*

After reading the message, CC connected to the encrypted comms gear and sent his request. He stood, picked up his cup, and sauntered into the kitchen area in search of more coffee.

Jake topped up CC's mug before refilling his own. "So, who's going to be on standby?"

"How did you know?" CC smiled.

"I haven't forgotten how your mind works."

"Aye. I've requested Pun, Ollie, and Gordon."

Jake nodded. "Good backup team—a Gurkha, a counter-terrorism specialist, and a SEAL."

"Aye. Ollie will be their team lead if we need them here."

New voices signaled the arrival of the others from their Béche tents. Before long, everyone held a mug of coffee.

Except for Carlos, who drank water. "Coffee makes me want to pee. Not a good thing to do when I'm flying on my own. Never did trust autopilots, and can you imagine what might happen if I'm in the toilet and the plane tilts? I could end up peeing on myself."

Everyone laughed.

"Five more minutes and all the hash and scrambled eggs you can eat." Jake laughed. "Grab your plates and form a line—you can dish up your own. This ain't a hotel."

After grabbing their food, the men sat wherever they could find a level space within the cramped hut. When they finished eating, everyone bundled back up in their Arctic gear and followed Carlos to the Basler BT-67.

CC turned to Gerhard and David. "Can you grab three more of the Béchervaise tents from the back?"

"Expecting company?" David raised a brow.

"Aye—perhaps. I've requested three more Bedlam operatives be deployed to Punta Arenas—in case we need them."

David nodded. "A wise precaution."

Carlos started the twin turboprop engines, and within minutes the aircraft appeared ready to leap into the sky.

Rufus and Alfie removed the chocks for takeoff.

With a wave out the window, Carlos nudged the plane forward along the runway. Reaching the other end, he turned around, and the BT-67 roared back toward the Bedlam operatives and into the sky.

He dipped his wings before turning in a wide arc and heading toward the northern coast.

"Aye. Okay, gents. Back in the hut. Time to set up a schedule."

Once inside and with new mugs of steaming coffee, Alfie, Gerhard, and David leaned against the crates of weapons while CC, Jake, and Rufus inclined against the outer wall.

"First order of business is to set up an observation post within sight of our camp but as far out as possible. Perhaps no more than eight hundred meters away." CC glanced around. "Any volunteers?"

David, Gerhard, and Rufus nodded.

"Thanks, guys. You know what's required, so there's no need for a discussion. This morning I received a message from the *Aquavit* indicating a storm front is heading our way. When you're outside, keep an eye on the sky."

"Ag, man." Gerhard rolled his eyes. "Just what we need—more snow! Why didn't they build their hideout in a desert?"

Alfie nudged Gerhard. "Then you'd be complaining about the sun, the sand, scorpions, and whatever else you could think of."

"But at least I'd be warm."

"I'd like to suggest a flagged route from the OP to the camp." Rufus glanced at the others. "Some type of beacon would be even better, but I read somewhere that all available systems used in Antarctica are still reliant on GPS and Iridium architecture which can fail when there's excessive sun-spot activity like in the eleven-year solar cycle we're in now."

"Aye. I read that, too." CC nodded. "That's why we ruled them out. One day they'll be practical to use in place of a flagged route, but not now. However, everyone has an Iridium tracking beacon embedded in their clothing as a precaution. David, why don't you and the others head out? The rest of us will restack our supplies in the hut and create a more useable space."

While David, Gerhard, and Rufus headed outside, the others drained their cups and cleaned the kitchen area.

Alfie and Jake pushed several crates of supplies against the wall before stacking the weapons crates on top so they would be within easy reach.

Meanwhile, CC started with the food supplies and created a path into the kitchen area, cramming boxes, barrels, and crates into all available space. Moments later, he donned his Arctic gear.

Alfie gestured to CC's clothing. "Where are you heading?"

"Thought I'd check out the outhouse."

Jake chuckled. "Bugger that. Don't fall in. We have a high-tech two-seater. Just remember—one hole is for peeing, and the other is for solid waste. There should be a bag in each one. When you finish, remove the bag, tie it closed, and deposit it in the barrel outside."

"Yeah, yeah. Not my first time using a cold-weather outhouse."

Jake and Alfie laughed.

As they left the hut, Gerhard, Rufus, and David grabbed their weapons and backpacks. Loaded down, they dipped their heads against the biting wind.

Rufus stood guard while Gerhard hammered the first marker into the ice.

David took the spool of rope and flags and headed away from the camp, pounding the next one into the ice about fifty meters away.

The men continued to leapfrog until they were about eight hundred meters from the camp. Using collapsible shovels and axes, they dug into the snow and ice to hold a tarp they brought with them to create a windbreak.

Forty-five minutes later, they had a usable OP with places to sit and gun ports cut into narrow slots in the sides of their shelter.

David yanked a thermos from his pack and poured each of them a coffee.

"Ag, man!" Gerhard sipped from his cup. "What did you put in this? Anti-freeze?"

David laughed. "Just a dash of Amaretto to ward off the chill."

"Any left?" Gerhard drained his cup and held it out.

"Wait a—"

"Down, guys." Rufus aimed his H&K G36 assault rifle through one of the slits. "Someone's out there watching us. I spotted a flash of light off something—perhaps a weapon or binoculars."

Gerhard and David grabbed their weapons and mimicked Rufus' stance.

"About five hundred meters in front of us and a bit to the right." Rufus' finger tightened on the trigger. "Don't see anything now. Let's keep an eye out in case my mind and eyes weren't playing tricks on me."

* * *

Diablo Outpost
Near Prince Charles Mountains

Gerald ducked behind a piece of whitewashed wood used to create the sides of his observation post. *Did someone spot me? They jumped in a hurry.* He swung his binoculars back to the right. *Was that a flash of movement?* He steadied the binoculars on the edge of the cutout in the whitewashed wood that formed the sides of his observation post. *Don't see anything now. Did I imagine it? Sawyer will get pissed if I don't check it out, but if I go by myself and run into someone, I could be in trouble.* He shook his head. *Ain't paid enough to risk my neck.*

# Chapter Thirty

F inbul Ice Sheet
Antarctica

Carina and Ailsa pulled their Sno-Cats to a stop about fifteen meters away on either side of Rona's stricken machine and shoved the engines into idle.

Gunner climbed out of Carina's vehicle and trudged through the snow to the front and grabbed the winch cable while Bertelot did the same on Ailsa's Sno-Cat.

Unable to open the frozen windows, Rona and Eggert cracked open the doors enough for them to grab the alloy safety hooks.

"Grab the hook and pull the cable through and pass out the other side." Gunner gestured toward Bertelot. "He will take the end and secure it to the other Sno-Cat. Then push his cable through to me, and I will do the same on this side."

"Okay, Gunner." Eggert pushed the cable out the open window. "Please hurry before we fall deeper into the crevasse."

Bertelot and Gunner continued to feed the cables to them, and soon each was connected to the opposite Sno-Cat.

"Move into the back if you can." Bertelot pointed to the rear. "The cables will stop your vehicle from falling further. Cover your faces. We will break the front window so you can climb out."

Gunner approached carrying axes from the other Sno-Cats.

Rona and Eggert grabbed the cables and climbed onto the hood. With measured but powerful swings of the axes, the window collapsed.

"Hurry." Gunner waved Rona and Eggert forward. "We must leave here as soon as possible before the chasm widens." He followed Bertelot, who was already back next to Ailsa's Sno-Cat.

Together, Bertelot and Gunner steadied the cable as Rona and Eggert climbed out the broken window and made their way to the edge of the Sno-Cat. With a leap, they jumped off the hood, landing in deep snow a couple of meters away.

Carina and Ailsa climbed out of their vehicles, ran to Rona, and hugged her.

Bertelot glanced around the group. "I do not want to risk trying to pull the Sno-Cat from the crevasse as it is too dangerous. Pick up any supplies that did not follow the trailer into the hole, and we will continue our journey. Rona and Eggert, you ride with Ailsa and me, and Carina and Gunner will take the lead. Carina, please be careful."

Carina grinned. "Of course. Aren't I always?"

"When it suits you." Bertelot pursed his lips. "Let us disconnect the winch cables and get moving."

After rewinding the cables onto their drums on the front of each vehicle, Carina and Gunner climbed into their Sno-Cat, leaving the others to board the second one.

With a scrape of metal and a groan, the third one settled deeper into the crevasse.

"That was a close call for Rona and Eggert." Carina engaged the Sno-cat's gears, and they continued to trundle across the snow and ice. "Keep a sharp eye out for any potential dangers."

Gunner nodded as he stared at Carina.

"What's the matter, Gunner? Something on your mind?"

"Yes, there is. Our time together in Ushuaia—I thought we had something special. Was I just another conquest?"

"What on earth are you talking about?"

"CC. You seem to drool over him every time he is around. Will he be a new conquest?"

"Gunner!" Carina shook her head. "What's got into you?"

"I-I love you, Carina." A tear trickled down Gunner's face. "I hoped to one day marry you."

She reached out and put a gloved hand on Gunner's knee. "How very sweet, Gunner. But I told you I don't make commitments. What we had was fun and helped to pass the time. However, I'm not ready to settle down yet."

"So, what about CC?"

"What about him? We're acquaintances at the moment—that's all. Time will tell if things change between us. However, we both have important jobs that take us to different parts of the world, and I can't see either of us giving up our careers for the other."

"So there is still a chance for me in the future?"

She smiled at him. "Anything's possible." She shrugged.

"Thank you." He gave her a half-smile.

"Let's concentrate on our tasks. Perhaps later, we can talk."

"Yes. I would like that."

"Check the GPS coordinates. I think we should be getting close to the first location."

Gunner pulled the GPS locator from his pocket and nodded. "Yes, you are correct. Keep going until I tell you to stop."

* * *

First Ice Drilling Camp
   Finbul Ice Sheet

. . .

Five minutes later, Gunner waved a hand in the air. "Stop. We are where we should be."

Carina halted the Sno-Cat and glanced at Gunner. "Please don't say anything to the others about our conversation."

"I will not." *I do not want to embarrass myself.* He drew an X over his heart. "As the saying goes, 'Cross my heart and hope to die.'" A smile creased his face.

"Thank you." Carina opened her door and climbed out.

Gunner joined her moments later as they waited for the other Sno-Cat.

As the six SPA members formed a semi-circle, Bertelot checked the coordinates again and smiled. "Excellent. We shall set up our camp here. I want everything finished today so we can begin drilling our ice cores."

They unloaded the remaining two trailers and checked to see what was missing.

Bertelot shook his head. "We will have to shorten our core lengths. Some of the tubing was on the third trailer."

"How far will we be able to drill?" Rona stood near him, hands on her hips.

"I think to a maximum of nine meters. Gunner and Rona, start setting up the protective tent and windbreak, where we will begin drilling. I want to start now and cut as many samples today as possible." He turned to the others. "Organize our camp. I think we can all sleep in the Jamesway hut, which will make things easier as we will not have to erect any tents."

"What about the outhouse?" Carina pursed her lips. "It was on the other trailer."

"We shall have to improvise. Go through the supplies and locate what you can use. We will partition off a corner of the hut for our toilet."

"Ugh." Carina grimaced.

Bertelot shrugged. "Best we can do, but we will not be on the ice sheet for long." He clapped his mittened hands together. "Time to work."

Two hours later, a primitive camp stood on the ice sheet, ready to withstand the wind and weather. Nearby, the cutting area was in operation.

Bertelot operated the hand-powered drill, the bit slowly sinking into the ice.

As each core segment over one meter rose above the hole, Gunner and Rona separated the ice from the drill and carried it outside to a box designed to hold the samples. They continued to repeat this procession as new segments became available.

\* \* \*

Carina, Ailsa, and Eggert organized things inside the hut once it was assembled.

Ailsa unrolled sleeping bags and arranged them in a row along one wall.

Carina placed lanterns around the hut and turned them on.

Eggert declared himself cook. "I'll heat some vegetable soup. The guys and Rona will be cold and hungry when they come inside." He opened the lid of an institutional-sized can of soup. "Think three liters will be enough?"

"Yes." Ailsa laughed. "There are only six of us, so that's half a liter each. Should be plenty."

Carina nodded. "How much of the B&M canned bread should I open?"

Eggert grimaced. "None for me, thanks, unless you brought along a toaster."

"Open two of them." Ailsa put her hands on her hips. "It's okay at room temperature with plenty of butter, but I agree with Eggert about it being toasted."

"Butter, we have, so we're good to go." Carina smiled. "Soup and bread will warm us up. I'll put a pot of coffee on, too."

"Here's a thought." Eggert clicked his fingers. "We can use the soup cans in our new toilet. I found a couple of boxes of bags and tie wraps. Be better than using the outhouse as it'll be warmer in here."

"Good thinking." Carina poured the soup into a large pot and turned the heat to medium on the stove.

* * *

Bertelot continued to operate the hand drill, stopping from time to time to sip from his canteen. He glanced around the area and nodded with satisfaction at the way the others kept the space tidy. *Gunner and Rona work hard—I am glad they are with us.*

The windbreak opened as Gunner and Rona returned from dropping off an ice core. They approached Bertelot, who stopped the drill so they could remove the latest sample.

Gunner operated the jigsaw they used to remove the ice. Holding the saw at an angle, he began cutting when the ten-inch blade bounced off something in the ice. He turned to Bertelot. "How far down was this section?"

Bertelot studied the sample. "That is the piece from six to nine meters down in our fourth hole. Why?"

"The saw hit something. I can't tell what it is. It could be a rock. I'll try to cut around it."

"Be careful, Gunner. We do not want any mishaps."

"I'll help." Rona stepped forward with a metal rod in her hand.

Gunner shook his head. "Keep clear, Rona, in case the blade jumps again." He restarted the saw and resumed cutting.

Rona shoved the rod into the cut, trying to pry it open.

The saw hit the rod, throwing it back at her.

"*Ieeeeeah!*"

She screamed as she pulled her hand back. When the rod was thrown, it impaled Rona's hand through the fleshy part, cutting a ragged hole as it came out the other side.

"Gunner! Grab the med kit." Bertelot held her arm in the air to slow the blood loss, clamping his other hand on Rona's and applying direct pressure.

When Gunner returned, they wrapped her hand and wrist with gauze and tape.

"We will try to remove the rod in the hut. Too cold here." Bertelot gestured outside. "Let us go."

The men entered the hut in a rush.

"What's happened?" Carina put a hand to her face. "Let me help. Eggert, Ailsa, get some water heated and more bandages." She turned to Rona. "This will hurt like hell when we remove it."

Rona grimaced. "Understood. Help me, please—I do not want to lose my hand."

Carina glanced at Bertelot. "We'll do our best—now brace yourself." When Rona couldn't see her face, she gave Bertelot a slight shake of her head.

# Chapter Thirty-One

F ederal Bureau of Investigation
       Miramar, Florida

Chris alternated between twiddling his thumbs and cracking his knuckles as he sat in a green plastic chair at a chipped and stained laminated table in the cream-colored interrogation room. He feigned a yawn before taking a careful sip from the now-warm Coke an agent had given him earlier. *This is boring. What kind of game are they playing?*

A dim lightbulb hanging from the ceiling cast shadows on the concrete block walls. A single door stood closed in front of Chris, while on the wall to the right was a mirror. He glanced at it and waved. *I assume it's a two-way, and someone's probably watching me. Wonder if I should give them a show? Perhaps moon them?* He shook his head. *Naw. Might make it more difficult to be released.*

Voices and footsteps echoed in the hallway, ceasing when at least two people stopped outside the locked door of the interrogation room.

Chris smiled. *So, are the games to begin? Good cop, bad cop, like in the movies, or something more sinister?*

The door swung inward, and the two FBI agents who detained him at Costa's stepped inside. They sat across from him and folded their arms.

Chris mimicked them.

The one with short blond hair and blue eyes gestured toward his partner. "He's Mike Black, and I'm Ike Brown. We're both FBI Special Agents."

*Great. Wannabe comedians.* "So, why am I here? I didn't break any laws." *At least, none I'm aware of.*

"You aren't under arrest." Ike recrossed his arms.

"Good. I'm outta here." Chris stood.

Mike slammed a meaty fist on the table. "Sit down! Otherwise, we'll come up with a charge and keep you here."

"Okay." Chris sat. "You haven't answered my question. Why am I here?"

Ike hit a button on the table. "We're recording your interview. Do you have any objection?"

"Would it matter if I did?"

"No, but we're required to ask. Are you Christopher Chandler?"

"Nope." Chris shook his head. "You have the wrong guy."

Mike smirked. "We have the right person. So, what's your name, wiseass?" He glared at Chris.

"You took my passport and wallet. Didn't you examine them?"

"Yes, I did. Now for the recording, what's your name?"

*Should I keep playing with these jerks?* Chris shook his head again. *Better not.* "As my documents show, my name is Chris Handler. My first name isn't shortened from Christopher. My parents didn't like Christopher—they thought it was too formal and didn't fit with their image. They were part of the hippie generation."

Mike nodded. "Your name matches."

*How about that? Guess I know who I am.* "So, now what?"

207

Ike glanced at Mike before looking at Chris. "Who did you call on your phone before we picked you up?"

"You should know. It was someone at the Pentagon. He was my former roommate at MIT."

"Yes, we confirmed this with Mr. McMasters. We also spoke with Admiral Blakely to find out if he had ever heard of you, which he had."

*Thank you, Matthew.* Chris cracked his knuckles. "What do you want from me?"

"We're looking for Walter Brown, CEO of Diablo Corporation. You work for him, so where is he?"

*As if I'd tell them.* Chris tilted his head from side to side. "Mister Brown is a private individual and doesn't like to be disturbed. All of his employees sign a non-disclosure statement when they're hired, which covers all information regarding his corporation and him. I'm sorry, gentlemen, but I can't help you. Perhaps you should speak with his lawyers."

"Can't or won't?" Mike glanced at the ceiling in apparent frustration.

"Unless you're prepared to pay all my costs when Brown sues my ass for breaking the NDA, I can't help you. Otherwise, you'll have to find him on your own." Chris stood. "If you have nothing else, I'm leaving."

Ike nodded. "You're free to go—for now."

Chris grinned as he walked toward the door. "Gentlemen, it's been my pleasure. Perhaps next time we can be a bit more informal and enjoy a meal together ... at Micky Dee's. I'll buy."

Ike and Mike glared at him but remained silent.

After leaving the building, Chris stopped a passing taxi. Twenty minutes later, he was dropped off at the Diablo Corporation offices and headed inside. He showed his identification to the security guard and was given access to the penthouse suite.

Before entering, Chris sent a text to Matthew: *Approximate base coordinates: 73.5000° S, 61.8333° E. Nearest peak is Mount Menzies. Base underground.*

He used his key and entered the penthouse. Stopping in the kitchen, he grabbed a bottle of water and headed to Brown's communication center. He logged into the computer and composed a message to Brown:

*Secured Doctor Stine and Doctor Rhude (specializes in neurology) per your request. Departing tomorrow. Please advise if there is anything else I should bring. Otherwise, see you in two days.*

After sending his message, he picked up the desk phone and dialed.

A female voice answered. "Doctor Stine's office. How may I help you?"

"Hello. This is Chris Handler. Is Doctor Stine available? He's expecting my call."

"Just a minute, sir."

Moments later, Stine came on the line. "Hey, Chris. Are we all set? Doctor Rhude and I'll be ready to depart in the morning. Since we have our gear sorted out, we'll meet you in front of the building."

"Excellent. I'll be waiting in a Diablo Corporation van by 09:30."

"Okay. See you tomorrow."

Breaking the connection, Chris wandered back into the kitchen. He pulled a pepperoni pizza from the freezer and turned on the oven. After taking the pizza from the box, he put it on a cooking tray, shoved it in the oven, and set a timer, adding a few extra minutes since he didn't wait for the oven to heat up.

Kicking off his shoes in the bedroom he used when staying in Miami, he turned on the TV and searched for a baseball game. He found one. *Perfect. Miami Marlins versus the Detroit Tigers.*

Twenty-five minutes later, the timer dinged. He dashed into the kitchen, slid the pizza onto a platter, grabbed a cutter and a bottle of beer, and headed back to his room.

Chris ate, finished the beer, and dozed as the game stretched into the fifth inning.

\* \* \*

Diablo Headquarters
Miami

The following morning, Martin, one of Diablo's drivers, met Chris outside with a van. "Morning, Chris. Ready to head back to the deep freeze?"

"Hey, Martin. When are you going to join us?" Chris climbed into the passenger seat.

Martin shook his head. "Uh-huh. Not for me. Give me Miami's weather any day." He pulled into traffic, and they headed to the building where Doctor Stine maintained his office.

When they pulled up out front, two men waited next to a pile of luggage.

The doctors were polar opposites. While Stine was tall and lean, Rhude was short and heavyset. Stine sported a tidy mustache, while Rhude sported a walrus mustache—thick, bushy, and drooped over his mouth. Both men wore lumberjack-style shirts and jeans, along with all-weather boots.

Chris and Martin jumped out of the van.

While Martin opened the rear door, Chris approached the doctors. "Did you leave anything behind?" He laughed.

Stine wiped the perspiration from his forehead as he gestured toward the luggage. "Better to be prepared than forget something. Don't think there'll be too many opportunities to go shopping."

"That's true. But I don't think you need those heavy shirts right now."

Stine glared at Rhude. "See! I told you we should have packed these as well."

Everyone grabbed a piece of luggage and carried it to the rear of the van, where Martin waited. Soon, everything was aboard, and the men climbed inside the vehicle.

After a short drive to the General Aviation Center at Miami International Airport, Martin weaved through several privately-owned planes until he reached Diablo's.

Rhude whistled. "I thought we'd be flying commercial."

Chris turned in the front seat and grinned. "No, we'll be using Mister Brown's planes. Better get used to a few changes as in addition to what he's paying you, there'll be plenty of perks to enjoy."

\* \* \*

Once the luggage was stowed, Chris and the two doctors boarded the plane. Chris pointed to chairs and grabbed a third one for himself. Picking up a handset, he hit a button. "We're ready to go, Godfrey."

"Yes, sir."

Godfrey engaged the engines, and the plane began to taxi.

Chris turned to the latest Diablo employees. "It'll take a couple of days to reach our destination. There'll be two stops to refuel and pick up anything waiting for us."

Rhude grinned. "Any chance of some sightseeing on the way?"

Chris shook his head. "No, 'fraid not. This isn't a pleasure trip. We'll stop in Santiago, Chile, and Punta Arenas with this plane before switching to one designed to land in Antarctica."

\* \* \*

General Aviation Center
  Miami International Airport

. . .

Mike took final photos of Brown's plane departing. He pulled them up to check the quality.

Ike kept his binoculars focused on the front of the aircraft. He dropped them in his lap and glanced at his partner. "Well, we know their flight plan says they're going to Punta Arenas via Santiago." Ike rubbed his chin. "From there onto Antarctica? Wonder who the two guys were?"

Mike shrugged. "The agents checking out the office building took photos of them, and they'll ask the security guard. We should have that information later."

"When we return to headquarters, I'll send a message to the legal attaché office in Santiago. Perhaps they can follow up."

"Good thinking."

\* \* \*

Enroute from Punta Arenas
   To Antarctica


Chris slathered mayo on one half of four hoagie buns neatly positioned on wax paper. He placed honey mustard on the other half before layering roast chicken, fresh tomatoes, and lettuce on the buns. When he finished making the sandwiches for himself, the pilot, and the doctors, he placed them on trays along with single-serving bags of chips. After giving them each a tray, he returned from the galley, pushing a cart of drinks. "Help yourselves, gentlemen. Sorry, we don't have something better for lunch, but since the chef didn't fly with us, you're stuck with what I can make."

Stine bit into his sandwich and smiled before speaking with his mouth full. "Best airline food I've ever had. So, what's the plan for when we arrive? Will we meet with Mister Brown right away?"

"I'll put you on his schedule." Chris shook his head. "No one meets with him without an appointment, even at the bottom of the world. I'll show you around tomorrow, and you'll get to inspect the modern surgical unit Mister Brown had installed when the facility was built."

"What will our working hours be?" Rhude glanced at Stine.

"You'll set your own hours as you deem necessary. However, you'll both be on call twenty-four hours a day. Other than the occasional accident to deal with, there won't be much for you to do unless Mister Brown has another attack. Before we arrive, you'll have to surrender any devices which can be used to communicate. You'll have full access to the facility's communications system and will be issued new phones since Mister Brown doesn't allow anyone to use devices they brought with them. The numbers are already programmed into his Quicksafe V3 Man Down alarm system. Until you learn your way around the complex, should you be summoned, either Dianne, our nurse, or I will take you to his quarters."

Chris glanced at the clock on the bulkhead and began cleaning up after their lunch. When he finished, he returned holding two black masks. "I'm sorry, but you'll have to put these on soon. This is a security precaution, as you won't be able to describe our approach and landing to anyone after you depart."

An hour later, the plane landed and taxied into the facility's hangar.

Chris unbuckled his seatbelt and stood. "Welcome to Antarctica. You may remove the masks. Follow me, and I'll take you to your quarters. Your rooms are adjacent to each other."

They descended from the aircraft.

Both doctors gaped as they gazed around the vast hangar.

Chris grinned. "The size of this place hits everyone the first time. You'll get used to it. Follow me, and we'll find your rooms. A couple of the staff will bring your luggage."

"Can we take a peek outside?" Rhude grinned as if he was a boy with a free rein in a candy store.

Chris pointed to a green door. "That's one way outside. But please don't leave the compound without approval and an escort."

"What would happen if we wanted some fresh air? I sometimes suffer from claustrophobia even when I'm in large, enclosed spaces."

*Now he tells me.* "It's too dangerous to go outside on your own. At minus fifty-two degrees, it takes an unprotected human body seven minutes to freeze solid. It's no joke out there." Chris shook his head. "Contact me first, and I'll arrange something for you."

Rhude crossed his arms. "Don't treat us like we're children. If we want to go outside, who are you to tell us not to?"

"Security makes the rules, and everyone abides by them or faces the consequences. You'll meet with our head of security, Sawyer Johnson, tomorrow for a briefing." Chris shrugged. "Take it up with him. However, heed my warning. Otherwise, you could be shot by security personnel as an intruder unless you freeze to death first."

# Chapter Thirty-Two

Diablo Corps Secret Outpost
Near Prince Charles Mountains

Sawyer sat at one end of a rectangular table for eight in the staff canteen. He kept an eye on the door as he spoke to some workers and nodded to acknowledge other patrons. He glanced at his watch—*late. Wonder if they got lost?*

When he spotted Needham and his team of five, he waved them over.

Ned sat next to Sawyer and grinned. "Sorry, we're a bit late. We were checking out the map app Emmanuel installed on the phones you gave us. We found a couple of glitches but will pass the word."

"You're the first to test the application, so he'll be pleased with your feedback. Write up your comments and send them to me. I'll see that Emmanuel and the IT team receive them." Sawyer glanced at the other team members. "Welcome. I'm Sawyer Johnson, head of security. While you're with us, you'll remain under Ned's leadership, subject to any changes from me, which will be passed through him."

Everyone nodded.

Sawyer stood. "Let's grab some chow. After we eat, we'll head to the security offices and discuss your mission."

Forty minutes later, Sawyer led the mercenary team into the security conference room. "Sorry, no doughnuts."

"As long as we have our coffee, we're good to go." Ned raised his mug in the air.

"Excellent." Sawyer sat in front of a computer at one end of the table. He jerked a thumb over his shoulder toward a large projection screen hanging on the wall. Rugged terrain covered with ice and snow and nearby mountains was all that appeared.

"Here's an aerial view of the outpost. As you can see, there isn't much above ground to show our whereabouts. If you know how to check for air vents, you might find us. Otherwise, we're invisible."

Lucas raised a hand. "How many air vents?"

"Eight. They're well-hidden and covered with white camouflage netting. Two maintenance guys check them every few days and adjust the netting if necessary. Their visits are timed with expected storms, so any footprints are wiped out."

Hudson glanced at the others. "So, what do you want us to do?"

"I only have sufficient security personnel to cover one OP around the clock. I'd like you guys to set up two more. We'll break with tradition and only have one person on duty at a time." Sawyer pursed his lips. "I wanted a dozen of you, but Mister Brown cut my request in half."

"Since we're in the middle of nowhere, what are the threats?" Mateo rubbed his chin. "Seems to me you'd be able to spot intruders without any difficulty."

"In normal circumstances, you'd be correct." Sawyer waved a hand in the air. "However, there's a research ship on the coast with a stated goal of conducting an investigation into climate change. Two of my men snuck onboard the *RV Aquavit* a few days ago. They sent several SITREPs before contact was lost. Also, the guy manning OP-One reported a possible aircraft sighting not associated with normal Antarctic flights. It's probable someone has learned about Mister Brown's hidden outpost and is investigating."

He glanced at each man in turn. "Your mission will be to interdict any potential adversary."

"What are the rules of engagement?" Carter grinned. " I hope we're not going to monitor the situation and let any intruders do what they want just because they might be associated with the UN."

Sawyer shook his head. "The ROEs are simple—do onto them before they can do anything to us."

"Does that mean deadly force is authorized?" Lucas smiled.

"If necessary—yes."

Grins spread across the team's faces as they high-fived one another.

"I must warn everyone—this won't be a free-for-all. Every effort must be made to determine the identity of anyone approaching and report the details back to me. However, if intruders are approaching a base entrance with weapons in full view, use your judgment."

Sawyer glanced around the table. "A word of caution. You won't be covered by military protocol like you're used to, as it's forbidden under international treaty, and certain acts could be prosecuted as homicide. Make sure your actions are protected as well as the organization."

He studied the aerial view and gestured to a small hump in the landscape. "The existing OP is about a mile away and centered, so the new ones should be about the same distance, one to the left and the other to the right."

Lucas raised a hand again. "What will we make the OPs out of?"

"Good question." Sawyer nodded. "We have plenty of wood and PVC cladding sheets to build the frames, as well as sufficient white camo netting to hide everything underneath. You'll need pickaxes and shovels to remove the ice and snow so you can keep the OPs as low as possible to the adjacent terrain so they don't stand out. Do it the same way as we did for our mission near Severomorsk when we were monitoring Russian fleet operations."

Lucas nodded.

"What about comms?" Ned gestured to the projection. "Assume we don't require anything fancy for short distances."

Sawyer nodded. "Standard VHF radios for around the outpost. However, if venturing further afield with one of the Sno-Cats, they carry HF radios, so use them. Snowmobiles are available for the immediate area."

"That brings us to the all-important question." Ned smiled. "What weapons will we carry for this mission?"

Sawyer laughed. "I'm surprised this wasn't the first question. For pistols, everyone will be issued a Ruger GP100 .357 Magnum. For rifles, you can choose between AK-74s, Winchester Model 70 Extreme Weather SS, or M16s."

Lucas raised a hand for the third time. "Can I have one of each?"

"Lucas!" Ned rubbed his temples before shaking his head. "How many times must I remind you everyone gets the same number of weapons?"

"Why should I share?"

"Because I told you to."

"You know, whenever weapons are mentioned, I always take as many as I can get. Since I have two hands, I should at least get two." Lucas chuckled.

"Don't remind me. The mountains of Afghanistan are littered with the weapons you left behind."

Lucas turned red. "Can't help it if the chopper guys wouldn't let me bring all of them."

Ned shook his head. "I think you took every weapon seized from half a dozen Afghan villages to add to those you were issued."

"Better in our hands than in theirs."

Hudson glanced at his team leader. "Ned, give the poor guy what he wants. As long as he doesn't expect any of us to carry them for him, he'll learn."

"Right you are." Ned chuckled as he turned back to Sawyer. "When do you want us to get started?"

"The sooner, the better. Having you and your team watching for interlopers will be far better than Gerald, the guy in the OP right now. He's not cut out for armed guard duty."

"Works for me."

An hour later, the mercenaries were armed and dressed in Arctic clothing. Security provided each of them with snowmobiles and radios.

When they exited from an up-and-over white metal door in the security window, Ned, Lucas, and Mateo headed toward the left while Wyatt, Hudson, and Carter veered to the right. Two members of each team towed sled tubs behind them, loaded with material for crafting their OPs.

Weaving through snow drifts, rocks, and piles of ice, each team made their way to their designated locations.

Coming to a stop between two drifts, Ned yanked out his radio. "Merc-Two, this is Merc-One. We're in position."

"Roger, Merc-One. Same here."

"Keep your eyes peeled for any intruders while you set up the OP."

"Roger, Merc-One. Will do."

Ned stowed his radio and climbed off the snowmobile.

Lucas and Mateo, with rifles strapped over their shoulders, had already paced out a diagram in the snow for their OP.

Ned joined them.

They used shovels and pickaxes to break up the ice so they could dig down and keep the OP as low as possible. Before long, the three men laid out a six-foot by six-foot base using wood planks. Interlocking cladding sheets comprised the walls, and a double layer served as the ceiling.

When they finished, they covered the entire structure with the white camouflage netting, driving ice spikes onto the ends to keep the material in place.

Ned inspected the outside while Lucas and Mateo finished stocking the OP with field rations, a small propane-fuel stove, and plastic bags to be used for waste. A bucket was placed near the doorway for collecting snow to melt on the stove.

"Merc-One, this is Merc-Two. Come in please."

Ned responded to the call from Wyatt. "Read you five by, Merc-Two. How are things going?"

"Almost finished. I'll take the first two-hour stint and—"

A burst of static came through the radio.

"Come in, Merc-Two."

Silence.

"Merc-Two, this is Merc-One, SITREP over."

"Shit. Sorry, Merc-One. Someone took a potshot at us."

"Here? What direction?"

"Seemed to come from your area."

He glanced at Lucas and Mateo.

Both men shrugged and raised their hands as if to signal, what's up?

Ned shook his head. "Negative, Merc-Two. No one from here is shooting. Give me a sec—gonna check something with security." He switched to a pre-arranged channel. "Sec Base, this is Merc-One. Come in, please."

Another burst of static filtered through the radio.

"Merc-One, this is Sec Base. Status?"

"Both OPs are now functional. However, someone is shooting at Merc-Two."

"Must be Gerald. Let me reach out to him and get him to hold his fire." Sawyer groaned. "He can be a bit crazy at times and sometimes isn't too good with his decision-making ability. But he was never supposed to be out there on his own. However, the men who were supposed to assist him are the ones who are missing."

"Roger that. Get him to ease up on friendlies. Otherwise, Merc-Two will take him out."

# Chapter Thirty-Three

D iablo Corps Secret Outpost
     Near Prince Charles Mountains

Graham removed his earbuds and tossed them on the desk. The strains of Andrea Bocelli and Sarah Brightman's duet, "Time to Say Goodbye," echoed across the room from his earphones. He climbed out of his ergonomic chair, pushed the interconnecting door open, and strode to Emmanuel's desk, about fifteen feet away. "Hey, boss. Got a minute?"

Emmanuel turned from his screen and glanced at Graham. "Yeah. What's up?"

"I'm not sure, so I want to run it by you. I just finished hacking into an account at the Bank of Japan. While I was snooping around, someone or something threw me out. Not just out of the account, but from the bank's website." He shook his head. "Never happened before."

Emmanuel stood. "Follow your earlier hack so I can watch what happens."

"Okay." Graham returned to his desk, trailed by his boss. Graham replicated what he had done before. "Strange. I was knocked out at this point. It appears I can continue now." He shrugged. "Sorry, boss. Not sure what happened."

"Hmm." Emmanuel pursed his lips. "Inform me right away if it happens again."

Graham's fingers flew over the keyboard. "Hey, boss. I might be back in, but I can't access anything else linked to this account."

"I'll try from my computer." Emmanuel made a note of the details before returning to his desk and logging into the same account. Graham followed him. "I'm in—let's see what I can do." He frowned. "Same thing here—just got booted out. Move onto the next project and let me think about this."

* * *

Bank of Japan,
Tokyo

Hinata Takahashi thrust a hand in the air. "Got you. Keep out of my network." He smiled as he booted a hacker identified only as N3M3515 out of the Bank of Japan's system.

Moments later, another hacker, identified as Mo7H3R5H1P, entered the site. As with N3M3515, Hinata kicked him out. He tapped a button on his computer console and listened to the call connect.

"Hello, you have reached the desk of Matthew McMasters. Please leave your contact information, and I'll call you back."

"Hey, Matthew-san, it's Hinata."

A couple of clicks and Matthew came on the line. "How are you doing, Hinata? Any problems with the phishing account we set up for you?"

"That's what I'm calling about. I had two 'fish' today. One was called Nemesis, and the other was Mothership. Heard of either one before?"

"Neg, I haven't, but I'll pass the word to my friends. Perhaps they've come across them before. Were you able to trace them?"

"No, so sorry, Matthew-san. I followed both of them to Panama, but they hopped again, and I lost them."

"No worries. I'll put the word out to the others."

"Excellent, Matthew-san. That's all from Tokyo right now, so I'll get back to you later."

"Sounds good. Let me know if I can do anything else for you."

"Sayōnara." Hinata broke the connection.

\* \* \*

The Pentagon
Arlington, Virginia


Matthew hit two digits on his phone and connected to Admiral Blakely's secretary. "Hey, Susan. Does the admiral have a few minutes to spare for me?"

"He's on the line with the NSA right now. Come over, and I'll squeeze you in before his next appointment."

"Perfect." Matthew disconnected and headed to the admiral's suite. He smiled at Susan as he took a seat.

She returned his smile and nodded to a closed door. "The admiral just hung up, so you can go in."

Matthew stood, walked to the door, and knocked.

"Come in."

Matthew entered and took his regular seat.

"What do you have for me today?"

"Thought you might like an update from my 'hacker' buddies. Hinata, who works for the Bank of Japan, caught two guys in the bank's system when they logged into the phishing account we set up. He wasn't able to track them to a specific location. They took him all over the world, but he lost them in Panama. Hinata also said he booted the hackers out of the bank's system."

The admiral nodded. "Excellent work and perfect timing. I'm meeting with the president, the NSA, and the CIA director later. Anything else?"

"Yes. One of the hackers was called Mothership, and the other Nemesis. Since Hinata lost them in Panama, I wonder if they work for Diablo? My research showed Diablo had commercial interests in the country." Matthew stroked his chin. "We'll have to create some additional IT accounts to dangle in front of them with some of the major banking institutions."

"Should we ask the president to update the G7 leaders?"

Matthew shook his head. "I'd suggest holding off on that, Admiral. Until we have a better handle on the situation, I think it's better to keep what we know a close hold—in case there are other systems being hacked that we don't know about. Let's get the bigger picture before alarming anyone."

"Hmm." The admiral swiped a hand through his sparse hair. "I suppose you're correct. If anyone at the meeting suggests this, I'll head them off."

"Yes, sir. That's all I have at this time, Admiral."

"Please let your friends know I'm very grateful for their assistance. When the time is appropriate, I'd like to mention their names to the president—hacker handles if they only want to be referred by them."

"I'm sure it will be appreciated." Matthew stood and left the office.

* * *

Diablo Corps Secret Outpost
  Near Prince Charles Mountains

Identified as 4RCH4N63L, Klaus Müller clicked on an icon and entered the European Central Bank computers via his normal entry point. As he did so, he spotted a new employee account. *What's this?*

He clicked on the account and tried a myriad of logins and passwords without success. He closed his eyes before trying a simple login and password and was granted access. *Gott in Himmel! Is someone at the ECB slipping?* He shook his head as he reviewed the account information. *Ah. A new member of the ECB is taking shortcuts. I shall soon teach him a lesson he'll never forget.*

With a few strokes on his keyboard, Klaus made himself a secondary controller of the account. He also added a keystroke logger so he'd be able to read what the primary account holder was doing.

* * *

Bundeskriminalamt
  Weisbaden, Germany

Tobias Trinkenschuh, a member of the *Bundeskriminalamt*, also known as the German Federal Criminal Police Office, leaned back in his chair in his small office at the organization's headquarters in Wiesbaden. He grinned as he monitored the keystrokes entered by a hacker in the ECB computers. *I'll treat Matthew at the Sterinernes Haus restaurant in Frankfurt the next time he visits. Without his assistance, we wouldn't be able to catch these hackers.* He activated a tracer route program to track the hops used by the hacker.

"*Scheisse!* Lost him in Peru. I better pass the information to Matthew. Perhaps his other friends can trace the hacker." He typed a short email and sent it.

225

* * *

Diablo Corps Secret Outpost
    Near Prince Charles Mountains

M43STRo, the hacker handle for Finn O'Brien, logged into the Bank of England in London's Square Mile. His access had continued to grow ever since an unsuspecting individual triggered a malware download. Skipping from account to account, he wormed his way deeper into the inner workings of the bank until he stumbled across a new employee account he hadn't seen before. *What's this? Another newbie I can exploit?*

Intrigued by the new account, he put his database of leaked passwords and usernames to work. He leaned back in his chair and sipped his Thompson's Irish Breakfast Tea.

Before long, an alarm chimed.

Glancing at the screen, Finn smiled. *Works like a charm—every time.* He logged into the new account, installed his keystroke logger, and left the account. *I'll check later to see what's what.* He backed out, chuckling as he went. *Time to shut them down again.*

* * *

GCHQ's National Cyber Security Centre
    Cheltenham, England

Isla Robertson, a computer exploitation expert with GCHQ's National Cyber Security Centre, grinned when she spotted a hacker leaving a keystroke logger in the account she had set up in coordination with Matthew and his hacker friends. She activated her tracer program and watched the hacker as he bounced around the world.

All of a sudden, she frowned. "Damn! Lost him in Argentina. It seems to be pointing the way Matthew opined. Is this guy associated with the group in Antarctica?"

* * *

The White House
  1600 Pennsylvania Avenue
  Washington, D.C.

Admiral Blakely arrived at the White House at the appointed time. After clearing security, a Secret Service officer escorted him to the Oval Office. The officer knocked on the door and pushed it open, allowing the admiral to enter. After closing the door, the officer departed.

The president, National Security Advisor Jonny Meu, and CIA Director Amelia Collins sat around a coffee table in front of the Resolute Desk. They stood and shook hands with the admiral.

The president picked up a silver pot. "Coffee? It's my own special blend."

"Yes, please, sir."

The president filled a cup and passed it to the admiral before refreshing the others. "So, Jonny tells me you have an update on what's happening with the G7 banks?"

"Yes, Mister President. I asked Jonny and Amelia to meet with us as they are well-positioned to keep on top of things and protect our nation." The admiral cleared his throat. "I turned one of my men loose on the project. I've referred to him before as Grandson."

The president nodded and motioned for the admiral to continue.

"When he studied at MIT, he made friends with a number of individuals who are involved in what might be termed as nefarious activities." The admiral smiled. "Come what may, many of these individuals now hold important positions either in friendly governments or at some of the banks under attack. They created what

Grandson referred to as a phishing account and have lured in some big ones."

Everyone chuckled.

"By the time I departed to come here, two hackers using the usernames Mothership and Nemesis were caught in the trap. I suspect there might be more by this time. Anyway, tracing their whereabouts is proving problematic. We followed both to Panama before the trail disappeared. Grandson hypothesized this might be pointing to Antarctica, and I agree with his assessment."

A phone rang.

Jonny picked up the receiver and listened for a couple of minutes before hanging up. "Someone just hacked into the Bank of England again and brought them down."

# Chapter Thirty-Four

F inbul Ice Sheet
   Antarctica

Carina and Eggert strapped Rona's arm in an upright position to minimize any blood loss from the injury to her hand. They helped her into the passenger seat in one of the Sno-Cats.

Bertelot took Ailsa and Gunner aside. "Ailsa, I'm leaving you in charge until I return. Gunner will continue to drill the ice, and he will need help to cut the samples. Be careful!"

"Don't worry. We will." Ailsa laid a gloved hand on Bertelot's arm. "Drive safe and get Rona the help she needs. We'll be fine."

Bertelot nodded and climbed into the Sno-Cat. He engaged the vehicle's gears and accelerated into a turn, heading back to the *RV Aquavit.*

Gunner glanced at Ailsa. "If you are helping me with the ice core, we should make a start. I want to do as much as we can and wrap up here today." He shivered. "I feel like someone is watching over my shoulder."

"I understand what you mean." Ailsa scanned the horizon, searching for any sign of life among the snow and ice-covered peaks and rocks. She shook her head. "I've felt like that ever since we arrived. So what do you think was stuck in the ice?"

"Not sure. Perhaps it fell from a passing airplane years ago and became embedded in the ice. We better keep an eye peeled for any more debris."

Ailsa nodded. "I hope Tim can help Rona."

"If anyone can, it will be Tim. I understand he is a super nurse practitioner and knows his way around various injuries one can experience in Antarctica."

They headed into the cutting area.

Gunner maneuvered the hand-powered drill into the existing hole, slowly sinking it into the ice. As each core segment rose more than one meter above the hole, he stopped drilling.

Together, Gunner and Ailsa separated the ice from the drill, carried it outside, and added the piece to the others. Ailsa wrapped a tag around the end of the core providing details of the hole and the core's position.

Two hours later, Gunner called a halt. "This will be the last one from this hole as we have reached the maximum depth for the drill. What say we go inside for some hot chocolate to warm up after we cut this?"

"Works for me." Ailsa smiled. "I'm always ready for a hot chocolate."

"Afterward, we will start breaking down the camp."

\* \* \*

En Route to *RV Aquavit*

. . .

Despite Bertelot's attempt to avoid unnecessary bumps on the return trip to the ship, he hit several hidden rocks.

Each time, Rona groaned and glanced at Bertelot. "Please, try to miss the bigger ones. The jolts hurt like hell."

"I am doing my best. By my calculation, we should spot the ship in about an hour."

"It's okay with me if you go a bit slower." Rona winced as they dropped over another hidden clump of ice or rock.

"Sorry." Bertelot slowed the Sno-Cat. "I will not go as fast. How is your hand?"

"It hurts but not as bad as before. I think it's getting numb. I hope that's a good sign."

"Hmm." Bertelot gave a slight shake of his head. "Try to get some rest to help the time pass. I will wake you when we approach the ship."

"Okay." Rona leaned back in her seat, careful not to bang her raised arm. Before long, she appeared to either be asleep or had passed out.

As time ticked by, Bertelot kept glancing at his friend every few minutes as he maneuvered through the landscape of ice and rock.

Rona never moved.

At last, the ship came into view. "Hey, Rona, I can see the *Aquavit* now." He studied her frame.

"Rona? We are almost to the ship. Let me call them." Bertelot picked up the radio. "Hello, *Aquavit*. This is Bertelot. I have an injured woman. Please inform Tim. We shall arrive in less than fifteen minutes."

"Roger, Bertelot. This is the *Aquavit*. Tim will be standing by with an emergency team."

"Thank you." Bertelot tapped Rona on the leg. "Hold on, my friend. Help will be with us in a few minutes."

Her head lolled to the side.

"Hang tight. Tim and the others are heading down the gangway to meet us."

Bertelot stopped the Sno-Cat near Tim. "Hurry, please. My friend hurt her arm, and it looks bad."

Tim opened the door and glanced at Rona before he began checking her vital signs. He turned to one of his corpsmen. "Get the stretcher ready. I think she's passed out, but I don't want to take any chances with her injury. We'll leave her arm taped in position as it is. Vitals are a bit erratic, but overall okay."

Within moments, they had Rona out of the vehicle and laid her on the stretcher.

"Take her to the pre-op bay." Tim glanced up at the ship. "We'll check her condition there." He turned to Bertelot. "What happened?"

"We were harvesting the ice cores when the saw hit a metallic object. It swung from the ice and penetrated Rona's hand. Will she be okay?"

Tim nodded. "Yes. At least, I think so. When did this happen? Did she lose a lot of blood?"

"About two hours ago. Yes, blood was everywhere."

"Okay. She'll probably need some fluids, and we'll put her on a drip. We'll do our best for her."

"Thank you."

Ninety minutes later, Bertelot entered the recovery bay.

Rona lay on a bed with her arm extended in a sling above her body. Her eyes were closed, but her vital signs were normal, according to the monitor.

Tim turned as Bertelot entered and smiled. "Your friend will be fine. She'll have quite a scar on both sides of her hand, but there doesn't appear to be any serious damage. It was a simple puncture through the hand and didn't hit any ligaments or bones, so there shouldn't be any future problems. Whoever strapped her arm before you headed here did the right thing."

"Thank God." Bertelot crossed himself. "We were afraid she would lose her hand."

Tim shook his head. "Not in my sick bay. She'll need to rest for a few days, and I'll give her some light physical therapy exercises to do. No heavy lifting or exertion with the hand for at least eight weeks."

"Thank you again, Tim."

* * *

Bertelot met with Captain Smythe. "I must thank you for allowing Tim to take care of my friend. I understand Rona will be back in action after a lengthy recovery period."

"You're welcome, Bertelot. Is there anything else I can do for you?"

"Yes, Captain. Might I borrow a crew member to travel back with me and break down the camp? We will move to one of the other core drilling sites later."

The captain nodded. "Of course. I can spare Oskar since we're anchored. I'll send him with you."

"I will wait for him in the Sno-Cat."

"Give him fifteen minutes, and he'll be with you."

Bertelot left the ship and climbed into the vehicle. He maneuvered it to their refueling station and filled the tank. Afterward, he connected a new trailer.

Oskar joined him, and they headed toward the Finbul Ice Sheet.

"What is the plan, Bertelot?" Oskar held onto a panic strap as the vehicle sped over the ice and snow.

"We will close up the camp and bring everything here. On the way back, I want to stop and check out an area where the ice broke away."

"Okay. How long will it take to shut down the camp?"

"A couple of hours. Those who remained should already be working to remove everything."

When they approached, Bertelot pointed through the windshield. "It appears they have most of the work done for us. I hope there is something hot to drink."

Oskar smacked his lips. "Me, too. I could use something to warm me up."

Bertelot and Oskar joined the others around the camp stove, where a coffee pot simmered.

Eggert picked up with pot. "Coffee, anyone?" He glanced toward Gunner and Ailsa. "We ran out of hot chocolate."

Ailsa blushed. "It's my one weakness when on the ice."

After everyone finished their drink, they loaded the last of the supplies and equipment into the three trailers and secured the gear with bungee cords and tarpaulins. After checking to ensure every item was packed, they formed a convoy and headed back in the direction of the ship.

About an hour later, Carina followed Bertelot's directions and headed to the area they had spotted on the way out.

She pulled up with the other Sno-Cats following suit.

Bertelot climbed out, holding a camera. After attaching a rope around his waist and connecting the other end to the vehicle's bumper, he inched out on the ice. He took a few photographs before heading back. He shook his head as he climbed back inside the Sno-Cat. "The ice was broken away. But, there is evidence this was done by humans, not climate change."

# Chapter Thirty-Five

The Pentagon,
Arlington, Virginia

Matthew glanced at the caller ID and picked up his phone on the second ring. "Good morning, Georgia. How are things at Bedlam HQ?"

"Morning, Matthew. How is my favorite guy doing today?"

He laughed. "That's what I like about you, Georgia. You always put a smile on my face."

"All part of the service." She giggled. "Anyway, I thought you'd like to know Pun, Ollie, and Gordon depart this evening for Punta Arenas."

"Fantastic! Perfect timing. I'll inform CC when I send an update to him. Are we still on for bowling this weekend?"

"Sure thing. Bring plenty of money as I plan to whip you again."

"Okay, so I lost last time. Rub it in."

They both laughed.

"I better let you go, Matthew. I need to find out what Charles is doing in the 'Creativity Den.' He said something at breakfast in the canteen about trying to devise exploding snowballs."

"Explosive snowballs?" Matthew gave her a wry smile. "Would be a great follow-on to his action-figure toys filled with C-4."

"Never can tell what his mind is up to. See you on Saturday."

"Bye, Georgia." Matthew broke the connection and turned to his computer. He crafted a new email to the Bedlam teams:

*To: Alpha, Bravo, Charlie, QRF-1*
*From: Bedlam*
*Received approximate coordinates of target at 73.5000° S, 61.8333° E. Nearest peak is Mount Menzies. According to intel, facility located underground.*

*As earlier requested, Red, Nightjar, and Panther will depart CONUS for Punta Arenas this evening and will be in position to transfer to your location if reinforcements are needed. Additional equipment, weapons, and supplies are being sent separately via SWOOP and should arrive today. A second shipment is being prepared in the event it's required.*

Matthew picked up his ringing phone. "Hey, Georgia."

"Sorry, big guy. It's Charles. Just wanted to let you know that twelve of my action figures are ready for you."

"Excellent. I'll add them to the shipment heading to Antarctica today. If CC and the others find the underground outpost, your toys will make it easier for them to breach the facility."

"Always glad to help out the Bedlam guys."

A bang echoed through the receiver.

"Oops! Gotta run. One of my snowballs just exploded."

"No—" Matthew listened to the dial tone before hanging up. He turned back to his computer and scanned the list of items being sent to Punta Arenas for onward delivery by SWOOP Antarctica. After adding six Styrofoam packages containing two each of the red, white, and blue action figure toys to the inventory, he grinned. *Would love to see these used in action. Must pack a wallop.*

The intercom buzzed.

Matthew answered. "Yes, Susan?"

"Matthew, the admiral wants an update before he heads out for another briefing at the White House. He's on the phone right now, but if you hurry, I'll get you in before anything else pops up."

"On my way." He headed out of his office and entered the admiral's suite.

Susan stood. "Come this way—he just got off the phone."

She knocked on the door and opened it.

Matthew followed her into Admiral Blakely's office. "Yes, Admiral?"

"Hi, Matthew. Anything new I can share at today's meeting?"

"A couple more recovered hacker handles—Maestro and Archangel. As with the first two, we still haven't located them, but we believe they're working for Diablo in Antarctica. Archangel was tracked to Peru by the Germans, and the British tracked Maestro to Argentina."

The admiral nodded. "Anything else?"

"Not about the hackers. But, we're sending more equipment, weapons, and supplies to CC and pre-positioning three Bedlam operatives in Chile in the event they're needed."

"Perfect timing. Jonny will want to hear this. Tell everyone to keep up the good work."

Matthew grinned. "Will do, Admiral."

\* \* \*

Bedlam Base Camp
Near Prince Charles Mountains

. . .

Randall Krzak

Carlos lowered the landing gear on the BT-67 as he tipped the aircraft's wings before lining up on the makeshift runway. The plane bounced several times over ice protrusions and shallow snow drifts along the rough surface before he brought the Basler to a standstill. *Not much powdered snow today. Must not have snowed since I left.*

CC, David, and the other Bedlam operatives approached the aircraft.

While CC met with the pilot, the others opened the cargo area and began unloading.

"Welcome back, Carlos. It seems like you're clocking up loads of air miles ferrying things to us."

"Sí. I understand there will be another flight in two or three days."

"Aye. Our headquarters always ensures we have everything we need and then some."

Carlos nodded. "Good people."

"Aye. The best in the world—but I don't tell them that as I want them to work harder." CC laughed.

A grin creased Carlos' face. "Sí. Makes perfect sense." He turned toward the unloading. "They are working very hard. Is there time for a hot chocolate before I depart?"

"Of course." CC turned and led the way to the Jamesway hut.

An electric kettle rested near the two-burner propane stove. CC turned it on and pulled two mugs from a shelf, along with a can of powdered chocolate. He prepared the mugs and added the water when it was heated before handing one to Carlos.

"Gracias." Carlos stuck his face into the steam rising from the cup.

"Aye. Nothing like a hot drink to keep the chills away—especially in Antarctica."

The door opened, and David entered, followed by the Bedlam team.

A gust of frigid air followed them.

"Hey, shut the door—we're losing what heat we have." David shivered.

Rufus did as asked. "Sorry about that."

After they prepared hot chocolate or coffee, each member of the team found a place to get comfortable and enjoy their drinks.

Carlos drained the mug and patted his stomach. "Will keep me warm all the way back to Punta Arenas. I'll let you know when I have more to bring you."

CC shook hands with Carlos. "Aye. Thank you again for your help."

"Always, señor. See you again soon. No need to come outside. Stay where it is warm."

CC nodded. "Have a safe return, Carlos."

After the pilot departed, CC turned to the others. "Captain Smythe sent an update this morning. One of the SPA team members was injured in an accident, but the nurse was able to help her. When they were returning to the ship, they spotted an area where ice had crumbled. There were apparent signs of human intervention. The captain also said another storm is brewing."

"Not global warming?" David shook his head. "Or is someone helping to change the climate?"

"Remains to be seen. However, we must locate this Diablo outpost and put an end to whatever they have planned. As Carina from the SPA team said, 'Our mission is important to convince every country to support international efforts to reduce greenhouse gases and show how Antarctica is being impacted by climate change.'"

Everyone nodded.

CC pointed to a map taped to the wall, showing their base camp with several dotted lines stretching away from it. "We don't have the manpower to do an extensive search, but I want two two-man teams to begin short excursions away from the camp, following the lines on the map."

"Ag, man." Bernard glanced at Alfie. "We'll take the first line to the left."

"Jake and I will follow the one to the right." Rufus folded his arms over his chest. "What are the ROEs?"

"No shooting except in self-defense." CC pursed his lips. "Recon only for now, so if you find something of interest, check the GPS coords and make note of them. We'll investigate later."

Bernard studied the faces of the others before bursting into laughter. "I suggest the last team back has kitchen duties tonight." He rubbed his stomach. "I'll be ready for it."

"You better be able to cook." Rufus tilted his head. "We'll be back before you."

The men dressed for the Arctic conditions. When they were ready, they grabbed backpacks holding emergency rations, extra ammunition, and trauma kits. Each carried a H&K G36 assault rifle.

"Send SITREPs every thirty minutes. David and I will monitor the radio and make note of your progress on the map."

The four men waved in acknowledgement as they trudged into the vast whiteness.

CC looked at David. "Want another coffee while we wait?"

David picked up his mug. "Sure."

* * *

The two teams headed out on the agreed-upon vectors, keeping in contact via radio. Clouds thickened as the storm approached.

Rufus keyed his radio. "Recon-One, this is Recon-Two, over."

"Ag, man. This is Recon-One. Go ahead."

"Spot anything yet?"

"Negative. Nothing but snow and ice. Give me a beach any day— plenty of sunshine and all the cold beer I can drink."

Rufus chuckled. "Roger that. Recon-Two out."

Shots echoed in the distance.

The four men hugged the ground with their rifles pointed in the direction of the noise.

"Recon-Two, this is Recon-One. Who's shooting?"

"Dunno, Recon-One. It must be someone from the outpost we're looking for. Can't get a bead on the direction with the echoes bouncing off the mountains."

"Same here. Suggest we back off and return to base at this time."

"Roger, Recon-One. Recon-Two RTBing. Out."

* * *

The Pentagon,
  Arlington, Virginia

After picking up his lunch from the Pentagon food court, Matthew returned to his office. He logged back into his computer and dug into his plate of tacos, refried beans, and rice. One new message waited for him.

*To: Numerologist*
  *From: Knuckle Cracker*
  25220 42609 22270 81803 14220 92422 13260 91822 08260 90918 05222 30712 26061 42213 07082 22406 09180 70212 11220 92607 18121 30827

Matthew reread his conversion a second time. "Damn. I gotta warn CC!"

# Chapter Thirty-Six

T he Pentagon,
         Arlington, Virginia

Matthew shoveled his lunch into his mouth with his right hand, chewing while his fingers flew over the keyboard as he typed a message to the Bedlam teams. He stared out the window overlooking one of the parking lots. *Wish I had a decent view.* He turned back to his keyboard.

To: *Alpha, Bravo, Charlie, QRF-1*
    *From: Bedlam*
    *URGENT ACTION*
    *Please be advised six mercenaries have joined the security team at Diablo's hidden outpost. Engage with extreme caution once the facility is located and interdiction operations commence.*

*Red, Nightjar, and Panther will be forward deployed to your location ASAP.*

Matthew sent his warning and thrummed as his fingers beat a rhythm on the desk. He glanced at the wall clock. *The admiral will be at the White House by now. Should I pass this info on to him?* He pursed his lips before picking up the phone and dialing.

"Hello, this is Matthew McMasters. I work for Admiral Blakely, who should be meeting with NSA Meu. Would it be possible to get a message to the admiral? It's urgent."

"Yes, sir," a female voice responded. "I'll pass it on to him."

"Thank you. Let him know six mercenaries are now involved in the complex Bedlam is searching for. Reserve team en route. He'll understand."

"Yes, sir."

Matthew broke the connection and leaned back in his chair. *Nothing else I can do.*

* * *

Bedlam Base Camp
   Near Prince Charles Mountains

CC sat at the small table as he acknowledged Matthew's warning. He picked up the radio to advise the recon teams but set it down when the door to the hut burst open, and the Bedlam operatives piled inside.

"Ag, man." Gerhard shook his head as he peeled off his Arctic gear. "Heard gunfire and couldn't determine where it was coming from, so we didn't stick around to find out."

"Aye. Best for you to return until the weather clears and we get a better idea of what we're up against." He gestured toward his iPad. "I received a message from headquarters about mercenaries augmenting the opposition. Was just going to contact you when you RTB'ed. I think we should only send one three-person team out at a time, so there's more firepower with the three weapons. Any recommendations?"

The operatives shook their heads.

"Aye. The new Recon-One will be Rufus, Gerhard, and Alfie. Head back out along the first vector to the left and keep an eye out and ears peeled for anything that might be of interest. Assume the mercs are out there."

Jake glanced at CC. "Any chance of additional support?"

"Aye. Pun, Ollie, and Gordon are on the way to Chile. As soon as they arrive, SWOOP will bring them here, so we'll have three teams available." CC glanced at David. "Of course, I'm assuming you want to take part?"

David grinned. "You betcha."

* * *

Recon-One rechecked their gear, suited up, and headed into falling snow flurries, their weapons cradled in their arms.

Rufus gestured to Alfie. "Take point."

He nodded and led the others, following in the remaining footprints left during the first excursion that hadn't yet been covered over.

Before long, they reached the area where the first team had hit the ground.

The revised Recon-One did the same.

Rufus grabbed Swarovski Optik 15x56 SLC Series binoculars from a receptacle on his belt and scanned the area. *Can't see anything in this snow.* He pulled his radio from another pouch. "Base, this is Recon-One."

Static burst through the radio before CC's voice came through. "Recon-One, this is Base. How do you read over?"

"Weak but audible. Damn snow is playing havoc with the comms."

"Aye. Understood."

"We're at the location where the first team took cover. Will continue forward progression and will advise any contact."

"Aye, Recon-One. Happy hunting. Base out."

Rufus stowed his radio and took another sweep of the perimeter with his binoculars. He stood and took point with Gerhard in the middle and Alfie bringing up the rear.

Ten minutes later, Rufus raised a fist in a 'stop' gesture. He pointed to his right.

A metal pole with a red flag rose above the ground.

"Look. Must be the flagged route to OP-ONE, so we're about eight hundred meters from the base." He gestured to his left. "We'll shift away from the OP and continue for another ten to fifteen minutes max."

"Ag, man." Gerhard wiped snow off his face. "Can't see a blasted thing. Why not go to the OP and wait this out?"

Rufus shook his head. "I want to continue a bit before we head to the OP in case the mercs have established an outpost."

"Okay. Time for me to take point."

After thirty minutes, Alfie took over, with Rufus in the middle and Gerhard dropping to cover the rear.

As planned, Rufus moved up to Alfie and halted him. "Far enough. Let me take another look with the binocs." He pulled them out of the pouch and scanned from left to right. "Nothing. Let's head to the OP. I'll take point again." He returned the binoculars to the receptacle before cradling his rifle.

Gerhard remained at the rear, taking a final look into the snow before following the others.

They continued in single file, retracing their progress until they reached the flagged route and trudged through the deepening snow to the OP.

After they settled into the small enclosure, Rufus contacted CC.

"Base, this is Recon-One. We're in position at the OP. No sign of unwanted visitors, but visibility is down to fifty meters, and the snow's thickening. Will remain here for another hour before RTBing."

"Aye, Recon-One. Concur. Base out."

Alfie passed out chocolate bars as they heated snow over a sterno can and made coffee.

The wind increased, whipping the snow into a frenzy.

"Ag, man. Still can't see a blasted thing, which means any opposition can't see anything either." Gerhard took a bite of chocolate and sipped on his hot drink.

Rufus nodded. "At least we're out of the worst of the storm but still need to maintain distance between us in the event of incoming fire. I suggest we scoop out shallow trenches in the snow and be on high alert."

* * *

Diablo Corps Secret Outpost
  Near Prince Charles Mountains
  Merc-One OP

Ned yanked his radio from his belt as he peered into the snow. *Can't see anything.* "Sec Base, this is Merc-One. Come in."

Static greeted him.

He tried again with the same result.

As he began a third time, a raspy voice came through the speaker. "Merc-One, this is ... Base. Please ... peat.'

Ned shifted position. "Sec Base, this is Merc-One. Can you read me?"

"Got you fine now. Status?"

"Merc-Two is checking on your other OP. They'll approach Gerald with care and deal with him as necessary."

"Roger, Merc-One. I contacted him and told him to stand down as friendlies were on the way."

"Okay. We'll continue to maintain our position at this time. Merc-One out."

* * *

Merc-Two
Somewhere Near Diablo OP

Merc-Two approached security's original OP. Wyatt held up a fist, bringing Hudson and Carter to stop. He switched to the appropriate radio channel. "OP-One, this is Merc-Two. Come in, please."

"Hello? W-Who is t-this?"

Wyatt grinned. *He seems scared shitless.* "OP-One—Gerald. This is Wyatt from Merc-Two. Sawyer sent us."

"G-Great."

"Can we approach? There are three of us."

"Oh. Yeah."

As they entered the OP, Gerald had his weapon aimed at them.

"Do you mind pointing your rifle elsewhere?"

A half-grin creased Gerald's face. "Oh. Sorry. I've been out here on my own, and when I thought I heard something, I started shooting."

Wyatt waved away Gerald's comments. "We know. You shot at us. Didn't Sawyer inform you we were coming?"

"No." Gerald shook his head. "He tried to call, but the storm interrupted his words, and he never got back to me."

*Figures—REMFs always mess things up.* "We'll take over now, and you can return to the outpost. By the way, we have another team out here as well, so don't head forward, or you might get your ass shot off." Wyatt pointed toward the outpost. "Head that way and circle around past the entrance."

Gerald nodded, picked up his backpack, shouldered his weapon, and departed.

Wyatt shook his head. *What was Sawyer thinking of by sending someone so green out here?* He glanced outside again. *Was that a blue light, or did I imagine it?* He rubbed his face. *Must be too tired, and my eyes are playing tricks on me.*

\* \* \*

The Pentagon,
  Arlington, Virginia

Matthew hung up the phone after talking with SWOOP control. He lowered the blinds to block out the brilliant sunshine from outside, and scooted to his computer and began typing.

*To: Alpha, Bravo, Charlie, QRF-1*
  *From: Bedlam*
  *Inclement weather in your area has delayed the departure of Red, Nightjar, and Panther. Flight will depart as soon as weather improves.*

Matthew shook his head as he sent his message. *Nothing's going smooth with this mission.*

\* \* \*

Bedlam Base Camp OP
  Near Prince Charles Mountains

· · ·

Alfie tightened the grip on his rifle. *There it is again.* He peered through the falling snow, unable to identify anything. "Hey, Rufus. I thought I heard something."

The Recon-One leader approached. He turned his head toward the shooting slot and listened. "Don't hear anything. What was it?"

Alfie shrugged. "Hard to describe but almost like something clinking together. I suppose it could have been my imagination playing tricks on me. Whatever it was, it reminded me of watching World War One movies with men moving through the trenches. But everything would be deadened by the snow." *Hope I'm not losing it. Not like I haven't been in combat before.*

Rufus laid a hand on Alfie's arm. "Keep listening and shout if you hear it again. Wonder if the wind is shifting small rocks or pieces of ice, and that's what you heard?"

"Could be. But, it seemed more artificial rather than from nature."

*Blam! Blam! Blam!*

The sound of shots rode the wind as bullets thudded into the outside of the OP.

"We're taking fire!" Alfie aimed into the darkness and used controlled bursts in a sweeping arc to ward off anyone attempting to approach.

Gerhard poked his rifle out another shooting slot and fired several rounds.

Rufus grabbed his radio. "Base, this is Recon-One. We're under attack!"

# Chapter Thirty-Seven

D iablo Corps Secret Outpost
Near Prince Charles Mountains

Emmanuel thumped a fist on his desk. *What's going on? My team's been able to access anything we wanted across the globe. Now, we're running into difficulties. Has someone finally figured out what we're doing?*

He drained his Coke, crushed the can, and tossed it into a nearby recycling bin. He smiled at the resulting noise. *Two points.*

His earbuds pinged, and he accepted the call.

"Where are you? You were supposed to update me an hour ago. I hope you've achieved what I wanted."

*Shit!* "Sorry, Mister Brown. I got tied up with computer issues."

"Well, hurry up and get over here. I don't have all day." He broke the connection.

Emmanuel took his time heading to Brown's office. *He can just wait. I'm tired of jumping every time he wants something.* He shook his head. *Perhaps a seizure will end his rants.*

\* \* \*

Brown pounded a fist into his palm. *Where is he? Emmanuel should be here by now. I've timed him before—only takes two minutes to get here.*

A knock sounded.

"About time! Get in here!"

Emmanuel opened the door and stepped inside. "Are you feeling okay, Mister Brown? Your face is covered with blotchy, red-purplish marbling."

"I'm fine—it's your nonchalance to my orders that's causing my skin to mottle." Brown glared at Emmanuel as he pointed to a chair. "Sit and give me your report."

He sat, crossing his arms.

"Well? I've been checking the news feeds, and there's nothing new about the G7 banks being hit again. What's your team been doing? Goofing off? I pay you too damn much to sit and twiddle your manicured thumbs."

"But—"

"No buts. You're paid to do a job, and as far as I can tell, you haven't done squat lately."

Emmanuel frowned. "If you must know, we've run into difficulties. I think—"

"What kind of problems? Must I do everything?"

"My team recently accessed the Bank of Japan, the European Central Bank, and the Bank of England. Each time they were booted out as if someone was onto them."

Brown shrugged. "So? It's your job to sort out any issues—not mine. I think it's about time to re—" He grabbed his chest as his other hand sought his pocket. "P-Pills."

Emmanuel jumped to his feet, shoved Brown's hand out of the way, and pulled out a bottle of pills. "How many?"

"T-Two."

Emmanuel pushed them under Brown's tongue and grabbed a water bottle from the desk.

Brown sipped from it before he clutched his chest again as he tipped to his left.

Emmanuel reached for the cord around Brown's neck and located the Quicksafe V3 Man Down device. He pushed the alarm and eased Brown onto his back.

Moments later, Stine and Rhude rushed into the room, followed by Chris, Dianne, and another member of the medical staff pushing a crash cart.

Stine took Brown's vital signs while Rhude loosened Brown's clothing.

Stine glanced at Rhude. "His blood pressure is sky-high while his beats per minute are less than fifty."

Stine turned to Emmanuel. "What happened?"

"He was shouting at me like normal when he clutched his chest. But, when I entered the office, his face was covered with blotches."

Stine nodded and gestured toward Brown's face. "Yes. He's been prone to mottling for years, but it's usually worse before the onset of an attack."

"We need to run more tests, but I think he's a candidate for a pacemaker." Rhude stroked his walrus mustache.

"I concur." Stine turned to Dianne. "Get him to the med center and hook him up to the monitors. I want a continuous EKG so we can find out what's going on."

Dianne nodded. "Right away, Doctor." She turned to Chris. "Grab the wheelchair from his bedroom, and we'll move him."

After the medical staff departed with Brown, Chris turned to Emmanuel. "So what happened?"

"Just as I said. He was on the warpath because we aren't moving fast enough in taking down the G7 banks." Emmanuel shrugged.

"One of these days, he'll have a heart attack or a stroke, and that'll be it. Couldn't happen soon enough if you ask me."

Chris nodded. "I think most of the staff is of the same opinion. Keep doing your job, and when the docs stabilize him, I'll try to talk some common sense into his thick skull."

"Good luck with that." A slight frown creased Emmanuel's face. "He's the worst boss I've ever had—no doubt about it." He headed to the door.

\* \* \*

Back in his own spaces, Emmanuel studied the most recent reports from his hackers. *Hmm. Each one reported similar activity before they were tossed out. Someone's definitely on to us.*

He tried logging into the Bank of Japan. While making initial headway, moments later, he ran into the same issue as Graham had experienced earlier. *I've had enough of this.* He called Graham, Klaus, and Finn to his desk.

Graham lowered his earbuds—the sounds of classical music filled the room. "What's up, boss?"

"I'm making a command decision. Brown hasn't been informed yet, but as of this moment, our hacking efforts are finished. We won't always be working for Brown, and based on his medical condition, he might not be around much longer. I think we need to be cognizant of our future beyond his mad scheme, and I have no interest in going to jail for this."

Klaus nodded. "What do you want us to do?"

"For now, keep doing the tasks I gave you." Emmanuel scratched the back of his hand. "Make note of everything you do. We might need this information as bargaining chips in the event we're caught."

\* \* \*

Merc-Two

Somewhere Near Diablo Original OP

Merc-Two, led by Wyatt, headed in the direction from where Gerald thought he had heard gunfire. They found a small rocky promontory and ducked behind it.

*Splat! Zing!*

A round ricocheted off the rock in front of Wyatt. He lowered his head and switched his weapon off safe. Kneeling to aim over the ridge, he fired a three-round burst in the direction from where he thought the shot came.

Hudson and Carter joined in, also firing controlled bursts along the same vector.

Wyatt grabbed his radio. "Merc-One, this is Merc-Two. Come in, please."

Static burst through the radio, along with the response. "Merc-Two, this is Merc-One. Status, over?"

"Taking fire from an unknown enemy."

"Roger, Merc-Two. We'll converge on your location and attempt to fire from a different vector."

"Thanks, Merc-One. Merc-Two out." Wyatt dropped his radio and resumed firing until his magazine emptied. He grabbed another from a pouch on his belt, ejected the first one, and slammed the new one into position.

\* \* \*

Recon-One

Somewhere Near Bedlam OP

Recon-One continued to use controlled bursts against their unknown assailants. Having a general direction of where the incoming fire came from, they shot along a similar vector to try to keep them pinned down.

A round splintered the side of the shooting slot near Gerhard's head. "Ag, man. These guys mean business." He poked his rifle through the space and fired three more rounds before ducking back.

Rufus glanced at Gerhard. "You hurt?"

"No." He spat on the snow. "Just pissed off. Why don't I head outside the OP and try to get a different bearing on them? Make them think we have reinforcements."

"Excellent idea. Go for it. Alfie and I will provide covering fire until you're in position."

Gerhard tapped both men on the shoulder as he departed. "Be back in the fight ASAP." He crabbed through the snow to his right, moving away from the OP. Finding a small cluster of ice and rock, he reloaded his rifle and aimed at a gun flash.

*Rat-a-tat!*

He let loose with a three-round burst, followed by a second one. He grinned as he heard Rufus and Alfie increase their response.

* * *

Merc-Two
Somewhere Near Diablo OP

"Hey, Wyatt." Carter emptied his magazine, discarded it, and reloaded. "Where's Merc-One?"

"Dunno. Ned said they were coming our way."

"Hope they hurry. Incoming fire from the enemy is increasing. It seems like they already have reinforcements."

"Damn!" Hudson clutched his left shoulder.

"You okay?" Wyatt rushed to his side.

"Yeah." He winced as Wyatt applied pressure on Hudson's bloody shoulder. "Lucky shot. Didn't see where it came from, but I think it was from a different direction than most of the incoming fire." He shook his head. "No worse than what happened to me in Afghanistan. Didn't expect to be shot in Antarctica, but that's what I get for thinking."

"Yeah, but you won't get a purple heart for this one. At least we're better paid than when we were in the army." Wyatt took Hudson's right hand and pressed it on the wound. "Hold it tight. I'll get a bandage on it real quick and get you back in the fight." Wyatt grabbed his emergency kit from his belt. After removing the bandage's outer protective wrapper, he pushed Hudson's hand out of the way. He smacked the dressing over Hudson's clothes and secured it. He gave the area a tap.

"Ow! What'd you do that for?"

Wyatt grinned. "Wanted to make sure you were still with us. When we get you inside, I'll check it over and rebandage it."

"You'd never make a medic. That hurt like hell."

"I'll have you know I was a medic—never lost a patient, and I won't be losing you. After all, all you received was a bullet graze, so you can still shoot."

"Just point me in the right direction, and I'll continue firing. Might need some help reloading, though."

"Let's end this now." Wyatt let loose with another burst from his rifle. "As soon as Merc-One arrives, I want to take a better look at your wound."

"Never mind that. It can wait until we return to the outpost." Hudson winced from the recoil as he fired. "Let's end this."

# Chapter Thirty-Eight

M erc-One and Merc-Two
        Somewhere Near Bedlam OP

Ned studied the landscape through the thickening snow. He shook his head. *Can't see anything in this blizzard.* He yanked the radio from his belt. "Merc-Two, this is Merc-One. Snow is making it impossible to locate you. Pull back, and we'll reconsider our options."

No response.

*Weather creating havoc with comms.* Ned tried again. "Merc-Two, this is Merc-One. Come in, dammit."

"Merc-One, ... Two. You're breaking up."

Ned shifted position. "I say again. Pull back to original OP. Acknowledge." *Don't want to lose any of my men against an unknown force.* He pursed his lips. *Best to pull back and protect the outpost.*

"This is Merc-Two. Order confirmed. Still taking incoming fire. Pulling back to OP ASAP."

* * *

Aboard *RV Aquavit*
    Off the Coast of Sanae IV
    South African Research Station


Bertelot stood in front of the table in the mess, studying the faces of the other SPA team members. "I tell you, I saw with my own eyes what appears to be the work of man to calve the ice. We must go back and obtain photographic evidence so we can show the world. It is bad enough that burning fossil fuels and cutting down forests are increasing their influence on the climate without someone intentionally doing this to make it worse."

"Talk to CC and find out if it's safe to go back out." Ailsa glanced at the others. "We can't take anything for granted. Wherever the two that attacked me came from, there could be more."

"I agree with Ailsa—it's for the best. We should wait until CC says it's safe to go." Carina touched Ailsa's arm.

Bertelot sighed. "I suppose I will not have any peace until I do so."

"Thank you, Bertelot." Ailsa hugged him. "I don't want anyone else hurt. Bad enough with the attack on me and the injury to Rona."

He nodded. "I will ask the captain to allow me to call CC." He rose and headed out of the mess to the bridge.

When he arrived, he scanned the room before approaching Captain Smythe. "If I may, Captain, I have a request. Would it be possible to speak with CC on the radio? I want my team back on the ice, but two of them recommended I talk with him first."

"Of course, Bertelot. As the SPA team leader, you don't need my permission to contact him, but thank you for checking." The captain turned to one of the crew. "Take Bertelot to the radio shack."

The crewman showed Bertelot the way to the radio room and helped him establish contact.

"Bedlam, this is *RV Aquavit*. Come in, please."

"Ag, man, this is Bedlam. Go ahead."

"Bertelot wants to speak with CC."

"Just a minute, and I'll find him."

Moments later, CC responded. "Go ahead, Bertelot. This is CC."

"I am sorry to bother you. As you know, the women on my team are very persuasive. We found possible evidence of man interfering with the ice and forcing a calving event. I want to go back to the area and take photographs so we can show the United Nations, but my team thinks it is too dangerous."

"Aye. I agree with them, Bertelot. We learned there are at least six mercenaries now in Antarctica working for Diablo. It's too dangerous for you and your team to leave the ship. When things quiet down, I'll help you obtain the evidence you require."

"Thank you so much, CC. It warms my heart to hear you say this. I will let you return to your duties."

"Talk with you later. Tell Carina I said hello and thanks. I know it was her."

"I shall do so. Goodbye."

\* \* \*

Merc-One and Merc-Two
  En Route Diablo Original OP


The mercenary teams found their way back to Diablo's original OP, where Gerald remained cowering in a corner.

Ned glanced at the security officer. "Take it easy, man. As soon as the snow lets up, we'll head back to the outpost. Two of my men will remain here."

"T-Thank you. I'm not cut out for this fighting stuff. They hired me to do admin stuff for the security office. I'm not a gun-toting member of society. In fact, I don't own any weapons back in the U.S."

Ned laughed. "Not to worry." He turned to Wyatt. "Sorry, mate, but we couldn't find you in the storm."

"Understood." Wyatt rubbed his face. "I took GPS coords of where we established contact. We can return later and rout them out. I just hope no one followed us."

Ned shook his head. "I kept watch as we made our tactical withdrawal. Didn't spot anyone following us. Of course, with this weather anything's possible. I just hope they didn't depart under cover of the storm and aren't lined up outside waiting to blow us away the moment we show our faces."

* * *

Recon-One
    Bedlam OP
    Near Prince Charles Mountains

Recon-One ceased firing when it appeared no one was shooting at them. Rufus cupped his hands and called to Gerhard. "Green, this is Condor. Merge back on us."

"Ag, man. On the way, assuming I don't get lost in the snow."

When Gerhard returned, Rufus and Alfie had already packed their gear.

"It appears the snow is easing up." Rufus gestured to Gerhard. "I want to return to base before whoever has been shooting at us realizes we're gone."

Alfie nodded. "Agreed. I think they departed under cover of the storm like we did. Since we can assume the opposition is prior military like us, they won't like fighting in snowstorms any more than we do. Bad enough in windy conditions, but hard to do in a blizzard."

Thirty minutes later, as the snow diminished, Recon-One took all ammunition and comms equipment with them. Along the way, they removed the rope and flags so the enemy couldn't use them to locate their base. Slogging their way through six inches of fresh snow, they arrived back at the camp. Pounding their feet and shaking their bodies to remove as much snow as possible, they entered the Jamesway hut.

CC, David, and Jake met their colleagues, each holding a steaming mug of hot chocolate for them.

Rufus, Gerhard, and Alfie peeled off their Arctic clothing before accepting the drinks, wrapping their hands around the mugs to warm them.

While the others gathered around the map of the camp and the surrounding area pinned to the wall and discussed the attack, CC logged into his email.

He smiled when he read a new message. He turned to the others. "Fantastic news. Carlos has been monitoring our weather patterns and is en route from Punta Arenas. He'll be here in a few hours. Best news—he has Pun, Ollie, and Gordon with him."

* * *

SWOOP Antarctica Flight
    En Route Bedlam Base Camp
    Near Prince Charles Mountains

Several hours later, Carlos switched his radio to the previously-agreed upon frequency. "Bedlam, this is SWOOP. Inbound your position. Will be with you in fifteen minutes."

"Swoop, this is Bedlam. Aye, your landing is approved."

The Bedlam operatives and David waited while Carlos landed the Basler BT-67. Like they did after the previous landing, everyone except CC rushed to the cargo area and unloaded several crates and fuel containers.

CC met Carlos and shook his hand. "Aye. Great to have you here again."

Carlos grinned. "I brought you additional men." He glanced around before leaning toward CC. Carlos whispered, "One of them is very strange. He grinned during the entire flight and kept sharpening one of the wickedest knives I've ever seen."

CC laughed. "That was Pun. He's a Gurkha, and the knife is called a kukri. It's Pun's favorite weapon. I've witnessed him beheading enemy combatants with a single stroke, and he's always smiling."

"Remind me not to get on the wrong side of him." Carlos shuddered. "He speaks well of you and said he would follow you anywhere."

CC nodded. "The Gurkhas are very loyal. Do you have time to join us for something to eat?"

"No, not this time." Carlos pointed toward the sky. "Another storm front is moving in, so I better be on my way before the weather turns ugly and I can't fly. After I'm refueled, I'll stop by the *RV Aquavit* if the weather holds, as I have supplies for them. Otherwise, I'll return to Punta Arenas and come back again next week."

"Aye. Understood." CC glanced over Carlos' shoulder. "I see my men are refueling you now."

"Excellent. Next time, I will hold you to a meal and perhaps some of that delicious hot chocolate you have."

"Would you like to take some with you?"

Carlos shook his head and patted his stomach. "I better not— getting too big around the waist."

Both men chuckled as they shook hands.

Ollie, Pun, and Gordon climbed out of the aircraft with their bags and approached CC.

Pun came to attention and saluted as normal, which CC returned before clasping the other men on the shoulders. "Welcome to Antarctica. Let's get inside, and out of the cold."

As soon as the others finished unloading the plane, they secured the storage area and waved Carlos away.

With a roar and bits of ice and snow thundering out from the wheels, Carlos raced down the runway and climbed into the air.

Everyone traipsed inside the hut. While the newcomers were given coffee or hot chocolate, CC studied the map. "When you have your mugs, gather around."

Jake handed CC a steaming mug.

"Thanks." CC pointed to a small red X he had placed on the map earlier. "Based on the coordinates Matthew obtained, it appears we're about five klicks from our target. Now that we've been reinforced, and there are nine of us, I want four teams. Jake and Rufus will be team one, Gerhard and Pun will be team two, while Ollie and Alfie will be team three." CC pointed to himself. "I'll be team four, along with David and Gordon."

Everyone nodded.

"The first three teams will proceed to the general target area and search for the air vents we were told about. If I remember what Matthew sent me, there are eight of them."

"Thinking of smoking them out?" Gordon glanced at the others.

"No, as there are probably too many people inside and the area could be quite large. However, locating some of them will help us confirm our target's specific location."

"What about you, David, and Gordon?" Rufus crossed his arms.

"We'll be a roving team, ready to reinforce anyone who gets into trouble." CC turned to Pun, Ollie, and Gordon. "We know they've been reinforced with at least six mercs. There might be more, so the size of the enemy force is unknown."

"What are the ROEs?" Rufus grinned.

"As with any firefight, take care of yourselves first—if fired upon, don't hesitate to shoot back. But remember, there are probably noncombatants inside the facility as well. Make sure any targets are holding a weapon before you take them out."

CC sipped his brew. "At least one individual inside has been providing information to Beldam. His name is Chris. If you find someone cracking his knuckles, that'll be him. I've asked Matthew to contact Chris and get a list of noncombatants. Our primary objective is to put the outpost out of commission and capture the CEO of Diablo Corps—Walter Brown."

# Chapter Thirty-Nine

D iablo Corps Secret Outpost
       Near Prince Charles Mountains

After helping Brown into his wheelchair, Dianne and the medical staffer rushed down the long corridor, pushing him as fast as they could. Brown fidgeted and moaned during the transfer.

After speaking with Emmanuel, Chris raced after them.

Doctor Stine and Doctor Rhude met them at the medical center door. He pointed. "In there."

The medical staffer held the door open.

The doctors, Dianne, and Chris helped Brown onto the surgical table.

After Brown was connected to the monitors, the men stepped into the corridor.

The doctors looked at each other and nodded.

Stine turned to Chris. "Brown needs a pacemaker implanted

now. However, we don't have sufficient operating room staff. You'll have to assist."

"Me? What about the medical staffer?" Chris raised his hands as if to keep the doctor away and stepped back. "I can't stand the sight of blood."

Dianne glared at Chris. "You know he faints when he sees blood like that doctor in the British series *Doc Martin*."

"Oh, yeah. I forgot." Chris snapped his fingers. "Wait a minute. I reviewed the records of the men who arrived to augment the security office. One was a medic."

Stine nodded. "He'll have to do. Get him. I want to start the procedure within the hour."

"Yes, sir." Chris scampered from the medical center and rushed down the hall toward the security office.

Stine grinned. "Never ceases to amaze me when people say they're afraid of a little blood, and they hightail it."

"Yeah." Rhude chuckled. "Not like it's coming from him. Still, some people are squeamish at the sight of anything out of the norm."

"We better start prepping our patient." Stine gestured to the operating room. "Have you been involved in this type of operation before?"

Rhude nodded. "But only as an observer. Never actually got involved with the actual procedure."

"I've done dozens of them. It'll take an hour or so unless we run into unexpected complications."

The operating room door opened.

Wyatt entered, followed by Chris, and glanced around. "Understand you need a medic?"

The doctors shook hands with him.

"I wanted to ensure we had sufficient medical staff on hand." Stine gestured to the now-sedated Brown. "We're going to give him a pacemaker."

Wyatt nodded. "Never done one before—just tell me what you need me to do."

"Okay. Follow us. We need to scrub and change before we start. Chris, please stay with Mister Brown while we're gone, and give a shout if you need us. Once we return, you can go back to your duties."

"Okay, Doctor Stine."

Fifteen minutes later, the doctors, Wyatt, and Dianne returned to the operating room wearing green surgical scrubs and set up the equipment they'd need for the operation.

Stine turned to Chris. "I take it there weren't any problems?"

Chris shook his head. "He remained the same as before with a few jerks which appeared to be involuntary."

The doctor nodded. "Okay. You can go now, Chris. Thanks for helping out."

Chris gave a brief smile and rushed out the door.

Stine checked everything over. "Seems we're ready to go. Dianne, attach an IV line to one of Brown's veins. We'll add midazolam to the line to make him drowsy and keep him relaxed." He turned and picked up several needles, handing them to Rhude. "I'll mark a few locations on Brown's chest where you can administer the local anesthetic. He'll still be awake, but the injections will numb the areas."

Rhude nodded and began injecting the areas as Stine marked them.

Stine took a deep breath and exhaled as he looked into each person's face. "Ready?"

Everyone responded in the affirmative.

"Here we go." Stine picked up a scalpel and made a two-inch incision just below the left collarbone.

Dianne used wadding to soak up the blood.

"Doctor Rhude, watch the scans to ensure I feed the wires into the correct chamber of the heart."

"On it."

Stine picked up the pacemaker from a tray and inserted the pacing leads into a vein until they became lodged in the tissue of

Brown's heart. He connected the other ends of the leads to a device to test whether they were working.

After adjusting the pacemaker settings, Stine created a small pocket between the skin on Brown's upper chest and the chest muscle and placed the pacemaker inside.

"That should do it. Let's close the incisions." Stine turned to Dianne and Wyatt. "After we move him to recovery, we'll keep him connected to the monitors to watch how things progress, but everything should be fine. Wyatt, sorry to pull you away from other duties. It appears your assistance wasn't needed after all. If you can help us get Brown into a recovery bed, you can head back to your office."

Wyatt nodded. "Will do."

Dianne slid a rollable bed next to the surgical table.

They shifted Brown onto the bed and wheeled him into the two-bedded recovery room. Once he was on one of the beds, Dianne reconnected Brown to the monitor and sat in a chair next to his bed.

Stine clapped Rhude on the shoulder. "See? Said it was simple."

* * *

Chris reread the email he had received from Matthew. After pursing his lips and glancing at the ceiling as if he was seeking divine inspiration, Chris hit reply to the message and began typing.

To: Numerologist

From: Knuckle Cracker

Received your request for a list of noncombatants. Will forward it in a separate message, but it'll include over fifty people, all of them support staff. As you suggested, I'll create small yellow tags they can sew or pin onto their clothing to help your men identify them.

Understand when the raid occurs, anyone with a weapon, even if they have a tag, will be considered a threat and dealt with as appropriate.

*You didn't ask for it, but I'll compile a list of those who I would consider the biggest threat to the raiding force. This includes the regular security force, the six mercenaries who arrived, and the hackers, as I'm not sure about some of them.*

*As requested, Diablo's plane is a DHC-6 Twin Otter. It can only hold up to twenty passengers, so additional aircraft will be needed to evacuate everyone at the same time. The hangar is large enough to hold two other planes of the same size.*

*If you send word when the assault on the outpost will commence, I'll try to raise the hidden hangar door. No promises, as it'll depend on the situation at the time.*

Chris read through his response, making minor adjustments, before sending it. *I hope this all ends soon. I've had enough of Brown and Antarctica. I think he's becoming more schizoid by the day. He doesn't pay any of us enough to carry out the chaos and damage Diablo plans to bring to the world.* He gazed at the ceiling. *What happens if Brown finds out about what Emmanuel and I have been doing? Will we end up joining Samson and Felix under the ice?*

Dianne thumbed through her latest copy of the *American Journal of Nursing* as she shifted in the chair next to Brown's bed. *Wonder if the doctors and Mister Brown will allow me to submit an article on the insertion of a pacemaker in Antarctica for a future issue?* She shook her head. *The doctors might, but I can't see Mister Brown allowing it —he's too secretive.*

She studied Brown's vital signs on the monitor and shrugged. *Seems to be doing okay. Too bad—I made a mistake accepting this assignment, even though the money is excellent. I miss my family and friends. Perhaps after this operation, he'll want to return to Miami and remain there.* She shook her head. *Too much to hope for. Maybe I should resign and return to the States. Would have to find a new job but at least I'd be warmer.*

*Beep! Beep! Beep!*

One of the alarms was activated.

Dianne silenced the audio and glanced at the monitor before looking at her patient.

Brown's open eyes were fixated on her. "W-What happened?"

She smiled as she stood and adjusted Brown's pillow. "Hello, sir. You gave us quite a shock with another episode. You passed out. Doctor Stine decided enough was enough, and he installed the pacemaker he had mentioned earlier. You should be feeling better soon, and the device will help to regulate your heartbeat and stop future seizures."

"Good." He pointed to a pitcher on the bedside table. "Water —please."

*Please? Did Stine give Mister Brown manners as well as the pacemaker?* "Of course. Are you hungry?"

"I could go for a chili cheese dog with jalapenos."

Dianne laughed. "Not until the doctor gives the go-ahead. Today's menu for you includes oatmeal, wheat toast, or one scrambled egg. No sugar, butter, salt, or pepper. But you can have all the water you want to drink."

Brown frowned. "What is Stine trying to do to me? I can't live on that stuff—it's not fit for human consumption."

"You mean, healthy? Sort of, anyway."

"Humbug. At my age, who cares what I eat?"

Dianne smiled at him. "Mister Brown, I've heard you say you want to live until you're at least one hundred. If you keep insisting on eating things you shouldn't, how do you expect to live another twenty years?"

"Listen, Dianne. You might be my nurse, but I'm the boss—and don't forget it!" He swallowed as he glanced down. "I suppose I should thank you for saving my life and caring for me, but that's what you're paid to do."

*Oh, dear, the old Mister Brown is back.* "Yes, sir."

"So where is everyone? Goofing off, I suspect, while I'm laid up. Fetch Chris—I'll dictate instructions to him as my goals must be accomplished without further delay. The world's survival depends upon it!"

She glanced at the wall clock. "Chris will be here in about thirty minutes. Doctor Stine gave explicit instructions no one was to bother you for at least three hours. So, tell me what you want to eat. Chris can bring it for you."

Brown frowned. "Who put you in charge?" He glared at her.

"You're my patient, so the doctor put me in charge to ensure you do as he wants. When you regain your health, you may resume doing as you like." *And heaven help all of us.*

He crossed his arms. "I should fire all of you for your impertinence—but then I suppose I'd have to do everything myself." He pouted.

"Now, Mister Brown. Behave yourself." She poured him a glass of water. "Pretend this is champagne."

"Humph! I suppose I'd better drink it—can't see you bending the rules for me, even if I am the boss. So, when can I go back to my office and my own bed?"

She hid a grin with the back of her hand. "As soon as Doctor Stine comes back and checks you over."

"It better be soon."

# Chapter Forty

T he Pentagon,
Arlington, Virginia

Matthew studied the email from Chris and thrust a hand in the air. *I knew he'd come through.* He smiled as he typed a response:

*To: Knuckle Cracker*

*From: Numerologist*

*Many thanks for the information. Look forward to receiving the lists. I'll provide them to the assault team. Suggest putting KC on the tags so they'll know you've identified these individuals.*

*Will arrange for additional aircraft to be on hand by the time the attack is over. Make sure you're not holding a weapon—would hate to lose my best friend.*

*No need to raise the hangar door—might put you in jeopardy.*

*Team is equipped with sufficient explosives to take care of any impediment.*

Matthew sent his message and provided a follow-up one to CC. *Better send a photo of Chris to CC as well. If I know my old roommate well enough, he's likely to be brandishing a weapon at the most inopportune time and get himself blown away.*

Emulating Chris, Matthew cracked his knuckles before picking up his empty coffee mug and going in search of a refill.

* * *

Bedlam Base Camp
  Near Prince Charles Mountains

CC's eyes roamed over the satellite images he had received the previous day from Matthew. It showed the area where the suspected outpost might be. He shook his head. *Nothing here but rock, ice, and snow.*

Rufus stood next to CC and glanced at the photos. He pointed to a location that appeared to be at odds with the surrounding terrain. "Hey, CC. Spot anything strange in this location?" He stepped around him and tapped the image taped to the wall. "This steep area near the ground seems too smooth to be natural."

CC rubbed the stubble on his chin. "Aye, now that you mention it. Why didn't I catch it before?"

"Too busy looking for a sign saying, *Enter Here?*"

Both men laughed.

"Well done, Rufus. That must be the hangar door. The toys Matthew sent should be able to blow that to bits."

"Can't wait to use them. Wish I'd had a few of these toys filled with C-4 on some of my missions with the SEALs."

"Aye. You'll have your chance." CC turned to the others. "Listen up, guys. It appears Rufus identified our target." He glanced at him. "Go ahead and show them."

After Rufus pointed out his suspicions, everyone agreed he had found their ingress point.

"Hey, guys." Gordon gestured at two of the images. "Turn these on their sides and look at them. Seems to be faint markings of a runway."

"Ag, man." Gerhard removed the photos and replaced them as Gordon suggested and nodded. "It does, doesn't it."

CC tilted his head and studied the images before grinning. "Great work, guys. Here's what we'll do. As I mentioned before, the three teams will proceed to the area. Now that we have a better idea of our ingress point, I still want you to check for the air vents. Take some camouflage netting and shove it into the vents to reduce their air intake. It might take some time, but if their air gets cut off, someone might come to investigate, and we can get inside when they do. If you spot any door we can use instead of blowing up the hangar entrance, so much the better."

"What about you, David, and Gordon?" Rufus gestured to the three men.

"Same as before—we'll serve as a QRF if one is needed. Same ROEs as discussed before. We need to end what Diablo is doing before they cause too much damage to the world economy." CC glanced into each man's face. "Any questions?" *Don't expect any—these guys know what they're doing.*

Most shook their heads, but Pun just wiped a cloth along his kukri and smiled.

The men put on their body armor and layered their Arctic clothing on top before strapping on their web belts and picking up their weapons.

CC donned his Z Tactical ZcomTAC IV headset. "Let's move out. We'll have to hoof it all the way as sounds from the snowmobiles will travel some distance and might give us away."

As they stepped out of the hut, they shoved their feet into snowshoes.

Slow going due to the recent snowfall, the nine men covered the five kilometers of undulating ground in a little over four hours.

CC signaled a halt. "Grab an energy bar and a sip or two of water. We'll move forward in fifteen minutes. Be ready for action. Team One will lead the approach from the left, while Teams Two and Three will converge on the right. Team Four will cover team one's movements."

Everyone nodded.

CC reinserted the magazine and clicked off the safety of his H&K assault rifle, with the others following his movements.

As the teams separated, CC conducted a comms check. "Team-One, this is Team-Four. Come in, please."

"Five by, Team-One." Rufus waved a hand in the air.

"Team-Two, this is Team-Four."

"Ag, man. Got you loud and clear."

"Team-Three, this is Team-Four, status?"

"Team-Three ready for anything," Alfie said.

"Aye. Move in." CC shifted the pouch containing one of the action figures stuffed with C-4 to his back, allowing more clearance for his rifle.

Outside Diablo Corps Secret Outpost
Near Prince Charles Mountains

Jake and Rufus crabbed through the snow to the left, pausing behind any slight rise as they proceeded. When they reached the rocks, they began climbing, one advancing while the other kept watch.

Rufus slipped on an icy patch and started to fall.

Jake reached out and grabbed him, pulling Rufus back to safety.

"Team-One, this is Team-Four. You okay?"

Rufus keyed his mic. "Roger, Team-Four. Just a slippery patch, but we're past it now. Going to check something out—might be an air vent."

"Ten-four."

Jake gestured to what appeared to be an artificial object about fifteen meters in front and to the right of them.

They reached a round smokestack with wisps of white vapor rising into the air.

Rufus turned to Jake. "Yep—air vent." He reached into a pouch and removed a wad of white camouflage netting.

Together they shoved the material into the hole, plugging the top of the vent.

"Team-Four, this is Team-One. Found an air vent and blocked it. Heading up."

* * *

Stine and Rhude wandered around the inside of the gigantic hangar dressed in green surgical scrubs and carrying their Arctic coats. With no patients to deal with, they occupied their time examining their surroundings.

Rhude pointed to a red door with a sign stating, *Emergency Exit —Do Not Open*. He glanced around. "C'mon, let's grab some fresh air. No one will miss us."

Stine shook his head. "You heard Chris' warning. Better to wait until we can arrange an escort."

"What are we—children? Don't be a chicken. Follow me." Rhude pulled his coat tight around him, pushed on the crash bar, and opened the door.

*Beep! Beep! Beep!*

A blue and red strobe light activated along with the alarm.

Rhude opened the door and stepped out. "Check this out—it's stunning."

"Just a minute." Stine sighed. "I'm—"

A hand grabbed Stine's shoulder and yanked him back inside. "Where do you think you're going?" Sawyer's grip tightened. "Where's your escort?"

"Oops." A sheepish grin crossed Stine's face. "Forgot we needed one."

Sawyer shoved him away from the door and pulled out his pistol. "Don't move." He stepped outside and brandished his weapon in the face of the other doctor. "You—inside. Now, before I blow a hole through your head."

Rhude grunted before pushing past Sawyer.

Two armed security guards arrived, both huffing from the exertion.

Sawyer nodded to them. "Take these two idiots to the security wing and lock them in a cell."

Rhude crossed his arms. "Take your hands off us. We have a right to be here."

"Is that so? Well, I'm Sawyer Johnson, head of Diablo security, and I didn't authorize any sightseeing tours outside. You'll remain in the cell until I say otherwise." Sawyer turned to the guards. "Get them out of my sight."

* * *

Team-Two and Team-Three dived into the snow when the side of the mountain opened, and a man stepped outside.

Pun yanked his kukri from his belt and touched Gerhard's arm.

Gerhard shook his head. He mouthed, "Wait."

Pun nodded and sat back on his haunches.

Ollie and Alfie tightened their grips on the rifles and aimed toward the opening.

A second man stepped out and forced the first one inside before the door slammed shut.

Gerhard keyed his mic. "Team-Four, this is Team-Two. Ag, man, there's a door on the side of the mountain. Two men just appeared. Might be a better ingress point."

"Team-Two, this is Team-Four. Aye. Copy. Team-Two, check on your side."

"Roger." Moments later, Rufus reported back in. "Team-Four, this is Team-Two. Found a well-concealed door on this side as well."

"Can you blow it?"

"Yep—one of those action toys will do the trick."

"Team-Two, this is Team-Four. Can you get inside?"

"Ag, man. Piece of cake getting in, but who knows what will be waiting for us when we do."

"Team-Three provide cover for Team-Two. Team-Four will do the same on this side. Team-One and Team-Two, prepare your toys for a controlled explosion."

All three teams responded in the affirmative.

Five minutes later, Rufus came back on the air. "Team-Four, this is Team-One. Door is wired—await your countdown."

"Team-Four, this is Team-Two. We're ready."

"Aye. All teams, stand by. On my mark." CC charged his weapon and glanced at his teammates.

David and Gordon gave a thumbs-up.

CC keyed his mic. "Aye. Five ... Four ... Three ... Two ... One."

In unison, Rufus and Gerhard pressed their detonators.

*Ka-Boom! Ka-Boom!*

The doors blew off their hinges, with the one near Rufus and Jake landing close to them.

*Beep! Beep! Beep!*

A voice came over a loudspeaker that could be heard outside. "Intruder Alert. Intruder Alert."

The attacking force clambered inside the outpost, weapons aimed in front of them.

Red and blue flashing strobes created strange patterns on the walls, floor, and ceiling while the noise of a siren pierced the air. To one side stood a Twin Otter aircraft. Rows of aviation fuel lined the wall behind the plane. Overhead lights provided sufficient lighting.

The Bedlam operatives and David spread out in small arcs, with five men on the left side of the hangar and four on the right.

*Blam! Blam! Blam! Blam!*

Someone from deep inside the hangar fired in rapid succession, the rounds ricocheting off the concrete floor.

CC aimed in the general direction of the blasts and triggered a three-round burst.

The others did the same.

Tracer rounds lit up the hangar as the invaders were met with a barrage of pistol and rifle shots.

"Aaaaiieeh!"

One of the defenders screamed as he was hit.

CC spoke into his mic. "All teams. Pick your targets and move forward. Remember to watch for noncombatants, but anyone holding a weapon is fair game." He fired another three-round burst as he scampered to his left behind a stack of metal sheets.

*Zing!*

Incoming fire bounced off the metal, sending sparks into the air.

CC fired again and watched his target collapse to the floor.

# Chapter Forty-One

D iablo Corps Secret Outpost
Near Prince Charles Mountains

CC ducked as a round hissed by his head. *Where'd that come from?* He glanced around and spotted a shadow on the steps to the Twin Otter holding a weapon. He aimed and fired.

The man collapsed without a sound.

CC kept moving forward, firing controlled bursts. When his magazine emptied, he paused to reload. "All teams—keep moving. We have them on the run."

His men stepped from behind a pile of machinery they had used to provide cover.

Five bodies lying in pools of blood littered the area behind a stack of wooden crates.

CC examined them. Each body had wood splinters embedded in them, along with bullet wounds. He glanced up when he heard the echoes of someone running as the last of the opposition disappeared from the hangar and slammed a door shut.

CC approached and checked the handle.

*Locked.*

He turned to Rufus and nodded.

Rufus pulled some C-4 from a pouch and tapped it against the hinges and the handle. After connecting the three pieces with det cord, he added a detonator. Turning to CC, he gave a thumbs up.

CC nodded as he and the others shed their Arctic clothing.

Rufus scooted away from the door before pushing a button and thumbing the switch.

*Ka-Boom! Ka-Boom! Ka-Boom!*

Three sharp explosions ripped the door from the frame. It teetered to the side and fell with a crash.

Ollie and Alfie dove through the opening into the building. Ollie went left, and Alfie dove to the right, their H&K assault rifles pointed down the corridor.

The stench of blood and the smell of gunpowder filled the air.

Six more bodies lay in haphazard positions along the hallway.

Ollie and Alfie fingered the triggers of their weapons as they edged along opposite walls. They checked each body as they neared them.

*Dead.*

Some showed shrapnel wounds from the explosion, while others were killed by gunfire.

CC keyed his mic. "We need to check each door along the corridor to locate our primary target. Remember, he's in his eighties, so his appearance should stand out from the others. Check the photo I gave you. Also, watch for noncombatants—they're supposed to be wearing small yellow tags with KC on them."

Every team leader clicked their mics in response.

Room by room, the Bedlam operatives checked for occupants.

*Empty.*

They approached another door at the end of the hallway.

Rufus grabbed the handle.

*Unlocked.*

Gerhard and Pun stepped forward and nodded.

Rufus turned the handle all the way before shoving the door inward.

Gerhard and Pun rushed inside, bowling over a man huddled against the wall, hands raised. Near him, a woman cowered.

"D-Don't shoot! We're unarmed."

"Ag, man. Who are you?"

The man gestured to himself. "I-I'm Reginald." He pointed to the woman. "This is Maddie. We're engineers." He pointed to the yellow KC tag. "We were told to wear these."

CC checked the list Matthew had sent him and nodded. "Aye. Both names are on it." CC turned to David. "Will you take them to safety? Perhaps on the plane in the hangar—but make sure no one else is onboard. We'll have to secure it and the hangar. Then rejoin us as fast as you can."

David nodded. "Will do."

After David led them away, CC pointed toward the first door on the left. "Gerhard and Pun. Check it out." He turned to Reginald. "How big is the security force?"

"There were a dozen men in the original security office, but they brought in six mercenaries—all prior military—to augment them. Sawyer, the head of security, knew the mercenary leader from the army."

CC nodded. "Thanks." He hurried after his men.

Pun pulled his kukri as they approached the door. He tried the handle.

*Unlocked.*

Gerhard kicked the door in, and the two Bedlam operatives rushed inside.

"Yeeeeeah!"

A man screamed as he swung a rifle at Gerhard.

Pun twirled, his hand and arm a blur as the kukri sliced through the air.

The man's head toppled from his shoulders, the body falling in a heap.

After checking no one else was in the room, Gerhard picked up the man's rifle and examined it. "Empty. No wonder he didn't shoot."

Pun smiled as they returned to the corridor.

Jake and Rufus barreled into the next room on the right.

*Empty.*

The eight men reached the next door. It was open an inch.

Ollie nosed the door wide with the barrel of his rifle and scampered to the left.

Alfie scampered inside to the right.

They stood in the middle of a new corridor devoid of light.

As Ollie moved forward, an overhead light clicked on.

CC opened the first door to the right and stepped inside. He fumbled for a light switch. Finding it, he flicked the switch on and peeked around the door's edge.

In front of him stood one of the mercenaries, a pistol in his hand. His other arm was around the throat of a woman he was using as a shield.

"So, Cameron, we meet again. I should have killed you when I had the chance in Afghanistan."

"Needham, you were lucky to escape the charges for killing that Afghan captain." CC pursed his lips. "You won't escape justice this time."

"Ha!" Needham's finger tightened on the trigger. "No one here to save your sorry ass before I blow it away." He shoved the woman away from him as he aimed at CC and fired.

Keeping an eye on Needham's trigger finger, CC dove to the floor a split second before he fired.

Before Needham could shoot again, a shadow filled the doorway.

Rufus fired once, his shot giving Needham a third eye.

Without a sound, Needham collapsed.

CC turned to Rufus. "How did you know?"

"I recognized him from the mug shots of the guys wanting to join the QRF. I don't forget faces. When I saw him, I knew he was a threat to be eliminated."

CC winced as he held his right hand over his left shoulder. "He got me—a flesh wound—but nothing serious. Help me up, and we'll continue our advance."

The woman got up from the floor and approached CC. "Let me see—I'm Dianne. I work here as Brown's nurse."

CC glanced at the yellow tag she wore and shrugged. "Later, Dianne. Believe me, I've had worse injuries. I need to keep moving with my men." He pointed behind him. "It should be clear for you to head to the hangar. Join the other noncombatants on the plane, and we'll get you later."

She nodded and rushed away.

Gunfire echoed along the hallway as CC and Rufus entered. They hugged the floor, weapons in hand.

The rest of the Bedlam teams engaged with the remaining mercenaries.

One by one, the operatives silenced their opposition until one man remained standing.

He dropped his pistol and grinned. "Guess you've arrived in time. These mercenaries were trying to take over." He took a step forward. "I'm Sawyer Johnson, head of security."

"Stop where you are." Gordon leveled his pistol in Sawyer's direction. "Hands in the air and turn around."

Sawyer reached behind his back and pulled a second pistol. He snapped off a shot, catching Gordon in the throat.

Dropping his pistol, Gordon's hand flew to his neck as he attempted to stem the blood loss. With a gurgle, he fell to the floor.

Rifle and pistol fire from the remaining Bedlam operatives pummeled Sawyer's body. The onslaught drove him backward until he crashed against the wall.

Rufus stepped forward and pulled his pistol, sending a final round into Sawyer's brain.

Ollie and Alfie rushed to help Gordon.

Too late—he was dead.

A door further along the corridor eased open.

As the Bedlam team aimed their weapons, more than a dozen people came out, hands in the air. Each wore small yellow KC tags.

The operatives quickly checked them for weapons.

"Ag, man. They're clear."

CC nodded. "Aye. Take them to the plane and keep an eye on them. The rest of us will continue searching for our primary target."

Gerhard and Pun escorted the people toward the other end of the corridor.

CC gestured to another door, this one painted blue, unlike the others, which were gray. "Wonder if this is Brown's lair?" He tried the handle and smiled. "Locked." He turned to Rufus. "Care to do the honors?"

"You bet."

Moments later, with the door blown off its hinges, CC, Jake, and Rufus entered.

Ollie and Alfie entered the room where the group of people came from.

Inside, a tall and slender young man with a thick black beard held a gun on an elderly man. The young man, who wore a small yellow tag with KC on it, dropped the weapon and cracked his knuckles. "Don't shoot—I'm one of the good guys. M-Mathew knows me—I'm Chris, also known as Knuckle Cracker." He pointed at the older man. "This is Mister Brown—he's the one you want."

"Kick the gun away." Rufus gestured to the pistol. "Don't make any sudden moves."

Chris did as instructed.

Rufus scooped up the weapon and examined it. He laughed. "Empty."

Chris grinned as he cracked his knuckles again. "Guns scare me, so I removed the bullets."

Brown moaned. "You imbecile! How dare you threaten me with an empty gun?"

Chris shrugged. "It kept you under my control."

CC grabbed some zip ties from a pouch and handed them to Jake as he gestured toward Brown. "Take him to the plane but make sure he's tied up—nice and tight."

Rufus and Jake led the now-secured Brown into the hallway.

Brown wriggled as he tried to escape. "Dammit! I know my rights. You can't do this to me—you've broken into my property and killed my men. I'll see you in prison."

CC shook hands with Chris before they followed.

Alfie and Ollie stepped from the other room, both shaking their heads.

"Ten bodies—all shot execution style." Alfie knelt and examined a small yellow tag sewn onto the shirt of one body. A non-combatant." He checked the others. "All noncombatants." He ground his teeth. "Too bad we killed all the mercs. I'd love to shoot them again for this."

"Jake, Alfie, and Ollie. Do a final check through the facility and meet us in the hangar." CC took one of Brown's arms while Rufus held the other, with Chris following.

When they reached the plane, Gerhard stood at the bottom of the stairs. "Ag, man. Some good news. The pilot was one of the captives, so he can fly the plane. There were two doctors and a nurse. It turns out the two engineers are explosive experts. If you want my opinion, they could blow this place up."

"Aye." CC nodded. "Excellent idea. You and Rufus escort them to where they store their explosives and wire this place. Once we depart, we'll destroy it, assuming the admiral gives the go-ahead. But before we do that, we'll need to grab all the computers, software, communications equipment, and paper, as the authorities will want physical evidence of guilt by Brown and his minions."

After Rufus and Gerhard left with Reginald and Maddie, CC climbed into the aircraft, pushing Brown in front of him.

Brown tried to jerk away from CC's grasp. "You don't know who you're dealing with. I have a legal right to everything within this compound because I built it, and what you're doing is theft. When I'm free, I'll come after you and your men with every lawyer I have, dammit!"

"Aye. Good luck with that." CC shoved Brown into a chair. "Don't move, or my friend will take care of you." He pointed to a grinning Pun, who stood stroking the blade of his kukri.

"What do we do now, CC?" David sat in a seat, a pistol in his hand.

"I need to send a request to Bedlam before we can vacate this facility." He sat in another seat and pulled his iPad from his backpack.

To: *Bedlam, Alpha, Bravo, Charlie, QRF-1*
    From: *Haggis*
    *Objective now in our hands. Primary target secured. Multiple noncombatants killed or injured. Same with Diablo security forces and the mercenaries. One team member KIA and one wounded. Two doctors and a nurse among survivors. Grandson's friend is uninjured and providing assistance.*

    *Additional air support needed to evacuate facility. It's being wired for demolition. Request authority to demolish the building prior to our departure.*

After sending his message, CC met with the medical personnel. "Is there anything you need right away to help treat the injured? I can contact the *RV Aquavit* and request their nurse and any medical supplies they can spare."

Stine shook his head and gestured toward Brown. "He was so

afraid of death he had a fully stocked medical facility installed here, including more supplies than we'll need before we leave. We'll patch everyone up and be ready to depart when you give the word." He smiled. "I know Dianne checked out your injury, but you'll be our first patient."

After Stine patched him up and he checked on the other noncombatants, CC returned to his iPad to check for a response from the admiral.

*To: Haggis, Alpha, Bravo, Charlie, QRF-1*

*From: Bedlam Actual*

*Demolition not authorized per the president and secretary of defense. Leave explosives in place but disconnect any detonators to prevent accidental destruction.*

*Interrogation of Brown unnecessary before he is turned over, as the authorities will read him his rights. However, make note of anything he might say. Leave all possible evidence in place pending analysis by authorities.*

*FBI contingent will arrive within ninety-six hours to take over control of facility. Prepare for your departure but delay until arrival of FBI Special Agent in Charge.*

# Chapter Forty-Two

D iablo Corps Secret Outpost
Near Prince Charles Mountains

During the thirty-six hours while CC and the others waited for additional air transport, the doctors checked everyone over. Stine pronounced his verdict to CC. "As soon as you want to evacuate, we'll be ready. Even those with the most serious injuries have been stabilized for departure."

"Aye. Many thanks, Doctor. Two extra aircraft are inbound as we speak, so we'll depart as soon as they land and are loaded."

"Excellent, CC. I, for one, look forward to being back in civilization."

CC laughed. "What's the matter, don't like our surroundings?"

Stine shivered. "Money isn't everything. While there's a stark beauty to the continent, it's too cold for me."

"Aye. I know what you mean. What a contrast to other locations where I've been deployed." He chuckled. "Good food will help counter the cold. I understand we'll have steaks, baked potatoes, and corn on the cob for our pre-departure meal. Jean-Luc is putting together an excellent repast for us."

Stine nodded. "He's an outstanding chef. In fact, I'm going to bankroll him in setting up a new restaurant in Miami. He wants to call it Picard's."

"Where do I remember that name from?" CC shook his head. "It might come to me later. But before you can offer him a job, he'll need to talk with the authorities and explain everything he knows about Brown and the Diablo Corporation. Otherwise, he'll be liable for conspiracy charges."

Stine chuckled. "I've already thought of that and plan to hire a good defense lawyer to help him."

Rufus and Gerhard approached CC, with Reginald and Maddie following.

"Aye? What's up?"

Rufus waved Reginald forward.

He shuffled to the front with his head cast downward. He whispered, "We did it."

"What did you do?" CC put a hand in front of his face to hide the spreading grin.

"We have the entire complex wired." Reginald gestured toward Rufus and Gerhard. "They showed us how to bring a building down as we'd never done that before."

CC nodded. "Aye. They've had plenty of practice. So, why the glum faces?"

"I've spent a long time here, and it's like home. So, seeing it ready to be collapsed is a bit nerve-wracking."

"And unsettling." Tears formed in Maddie's eyes.

"Och aye. Understood."

Rufus chuckled. "Per your instructions, CC, we didn't connect the detonators. It would have been a treat to blow this place up, but I understand about the authorities needing to go through the facility first."

"Aye." CC nodded. "It's now a crime scene. There could be important evidence--papers, computer disks, hard drives, communication devices with records of transmissions, and more that will be needed in the trial of Brown and his accomplices. Having a facility such as this will be of great value to governments and scientists studying and working in Antarctica." He shook his head. "But like you, I'd love to have watched the place implode."

Maddie and Reginald smiled as they turned away.

* * *

An hour later, Godfrey stepped out of the cockpit of Brown's Twin Otter. He popped the ring on a can of Coke and guzzled before turning to CC. "Just received word two aircraft belonging to a company called SWOOP will be arriving. One, captained by a guy named Carlos, will land at your base, while someone named Salazar will come here. Both are flying Basler BT-67s."

"Aye. I've met both of them—great guys. SWOOP is the company supporting the *RV Aquavit* and brought me and my team to Antarctica. Carlos has landed at our base several times, but Salazar might need some guidance from you on the runway and how to enter the outpost."

Godfrey nodded. "As soon as they are overhead and ready to land, we'll open the hangar door, and I'll guide him in."

"Aye. Thank you."

Godfrey returned to the cockpit.

CC stood and stretched his legs as he scanned the interior of the aircraft before bounding down the stairs.

On the far side of the hangar, three baggage carts held multiple black body bags.

With his left shoulder bandaged, and his arm in a sling, CC

walked over and counted. *Twenty-four. How many were innocent victims?* He glanced at a burnished copper coffin on a separate cart and stepped to it, putting a hand on the top. Intended to hold Brown's remains if he passed away while in Antarctica, it now held Gordon's body.

CC said a short prayer, tears forming. He wiped them aside as he turned away. *Despite all the years involved in various conflicts around the world, it never gets any easier to lose a teammate.*

Beep! Beep! Beep!

As the alarm sounded, a red flashing light bathed the hangar's interior. The door rose into the ceiling as CC spotted one of the BT-67s landing.

Minutes later, the aircraft taxied into the hangar and parked near the Twin Otter. Salazar disembarked and strode to CC as the hangar door rumbled and closed. "As soon as we refuel, we can begin loading."

CC shook Salazar's hand. "Aye. Welcome back." He gestured to the body bags. "We'll keep them in the back of your plane. There are three people with serious injuries, so they'll be on stretchers in the front. Two doctors and a nurse will accompany them."

"Sí. Carlos told me." He shrugged. "To me, cargo is cargo, whether dead or alive." He glanced around. "Where is the *baño?* It's been a long flight."

CC grinned and pointed to a door. "In there."

As Salazar scurried away to find the toilet, David and most of the Bedlam team approached Gordon's coffin.

Only Pun remained on the Twin Otter, keeping a close watch on Brown.

After a salute and a moment of silence, the men turned to CC.

"Aye. Time to vacate. Let's get everyone and everything we're taking from here on board. Take two of the Sno-Cats and park them outside. We'll use them to return to our camp rather than walking. The sooner we're loaded, the sooner we can depart."

David and the others nodded as they shouted orders to those milling about the hangar.

CC returned inside the Twin Otter, opened his iPad, and typed.


*To: Bedlam, Alpha, Bravo, Charlie, QRF-1*

*From: Haggis*

*Additional aircraft have arrived. Loading to commence ASAP. Non-combatant survivors and captives will be taken to Punta Arenas in a Twin Otter and a Basler BT-67. Twenty-four body bags and one coffin will be accompanying them. Request authorities be on hand to take custody of the primary target and his henchmen.*

*Red is carrying a list of those identified by our informant here as directly involved in criminal activities. He has taken personal charge of the target and will hand him over upon arrival.*

*Medical facilities should be put on standby as there are three people with life-threatening injuries.*

*Bedlam operatives will return to our base camp and dismantle it, using SWOOP aircraft to remove our equipment, supplies, weapons, and all personnel while awaiting arrival of FBI contingent.*


Rufus approached as CC sent his message. "Hey, CC. We're ready to blow this popsicle stand."

CC grinned. "Aye. Let's do it."

An hour later, both aircraft taxied forward as the hangar door opened again. They headed to the far end of the runway and turned.

The Bedlam operatives climbed into the Sno-Cats and followed, moving to the side of the runway.

The aircraft engines accelerated, and the planes rolled along the makeshift runway, gathering speed until they soared into the air. With a dip of the wings, they headed north.

CC and the others waved before they headed toward the Bedlam base camp.

* * *

When the Bedlam operatives arrived at their camp, Carlos came out of the hut and greeted them. "About time, señors. I have sandwiches, tomato soup, hot chocolate, and coffee ready for you."

Gerhard rubbed his stomach. "Ag, man, what kind of sandwiches?"

"Only the best—Polish ham and cheese and Argentinian corned beef."

Gerhard's stomach rumbled. "I'm ready!"

After filling up on the food and drinks, CC gathered the men together. "I want everything that can be loaded onto Carlos' plane finished today. He'll take it to the landing strip by the ship, and the crew will help him unload before he returns for us."

"How long do you think it'll take us to remove everything?" David gestured around the hut. "We brought in a lot of equipment and supplies."

CC nodded. "Aye. I figure about two days. We're donating every-thing except the weapons and ammunition to Captain Smythe and his crew. When we finish here, there's one more thing I want to do with the SPA team while we wait for the FBI."

"What's that?" David grinned. "I saw how Carina was making eyes at you."

Everyone laughed.

CC's face reddened. "That's not what I had in mind. I promised Bertelot we'd help him prove there was human interference in some of the ice calvings rather than climate change."

* * *

Aboard *RV Aquavit*
    Off the Coast of Sanae IV
    South African Research Station

. . .

Three days later, four Sno-Cats set off from the *RV Aquavit*, each towing a trailer. The six SPA members and the remaining Bedlam operatives shared the vehicles as they followed Bertelot's directions.

When they arrived at the designated location, everyone piled out of the vehicles and walked to the water's edge.

Bertelot pointed. "This is where I took the photographs. You can see the blackened ice. Nothing in nature would do this."

CC nodded. "Aye." He turned to the others. "Break out the chainsaws and cut away as much of the damaged ice as you can manage with the winches on the Sno-Cats. Be careful not to fall in the water—you'll die before we can rescue you."

The roar of the saws shattered the peacefulness of the morning.

While Rufus and Gerhard cut the ice, the remainder of the Bedlam men, Bertelot and Gunner, shimmied chains into place around the chunks.

As the pieces of ice came free, the chains were connected to a winch on the front of one of the Sno-Cats and dragged toward the other vehicles. Using hooks to shift the chunks, they were loaded onto the trailers.

After three hours, Bertelot waved everyone to a halt. "The trailers are full, so we have enough evidence to show the world." He removed a camera from one of the Sno-Cats. "I must take more photographs before we return to the ship."

\* \* \*

On the ride back to the ship, Carina sat on CC's right, her arm linked through his. She smiled as she glanced into his face. *I wonder if he has a girlfriend? Hasn't mentioned one. Doesn't wear a wedding ring, so I don't think he's married.*

She clenched his arm tighter. "Hey, CC, a penny for your thoughts?"

"Aye." He shifted closer. "When I came to Antarctica, I was

drawn to a number of locations I wanted to explore. I studied archae-ology as part of my university degree program."

"Where did you want to go?"

He grinned. "I wanted to visit the Soviet expeditionary cemetery, the Inexpressible Island Ice Cave, Shackleton's Hut, the Terra Nova Hut, Wilson's Stone, Scott's Discovery Hut, and the González Pacheco Shelter."

She whistled. "That's quite a list."

"Aye. But now that our mission is ending, I must return to America and prepare for the next one." He shook his head. "Perhaps one day, I'll be able to return."

Her face beamed. "The SPA mission is contracted for another four weeks in Antarctica, and I'll be staying during that time. It would be fantastic if you could return while I'm still here—I could go with you."

CC pulled her close. "Aye. That sounds promising."

\* \* \*

Diablo Corps Secret Outpost
Near Prince Charles Mountains

The following day, the Bedlam operatives lounged near the open hangar door to the Diablo outpost as two Gulfstream IV aircraft landed outside. The pilots taxied into the hangar. The door closed as soon as the planes halted.

Men and women wearing heavy coats emblazoned with FBI descended from both planes. Many of them carried briefcases and black suitcases. Even in the hangar, several continued to wear sunglasses.

A man with short black hair and wearing a suit underneath his open Arctic coat approached the Bedlam operatives. "I'm looking for Colonel Cameron."

CC grinned as he stepped forward. "Aye. That's me, although I haven't been a colonel for years."

The man whipped out his ID wallet. "I'm Special Agent in Charge David Brady. I'll be taking over command of this facility until counterparts from around the world arrive." He sneered at CC. "My director said you're in charge of the mess here. Do you realize how many international laws you and your team have broken? You should all be charged and convicted." He sighed. "However, I follow my orders. You and your men are free to leave Antarctica."

"Aye." CC chuckled. "Never mind we stopped a megalomaniac from trying to take over the world for his own benefit. We'll get out of your way and leave you to do your work." He gestured to his comrades before turning back to the SAC. "One other thing—make sure you and your people are properly dressed for Arctic conditions when they venture outside, or they'll be returning to the States in body bags."

# Chapter Forty-Three

B edlam Headquarters
Joint Base Myer-Henderson Hall
Virginia

Two weeks later, Admiral Richard Blakely cleared Bedlam security and marched down the hall. As normal, he wore his bemedaled naval uniform. His gray hair seemed thinner than usual, and stress lines were evident under his eyes.

Overhead lights clicked on and off as he passed. Stopping in front of an unmarked door, he took a deep breath and opened it.

Every person seated around the rectangular table jumped to attention.

The admiral smiled. "Please, be seated." He took his own chair at the head of the table. He glanced around the faces, nodding as he did so. "Glad everyone made it. I appreciate your time and efforts."

Soft gongs activated on the Marconi ViPr secure video conferencing system perched on a roll-around cart in the corner of the room.

Georgia stood, walked over to the system, and accepted the incoming calls.

The screen split into four windows labeled *Bedlam, Bravo, Charlie*, and *QRF-1*.

"Good morning, Richard." Harrison's face beamed from Charlie's window. "I finally figured out how to connect without any major assistance."

The admiral laughed. "C'mon, Harrison. Out with it. Who set it up?"

Evelyn Evinrude, Charlie's team leader, appeared on the screen. As normal, her blonde hair was spiked. "I gave him a helping hand, but he did almost everything himself."

The camera adjusted to show Harrison, Evelyn, and the remainder of Charlie, while Bravo and QRF-1's cameras were already showing those teams.

The admiral cleared his throat. "I want to thank everyone for attending today. First things first—yesterday was a very solemn occasion as we bid farewell to Gunnery Sergeant Gordon Russell, who died in action in Antarctica. The president authorized his burial at Arlington National Cemetery with full military honors, including a twenty-one-gun salute and taps by a military bugler. I presented the folded flag to Gordon's parents while the president spoke with them later in the day. Georgia—" He glanced at her.

Georgia nodded and gave the admiral a thumbs up.

"Georgia arranged for the funeral to be recorded, and it'll be uploaded to your servers today."

"Thank you, Richard." Sir Alex wiped a tear from an eye. "Thank you, too, Georgia. If it would have been possible, I'm sure all of Bedlam would have been in attendance."

"Hear, hear." Harrison coughed. "When we receive the recording, we'll hold our own service for Gordon."

The admiral turned to CC. "We don't have purple hearts for the organization since we're not an active military unit. However, with your injury in Antarctica, had we a mechanism to award decorations, you'd be receiving your second purple heart."

"Aye, Admiral." CC rubbed his left shoulder with his right hand. "Please don't remind me. And none of the team's usual jokes today. It still hurts to laugh." New pain lines creased his face as he winced when he shifted in his chair. He reached up again and pushed the ends of the bandage beneath the neckline of his shirt.

Everybody laughed.

The admiral glanced at QRF-1's screen. "I'm glad to see you're back with us, Maverick. No worse for wear after your unpleasant accident on the glacier?"

"No, sir. Just sorry I missed out on going to Antarctica."

The admiral smiled. "I want to congratulate the teams for a job well done. The leaders of the G7 countries have all thanked the president for what you've accomplished. Activities in Antarctica come under the 1959 Antarctic treaty, which established the continent as a site of common scientific interest and bans military activity. The signing countries, which now number fifty-six, run the continent together, with each country having the right to be consulted about activities there. The activities of both Diablo and Bedlam were in violation of the treaty. Some countries wanted to charge Bedlam under international law, but common sense has prevailed." He sipped from a glass of water before continuing.

"The FBI identified a string of charges that Diablo's CEO will face, along with the three hackers and a couple of security personnel who survived. They gathered a treasure trove of evidence, including computers, drives, discs, and cellphones as well as papers, which will take them a long time to sift through before charges are finalized."

"Excellent news, Richard." Sir Alex grinned. "I know the prime minister was thrilled with the results, and the information Grandson and his fellow hackers put together is aiding various G7 banking institutions in enhancing their computer security programs."

The admiral nodded. "Of course, we provided that information to the U.S. Cybersecurity and Infrastructure Agency which works with counterparts around the world. Matthew didn't actually contact anyone, although the UK's GCHQ and the German Federal Police were notified through his friends who work for them."

"What about the noncombatants who worked for Diablo in Antarctica?" Georgia glanced around the table.

"Those who were confirmed as noncombatants by Matthew's friend, Chris, have been asked to sign affidavits attesting to what they know went on at the outpost." The admiral smiled. "Most have already accepted and are working with the FBI to create a complete picture of what Brown was attempting to accomplish. We've also confirmed with the FBI that Chris won't be facing any criminal charges as long as he testifies when called upon. Neither will any Bedlam personnel. Also, two of the three critically-wounded staff members will make a full recovery. Unfortunately, the other one succumbed to his injuries.

"The head of Brown's hackers, a guy named Emmanuel, has been singing like a canary. Chris has vouched for him as well, explaining Emmanuel was the 'concerned citizen of the world' who tried to warn the governors of the major banks." The admiral cleared his throat. "He'll still face jail time because of the hacking activities but will likely receive a reduced sentence from the U.S. for his cooperation. Of course, other countries might have a different idea.

"There was some late-breaking news yesterday. Brown had another seizure despite his new pacemaker. They were able to revive him."

The admiral looked upward as if appealing for divine inspiration. "He's been in contact with his lawyers and is writing a new will. He wants all of the surviving noncombatants to receive a million dollars each from one of his accounts before the end of the year. The account was referred to as Project Green Earth. He's also requesting the bulk of his estate, estimated at between forty to fifty billion dollars, be used to support worldwide climate change initiatives, although he specified no G7 country was to receive a penny. He wants it to go to less-developed countries, which will need financial assistance. Of course, everyone believes he's doing this to save himself from dying in prison —assuming he lives long enough to go to trial."

"Despite his attempts to take on the G7 countries and bend them to his will, he might go down in history as one of the world's greatest philanthropists. He won't be the last one caught doing something illegal." Harrison shook his head. "It seems like he's doing the right thing in the end."

"One last thing." The admiral glanced from screen to screen. "I had a call yesterday evening from NSA Jonny Meu. He participated in a conference call with the president and the American ambassador to the United Nations. It appears the photos provided to the UN by the SPA team are sending shockwaves through the delegations regarding Diablo's actions. No one can deny the blackened ice and drill holes. But the clincher was a damaged Sno-Cat and a body. The Russians and Chinese are demanding Brown be charged with crimes against humanity."

A ripple of surprised voices echoed in the room.

"Aye. So, another mission has turned out well, except for the loss of Gordon." CC turned to the admiral. "Anything on the horizon we should be worried about?"

"It appears Gordon didn't have any immediate family, so the proceeds of the government life insurance policy he took out when he joined us will be given to his estate." The admiral clasped his hands. "Things are quiet around the world, and the threat board is empty. Of course, we all know that can change in a hurry."

"Aye. So back to training in preparation for our next mission."

"Speaking of adventures, I heard the RV Aquavit and the SPA team will be remaining in Antarctica longer than anticipated." Jake raised a brow as he studied CC's face. "Any chance someone from Alpha will be heading back out?"

CC's face reddened as he shook his head. "I dinnae ken. I did have an invite from Carina, but it seems it's been withdrawn."

"Who's Carina?" The admiral gave CC an amused glance.

"Hey, that's my cousin you're talking about. You better be nice to her, CC." Rufus grinned.

CC shrugged. "I received a 'Dear John' email from her last night. Seems like Gunner, one of the SPA guys, has won her heart after all—her words. But I'm invited to the wedding."

"If memory serves me correctly, this'll be her fourth attempt at marriage." Rufus chortled. "For some reason, they all ended at the altar before they were finalized."

Laughter, whistles, and catcalls erupted from the Bedlam teams.

"Aye. So, in the interim, I'll remain with Alpha." CC tilted his head toward the admiral. "That is, assuming you don't have new plans for me."

The admiral shook his head. "Leaving you in charge of Alpha and within my sights is the best place for you to be—at least for the near term. I'm still waiting to hear what the president plans to do with me, so there could be a shake-up of the Bedlam program."

The teams became silent at this news, with most shaking their heads.

"If it would help, Richard, I can ask the PM to have a word with your president." Sir Alex pursed his lips. "The Bedlam program was your creation and has only been successful because of your tutelage."

The admiral raised a hand in acknowledgement. "Thank you, Sir Alex. I'm sure the president will do what he believes is in the best interest of everyone, in particular, protecting our respective nations. Whatever he plans to do with me is within his power, so I'll have to go along with it like everyone else.

"Enough about that for now. When I find something out, I'll let everyone know. In the meantime, Sir Alex, Harrison, and I were discussing our next teambuilding offsite. We're having it in two weeks. Richard, care to provide any details?"

"Yes. All of our Bedlam family is invited to my ancestral home—won't be any shooting competitions like we're used to, but there'll be plenty of things to keep everyone occupied."

Randall Krzak

"Sounds fantastic, Sir Alex." Rufus drummed a beat on the table in front of him. "Where will it be?"

Sir Alex grinned. "I've already sworn Bedlam Bravo to secrecy. The rest of you will find out when you arrive. A coach will be available to take you from RAF Mildenhall for Alpha and QRF-1, while Charlie will fly into RAF Brize Norton. From there, you'll be taken through the English countryside to my small estate, which has been in the family since 1580. I guarantee you'll have a splendid time."

The admiral nodded. "We'll arrive on Thursday and remain through Monday morning, so everyone will have plenty of time to enjoy English hospitality." He glanced at each monitor before turning his attention to those seated with him. "Anything else? If not, let's adjourn. See everyone in two weeks."

# Chapter Forty-Four

RAF Mildenhall
Suffolk, England

The C-21 Learjet touched down on RAF Mildenhall's runway and taxied to a hangar. Inside, the pilot parked next to another military passenger plane.

Admiral Blakeley led the Bedlam Alpha contingent off the plane.

They were greeted by the QRF-1 team, who had arrived on the other aircraft.

After a round of handshakes, everyone climbed onto a blue coach with an electric sign on the front indicating: *Private.* Except for the windshield and the front side windows, the remainder were tinted.

As the admiral boarded, he stopped by the driver. "How long will it take to reach our destination?"

"Unless new roadworks sprung up since I was on the road yesterday or any accidents, we should be there in about two hours."

He jerked a thumb over his shoulder. "There's a cooler full of iced soft drinks next to the toilet."

"Thank you." The admiral climbed into a nearby seat as the rest of the operatives boarded.

CC strode toward the back of the coach before sliding into a seat. On the back of the seat in front of him was a magazine holder filled with maps and brochures advertising local tourist attractions.

One caught his eye, and he pulled it out. The cover depicted a sprawling estate labeled *Elderberry*. The picture of a man dressed in a tuxedo adorned the left side of the pamphlet. CC opened it and began reading, a smile creasing his face.

"Hey, Admiral. I didn't know Sir Alex was an earl. This brochure says he's the sixth Earl of Redchester."

"That's correct, CC. The title was handed down from father to son. It originated with his third great-grandfather."

"So, why doesn't he use it?"

"He prefers to use Sir Alex after he was knighted by the queen for services rendered to the country. But he still retains the title of earl."

"Aye. I understand. So, now that we know this, how should we refer to him when we arrive?"

The admiral chuckled. "Keep calling him Sir Alex."

Gerhard had picked up one of the brochures and was reading. He whistled. "Ag, man! He owns almost six thousand acres of land, most of it forested. With one hundred twenty-eight rooms, Sir Alex's home is large enough to house my entire village."

"Hey, Gerhard. Check the rear cover." Rufus chuckled. "They're expecting you."

Gerhard turned the brochure over and laughed. "Ag, man. Just what I want—a safari park."

They all laughed.

"Aye. It says here most of the house is open for public tours, but Sir Alex and his family maintain a suite of private rooms." CC shook his head. "Must be nice."

The coach turned onto the motorway and accelerated. The countryside sped by, as one by one, the Bedlam operatives took advantage of the trip to catch up on their sleep after their initial journeys.

Two hours later, the coach left the motorway and continued along narrow roads winding through the undulating terrain covered with trees and fields, with houses dotted here and there.

Before long, the driver slowed, turned left, and crossed a metal cattle grid jarring everyone awake. As far as the eye could see, elder hedges, heavy with fruit, lined the fields, with cows and sheep the predominant inhabitants. He stopped in front of a three-story stately home.

Sir Alex, dressed in a tweed coat, blue shirt, and jeans, stood at the top of twelve steps and walked down as Admiral Blakely and the others disembarked. He smiled as he waved toward the building behind him. "Welcome to Elderberry Estate, my ancestral home."

He gestured up the stairs. "Come inside, and I'll mention a couple of things. Harrison and Bedlam Charlie are already having a bite to eat in the dining room. We'll join them in a few minutes." They strode up the stairs and into the building.

"This is the Elizabethan Great Hall." He pointed to the alcove above. "That's the minstrels' gallery where musicians used to entertain important visitors." He nodded toward a door. "Through there is the Red Library, which houses most of the forty thousand books in the house. You're free to wander throughout the house at your leisure. Should you find yourself lost, just ask one of the staff for assistance. They'll be happy to assist."

He headed through another door and along a corridor. "This is the State Dining Room. I thought it fitting for us to have our meals here as there is plenty of seating." He stepped inside and gestured at the walls. "They're covered with Spanish tooled leather with gold and silver." He pointed to the table where Bedlam Charlie sat. "Find a seat, and the staff will take care of your needs. We're having brunch right now to take into account the various time zones everyone came from."

"Hey, CC." Evelyn stood and waved at him. "I saved you a seat."

He strode over and sat next to her. "Aye. Thank you." He glanced around the table as the others sat. "What a spectacular setting. How did you manage to keep this a secret from me?"

She tapped the side of her nose. "I'm a guest here as much as everyone else, even though Sir Alex is my cousin." She grinned. "Of course, I spend hours here when I'm not working. My goal is to open every one of the books and try to read as many as possible. The problem I have is the massive range of activities available." She glanced at CC. "Would you like to go horse riding later? Assuming it won't bother your shoulder."

"Aye. I couldn't think of a better companion. As long as we keep to an easy jaunt." He smiled.

She blushed as she reached over and adjusted his collar over the bandage. "Excellent." She nodded as a waiter offered her some smoked salmon.

The servant turned to CC. "Salmon, sir? Straight from Scotland."

"Och aye. Can't resist."

Sir Alex sat at the head of the long table, with the admiral to one side and Harrison to the other. He stood and tapped a spoon on a glass to get everyone's attention. "Welcome to my humble home. Please treat it as your own while you're here and take advantage of everything that's available. I can't offer you a kill house to practice your skills, but there is skeet shooting and archery. For riding enthusiasts, we have a stable of geldings and mares for you to check out. If you want to practice your navigation skills, we have a massive maze for you to get lost in, which includes dead ends, false paths, subterranean offshoots, zip lines, and six raised bridges." He chuckled. "Who will we have to rescue?"

Once again, everyone laughed.

"My family is also prowling around the estate, so please speak with them should you bump into them. I promise they won't bite, and they delight in meeting our many visitors from around the world." He turned to the admiral. "Richard, before we go any further, I know you wanted to share some information with the teams."

The admiral stood. "Thank you, Sir Alex, for opening up your home to this unruly group of characters." He glanced down each row of operatives before looking up as if trying to control his emotions. "Two days ago, I met with the president. As of the end of the year, I'll no longer be the Chairman of the Joint Chiefs."

Groans echoed throughout the room.

He put up his hand for silence. "That being said, you aren't rid of me so fast. The president asked—no commanded—I remain as the Bedlam program overseer until such time when I'm ready to retire and can find a suitable replacement."

Everyone clapped.

"I agreed, subject to his granting me a request. I asked to have a deputy, someone I can trust and perhaps, one day, turn the reins of Bedlam over to. He asked me if I had someone in mind. I did. When I gave him the name, he agreed."

The admiral looked at each operative in turn before turning his gaze on who he hoped would be his deputy. "CC, would you be willing to give up your adventures around the world and be my deputy? You wouldn't be able to go into the field in the future, so we'd have to identify a new team leader for Alpha."

CC stood and studied Evelyn, who nodded. "Aye, Admiral. I'd be honored to be your deputy."

Every Bedlam operative stood, clapped, and cheered, even the normally stoic Pun.

The admiral nodded. "Just one thing, CC. You'll have to start calling me Richard."

~ The End ~

# Thank You!

Dear Reader,

Thank you! I hope you've enjoyed reading this story as much as I did in creating it. If you did, I'd greatly appreciate it if you could take a minute or two to write a brief review on Amazon. It doesn't need to be long, but your feedback helps other readers and me.

Reviews are so important to all authors. For me, I don't have the benefit of being supported by one of the major New York publishers, nor can I afford to take out ads in the newspapers and on television. Your review helps to get the word out, not just on Amazon, but also through various social media outlets as I use these to create posts on Facebook, Twitter, and LinkedIn. Many thanks for your support!
**Randall**

# Key to Knuckle Cracker's Code:

27.

    26A

    25B

    24C

    23D

    22E

    21F

    20G

    19H

    18I

    17J

    16K

    15L

    14M

    13N

    12O

    11P

    10Q

    9R

*Key to Knuckle Cracker's Code:*

8S
7T
6U
5V
4W
3X
2Y
1Z
0Space
00Space

# Cast of Characters

## Bedlam Alpha

Craig Cameron. Bedlam Alpha team leader. Also known as CC. Call sign: Haggis.

Admiral Richard Blakely. Chairman of the Joint Chiefs of Staff and Bedlam Alpha overseer. Callsign: Bedlam.

William 'Willie' Campbell. Callsign: Rebel.

Dr. Charles Edwards. Computer expert and master of the 'Creativity Den.'

Jake Martin. Member of Australian Army on extended duty. Callsign: Aussie.

Benjamin Reid. Doctor and former member of the New Zealand SIS. Callsign: Kiwi.

Matthew 'the grandson' McMasters. Research analyst specializing in tracking money. Referred to in emails as Numerologist.

Georgia White - Bedlam Alpha's logistics whiz.

Aiden Johnson. Former Canadian Mountie. Callsign: Mountie.

Janice – Admiral Blakely's secretary at Bedlam HQ.

Susan – Admiral Blakely's secretary at the Pentagon.

## Bedlam Bravo

Sir Alexander Jackson. British National Security Advisor and Bedlam Bravo overseer. Call sign: Topaz.

Colonel Trevor Franklin (Ret.). Bedlam Bravo team leader. Former member of British Paras. Also identified as Trevor Martin. Call sign: Black.

Gerhard Badenhorst. Former member of the South African Special Forces Bridge. Call sign: Green.

Agam Bahadir Pun. Former sergeant in the Second Battalion, the Royal Gurkha Rifles. Call sign: Red.

Nathaniel 'Nate' Webster. Former member of the Drug Enforcement Agency. Used cover as a freelance writer. Call sign: Blue.

Fergus Mulligan. Former member of the Irish Special Branch. Call sign: White.

## Bedlam Charlie

Harrison Robertson. Director-General of Security, Australian SIO, and Bedlam Charlie overseer. Callsign: Whistler.

Lady Evelyn Evinrude. Bedlam Charlie team leader. Former MI6 operative. Callsign: Skylark. Cousin of Sir Alex.

Barbara Battersea. seconded from New Zealand's Security Intelligence Service. Petite and athletic, she wore her usual cargo pants and a short-sleeved top. Callsign: Raven.

Oliver 'Ollie' Forsyth, former team leader in Australia's Counter-Terrorism Centre. Callsign: Nightjar.

Noah Appleman, the quietest team member, came from Israel's Sayeret Matkal. Callsign: Petrel.

Alfred 'Alf' Livingston. Former corporal with 16 Air Assault Brigade and former bodyguard to Prince George, heir to the British throne. Callsign: Falcon.

Mark Baker. Evelyn's aide and logistics specialist. Callsign: Kestrel.

# QRF-1

August Lewis. Callsign Offender.

    Rufus T. Chopin – QRF-1 Leader. Callsign Condor.

    Maverick Kingfisher – Quincy's cousin. Callsign Leopard.

    Quincy Kingfisher – Maverick's cousin. Callsign Cheetah.

    Gordon Russell callsign Panther – died in Antarctica. Prior Marine gunnery sergeant.

    Alexandria "Alex" Steele – African-American callsign Bobcat.

Brigadier General Frederick Rhinehart, Ramstein Air Base installation commander.

    General Claude Bouchet, Air Force Chief of Staff.

## Scandinavian Officials

Ailsa Dahl – Danish. Project manager and climatologist.

    Bertelot Gulbrandsson – Norwegian. SPA team leader and engineer.

    Carina Eklund – Swedish. Climatologist.

    Eggert Falkenberg – German. Engineer.

    Gunner Bengtsson – Swedish. Research and data analysis assistant.

    Rona Lundgren – Swedish. Meteorologist.

## *RV Aquavit* Crew

Paul Smythe – captain of the *RV Aquavit*.

    David Tennent – work for Captain Paul Smythe as security officer. Former SEAL.

    Oskar Johansen – works in the *RV Aquavit*'s engine room.

    Tim Roberts - *RV Aquavit*'s nurse.

## Diablo Corps

Walter Brown – Founder and CEO of Diablo Corps.

Helen – Brown's secretary in Miami.

Reginald - One of Brown's engineers.

Samson Brown – Walter Brown's nephew.

Chris Handler – tall, slender, bearded. Cracks his knuckles a lot. Referred to in emails as Knuckle Cracker.

Emmanuel Durand – Brown's hacker chief. Known as Mothership ($Mo7H3R5H1P$).

Felix Zimmermann - another of Brown's hackers who meets with a deadly accident.

Graham Tuffin – another of Brown's hackers. Known as Nemesis ($N3M3515$).

Klaus Müller – another of Brown's hackers. Known as Archangel ($4RCH4N63L$).

Finn O'Brien – another of Brown's hackers. Known as Maestro ($M43STRo$).

Jean-Luc Picard – Brown's chef.

Sawyer Johnson – Brown's head of security.

Madeleine Fingerhut – Brown's new demolitions expert.

Winston Applegate – member of Brown's security team.

Liam Dawson - member of Brown's security team.

Gerald Jerry – member of Brown's security team.

Xavier Alpine – Brown's accountant covering elicit operations.

Godfrey Fenton – Brown's pilot.

Diana – Brown's nurse.

Dr. Theodore Stine – Brown's cardiologist in Miami.

Dr. Richard Rhude – Brown's epilepsy specialist.

Queenie – Marketing & Promotion VP.

Rachel - Finance & banking VP.

Wendy - Insurance VP.

**Mercenary Team**

Ben 'Ned' Needham – Brotherhood of Vengeance team leader and Sawyer's former army buddy. Tried to kill CC in Afghanistan.

Lucas Taylor – BV member.

Mateo Garcia – BV member.

Wyatt Moore – BV member.

Hudson Clark – BV member.

Carter Williams – BV member.

## Others

Ray - Albany/Boston police officer.

Lou – Albany/Boston police officer.

Ted Nicholson – Chairman, U.S. Federal Reserve.

Bruce McDermott – Governor, Bank of England.

Jonathan 'Jonny' Meu – National Security Advisor.

Amelia Collins – CIA Director.

Hortense Stonemason – U.S. treasury secretary.

Douglas Walliams – President, World Bank.

Carlos Alvarez – SWOOP pilot taking CC to Antarctica.

Salazar Alvarez – another SWOOP pilot and cousin of Carlos Alvarez.

Mârio – police officer in Ilulissat, Greenland.

Ike Brown - FBI agent who detained Chris in Miami.

Mike Black – FBI agent who detained Chris in Miami.

Hinata Takahasi – Japanese hacker friend of Matthew.

Tobias Trinkenschuh – Member of German and hacker friend of Matthew.

Isla Mc Robertson – Member of the UK National Cyber Security Centre (NCSC) and a friend of Matthew.

David Brady – FBI Special Agent in Charge.

# About Randall Krzak

Randall Krzak is a U.S. Army veteran and retired senior civil servant, spending thirty years in Europe, Africa, Central America, and the Middle East. His residency abroad qualifies him to build rich worlds in his action-adventure novels and short stories. Familiar with customs, laws, and social norms, he promotes these to create authentic characters and scenery.

His first novel, The Kurdish Connection, was published in 2017, and the sequel, Dangerous Alliance, was released in November 2018. Both placed in the 2018 Global Thriller Book Awards sponsored by Chanticleer International Book Awards, with The Kurdish Connection finishing as a semi-finalist and Dangerous Alliance being selected as one of seven first in category winners. The third novel in the series, Carnage in Singapore, was released in August 2019, and is one of six first in category winners in the 2019 Chanticleer International Book Awards. Colombian Betrayal (A Bruce and Smith Thriller Book 1), released in 2020 is one of seven first in category winners in the 2020 competition. It is also the 2022 Next Generation Indie Book Awards winner in the action-adventure category.

Mission: Angola (Xavier Sear Thriller Book 1) was released in January 2021 and was a finalist in the 2021 Page Turner Awards. It was one of six first in category winners in the 2021 CIBAs in their Global Thrillers category. Revenge (A Bruce and Smith Thriller Book 2) was released in October 2021 and was one of seven first in category winners in the 2022 CIBAs. The Kurdish Connection, Dangerous Alliance, and Carnage in Singapore were a finalist in the 2021 CIBAs in the Fiction series. Ultimate Escalation was released in November 2022 and will be competing in the 2023 CIBAs.

His first non-fiction article, 'Black Ops in Fiction,' is featured on the web daily, https://www.mysteryandsuspense.com/black-ops-in-thrillers/

He holds a Bachelor of Science degree from the University of Maryland and a general Master in Business Administration (MBA) and a MBA with an emphasis in Strategic Focus, both from Heriot-Watt University, Edinburgh, Scotland. He currently resides with his wife, Sylvia, and four cats in Dunfermline, Scotland. He's originally from Michigan, while Sylvia is a proud Scot. In addition to writing, he enjoys hiking, reading, candle making, pyrography, and sightseeing.

# Other Thriller Novels by Randall Krzak

**Bedlam Thriller Series:**

- The Kurdish Connection
- Dangerous Alliance
- Carnage in Singapore
- Ultimate Escalation
- Frozen Conquest

**Xavier Sear Thriller Series:**

- Mission: Angola

**Bruce and Smith Thriller Series:**

- Colombian Betrayal
- Revenge

# The Kurdish Connection

A semi-finalist in the 2018 Chanticleer International Book Awards (CIBAs) in the global thrillers category.

In their daily struggle for survival, Iraqi Kurdish scavengers uncover a cache of chemical weapons. They offer the weapons to fellow Kurdish rebels in Turkey and Syria to assist in their quest to free an imprisoned leader and create a unified homeland. After receiving a tip from an unlikely source, the newly formed Special Operations Bedlam team is called to arms!

Travel with Craig Cameron and his international team on their covert operation as they weave their way through war-torn regions seeking to locate and recover the weapons before they can be used to cause irreparable harm and instigate a world crisis.

The odds are stacked against them. Can they manage to keep their operation hidden and prevent further clashes before it's too late?

Universal Link - books2read.com/u/bovxOZ

Chanticleer Editorial Review - https://bit.ly/3zInlLm

# Dangerous Alliance

One of seven First in Category Winners in the 2018 CIBAs, global thrillers category.

United Nations' sanctions are crippling North Korea. China has turned her back on her malevolent partner. The North Korean military machine is crumbling, unable to function. Oil reserves are minimal and the government seeks new alliances.

Cargo and tourist ships are disappearing along the Somali and Kenyan coastline at an alarming rate. Speeches abound, but inaction emboldens Al-Shabab to seek their next prize: Kenya. The terror organization controls land but requires weapons.

Bedlam Bravo team leader Colonel Trevor Franklin (Ret.) leads the small international team into East Africa. Tempers flare as the team is embroiled in a political quagmire. The axis must be stopped to avert an international crisis but at what cost?

Universal Link - books2read.com/u/bzoxRj

Chanticleer Editorial Review - https://bit.ly/3AvQBpR

# Carnage in Singapore

One of seven First in Category Winners in the 2019 CIBAs, global thrillers category.

Terrorist groups such as Abu Sayyaf and Jemaah Islamiyah have flourished in recent years with new recruits joining them and ISIS-affiliates at an alarming rate. Blended operations by various Asian countries have forced the groups to work together to identify a new operational base.

They seek an island nation to call home, one where they can plot against countries who oppose their ideals. They found a target, a small nation-state, perfect for their needs: The Republic of Singapore.

Before anyone can respond, the ambassadors of the United States, Great Britain, and Australia are kidnapped from their residences in Singapore. Right index fingers of each victim are sent as a warning. Any attempt to recover the ambassadors will result in the removal of additional body parts.

Bedlam Charlie team leader, Evelyn Evinrude, leads the group to rescue the ambassadors and capture the local leaders of Abu Sayyaf and Jemaah Islamiyah. Can Bedlam succeed or will events escalate, resulting in more deaths?

Universal Link - books2read.com/u/3LD2vw

Chanticleer Editorial Review - https://bit.ly/3tZtJwB

# Colombian Betrayal

One of seven first in category winners in the 2020 CIBAs, global thrillers category. It was also the 2022 Next Generation Indie Book Awards winner in the action-adventure category.

Colombian drug lord watched her profits diminish over the years. Unable to increase market share because of a shrinking consumer base and a new international competitor, she formed an unholy alliance.

Olivia Moreno, head of the Barranquilla Cartel, struck a deal with a regional leader within the Revolutionary Armed Forces of Colombia. Little did she know but she initiated her own death warrant. FARC had an unknown support group who wanted a foothold in South America – Islamic State.

Forced to flee, Moreno is captured by a small CIA team. Fearing for her life, she spins a tale about using her money and manpower to destroy ISIS. Laws and rules of engagement mean nothing to her, only her life and family matter.

Will team leader AJ Bruce strike a deal to turn the tables on ISIS and stop them from launching a concentrated attack on the United

States? Or will they be too late? If successful, will Moreno's reward be total control of Afghanistan's poppy fields, or will she be doubled-crossed?

Universal link - books2read.com/u/4Azojo

Chanticleer Editorial Review - https://bit.ly/43Kve2T

# Mission: Angola

One of six first in category winners **in** the 2021 CIBAs, global thrillers category. Also a finalist in the 2021 Page Turner Book Awards.

Joao and Caterina Regaleria's twentieth wedding anniversary celebration was fast approaching when a contact from the past reaches out for his assistance.

Colonel Theodore Mwelewe, a former enemy commander during the Angolan war and now an important politician, requests Joao's help. The colonel's adult son, Peter, was kidnapped while working as a doctor for the Christian Aid Mission in the Democratic Republic of Congo.

Reluctant to get involved, Joao contacts Xavier Sear, a former CIA operative. They became friends when Joao served as a member of the United Nations Peace-Keeping Forces in Angola and Sear was an observer.

After Caterina's persuasive intervention, Joao and Sear head to the DRC to rescue Peter. Treachery abounds at each step of the way.

Will they be successful or will the situation deteriorate even further as various players follow their own agendas.

Universal link - books2read.com/u/3LRV71

Chanticleer Editorial Review - https://bit.ly/3XcMdZg

# Revenge

One of seven first in category winners in the 2022 CIBAs, global thrillers category.

Relegated to a desk job at the Pentagon despite his last field mission being a success, Colonel Javier Smith submits his retirement papers. He moves forward with his plans to create a security and investigative agency called the Brusch Agency. The focus will be aiding international clientele.

AJ Bruce, who co-led the mission with Smith, finds herself rooted at CIA Headquarters. Although now in charge of the division responsible for tracking terrorist groups in Latin America, she misses the action from being in the field.

Meanwhile, Alberto Cabrera was one of four terrorists who survived Bruce and Smith's mission. Also known as Abdul Rahman, he enlists the assistance of the others who escaped and vows to track down those who killed his friends and comrades.

As Javier and AJ grow closer together, will the future hold wedding bells or funerals? Hang onto your hats as the story unfolds.

Universal Link - https://books2read.com/u/mYQ5qP

# Ultimate Escalation

Punjabi militants seek to distance themselves from Indian and Pakistani dominance and interference. With the dissolution of British India in 1947, families were ripped apart as the Punjabi region was split between the two countries. Limited attacks within each country caused further persecution and heartache.

The militants have no idea how to achieve their desires--until the appearance of Vladimir Aleksandrovich Nikolaev, a disgraced Spetsnaz colonel. He offers the militants a means to spark a conflict between the two nuclear powers.

Russian subs sold on the black market and manned by Iranian and Russian sailors will surface off the coasts of the two countries and destroy Karachi and Mumbai. Propaganda machines will levy accusations against each country, leading to escalation of hostilities, pushing the countries to the brink of nuclear war.

The Bedlam organization fields their three teams to counter the violence and seek to restore calm before it's too late. Will they be successful, or will South Asia become a smoking ruin?

Universal Link - https://books2read.com/u/b6WqG6

# "Black Ops in Fiction"

Randall's first non-fiction article, "Black Ops in Fiction," was featured in the March 2021 edition of the web daily, *Mystery and Suspense.*

https://bit.ly/3tZX3Ty

www.ingramcontent.com/pod-product-compliance
Lightning Source LLC
Chambersburg PA
CBHW050659290626
47170CB00016B/2477